Fluent in Hebrew and Arabic, FBI agent Jake Bernstein goes undercover to infiltrate an Islamic terrorist cell in Silicon Valley. If he fails, thousands will die. But what price will Jake have to pay in order to serve his country? Will it cost him his newly rekindled relationship with Meg?

Undercover In Silicon Valley
Copyright © 2024 Donna Del Oro
ISBN: 978-1-4874-4138-8
Cover art by Martine Jardin

Published by eXtasy Books Inc

Look for us online at:
www.eXtasybooks.com

Undercover In Silicon Valley
A Jake Bernstein FBI Thriller

By

Donna Del Oro

DEDICATION

Doing the research into Islam took time and effort, and a level of guts I hadn't used before. Thanks to my big, tall Spanish-American cousin, Frank Rodrigues, we toured a mosque and attended a service that was both enlightening and disturbing. I had read many books about Islam, including the Qur'an in English. In my opinion, every civilized Westerner should read and learn about Islam, its history, its ideology, its objectives. As the Qur'an says, "War is deceit."

A sentiment which, ironically, underlines this story.

Additionally, I must thank my son, Todd, a biotech engineer in Silicon Valley for inspiring this story. His expertise, help, and advice were invaluable. I could not have written this story without him.

"Fight and kill the disbelievers wherever you find them, take them captive, harass them, lie in wait and ambush them, using every stratagem of war."
—Verse of the Sword, The Qur'an

PROLOGUE

Venice, Italy
August 2005

A mad kept the boy in his line of sight. The youth walked
stiffly, as if he had a rod holding his back straight. The
weight of the vest, no doubt, caused him discomfort. Fifteen
pounds of Sem-Tex and ten pounds of steel ball bearings,
tightly packed with wires attached to a detonator that
weighed another pound. The boy's hands never left the pockets of his bulky jacket, just as he'd been instructed. Good thing
cool breezes from the Adriatic forced people to bundle up. No
one would give the child a second look.

A good boy. Simple minded but devout and brave. A poor
villager from north of Kandahar, a madrassa graduate who
rarely spoke. His hooded brown eyes bespoke a short, miserable life. Today the boy would kiss the hem of the Prophet
and be rewarded for his sacrifice.

Peripherally, Amad noted the great shipping channel on
his left as he climbed the steps of a pedestrian bridge. Jet black
gondolas, leashed to their colorful poles, bobbed and swayed
in the brisk sea breeze. A gigantic white cruise ship sailed into
view, rounding the bend of the docks. How he would love to
blow that vessel up and send thousands of Satan worshippers
to a watery grave. Ah well, perhaps — *Inshallah*! Allah willing,
that would happen someday.

Although it was windy, the sun bathed his face with a
strange warmth. He exulted in the warmth, for that meant St.

1

Mark's Square, Piazza San Marco, would be filled with tourists as well as Italians scurrying about to wait on the spoiled Infidels. In the distance, the soft strains of an orchestra drifted out to the channel via the broad walkway to his right as he approached the walkway of the winged lions.

The two columns of winged lions, symbols of Renaissance Venice, towered above the crowd as it moved along with him toward the square, their destination not quite the same as his. Amad held the vain Venetians in silent scorn. Long before their Renaissance, the city's Jews had loaned money to the Devil Crusaders while the Venetian merchants gladly stocked their traveling coffers. Today they all would pay for past and present sins against Allah.

Of course, that was not his only motive for revenge. Many ghosts filled his mind, all crying for retribution, including that of his beloved brother. Mostafa lived inside Amad's head, a voice among thousands, strengthening him, making him resolute and hard. One infidel's death for every Muslim death. That was the righteous motto of a true *ikhwan*. A brother of Allah.

Amad, dressed in the high turban and polished suit of a Sikh businessman, stopped at the outer corner of the Doge's Palace. Around the corner, the vast Piazza San Marco fanned out to the west of Saint Mark's Church. *Time to get down to business.* In one hand, Amad held a mobile phone, specially programmed so that a certain sequence of numbers would set off the detonator inside the youth's vest. With feigned care, he studied an English-language tourist map while remaining at the corner. From his vantage point, Amad could peer over the map and track the young martyr's progress toward the center of the piazza. Another *ikhwan*, the boy's recruiter and handler, had rehearsed the youth the day before and thus far he showed no signs of hesitation. The boy, as instructed, walked among the milling crowd in front of St. Mark's

Church and halted.

Amad briefly wondered how much damage the church would suffer. No matter. He'd already estimated the fatalities would range between fifty and sixty, the wounded perhaps another fifty. One never knew. Due to the crowded conditions at this time of day, and the added weight of the vest, the numbers killed and maimed would be high.

Let the power of the Believers reign and let terror strike the hearts of the Infidels.

The youth gazed up at the four horses on the front façade of the cathedral. Amad watched as the boy then closed his eyes. In all his purity and trust, the boy waited. Mustn't make him wait too long.

Amad retreated to the other side of the palace wall, the side that faced the shipping channel. A gondolier waved to him and shouted something in Italian. Ignoring the man, he held up both the map and the mobile phone, the former to conceal his face as he muttered a prayer in Arabic. When he was ready, his right thumb pressed the sequence of numbers. Amad counted five seconds for the signal to bounce off the nearest cell tower, which he'd located south of the shipping channel.

Silence followed as the explosion seemed to suck the air out of the vast square. A moment later, the sudden eruption of sounds was indistinguishable, one from another. The only one that stood out for Amad was the bell in the clock tower which bonged once loudly.

Screams pierced the afternoon air.

Amad shuddered, then opened his eyes and looked up. His gaze met the gondolier's a moment before the man dove into the well of his boat.

An elderly tourist couple flung themselves on their knees in front of him. Amad hadn't noticed them before. Their proximity shocked him.

"*Qu'est-ce que c'est?*" the woman cried, her eyes wild with terror. The man and woman looked up at him.

"I don't know," said Amir in perfectly accented British English, "The square. Something happened."

"*Mon Dieu!*" The couple helped each other rise and then hurried around the corner. Amad had the impulse to yell at them. *No!* But why should he? They were infidels, just like the ones cut down in the square. Old, young—what difference did it make? Nevertheless, the woman's long wail sliced through him and he shivered.

Amad shook the feeling off, turned his back, and retraced his steps down the sidewalk and back across the pedestrian bridge. To his left, he acknowledged the Bridge of Sighs but kept walking. He had to check out of his hotel as soon as possible. Then he would meet Ali and take a *vaporetto*—water taxi—to the airport. Their Sikh disguises and British passports would not be a hindrance, and they were on no country's watch list.

The facilitator's work was done for the day, but there was more work to be done. Three more willing martyrs for decadent Europe before summer's end. Then the Great Satan.

Ah yes. For America, he would plan something special. The challenge filled him with great purpose and excitement.

CHAPTER ONE

FBI Headquarters, Washington, D.C.
Two months later

Jake Bernstein turned off Pennsylvania Avenue onto Tenth Street, the 2.5 million-square-foot, tetrahedron-shaped Hoover Building looming on his left. The rear of the building held eleven stories, the front facing Pennsylvania consisting of seven, lending it a strange, lopsided appearance.

Although intimidated four years ago by the unorthodox structure, and all that the Bureau represented, now Jake felt only impatience at returning. His new assignment awaited him and he was eager to get started. The past two months had consumed him, both intellectually and physically. Eight weeks at Quantico in a total Arabic immersion program during the day, evenings of lectures on Islam and the various cultures and history of Middle East countries and tribes. Not to mention the early mornings filled with weaponry and close combat refresher practices. The total mental and physical preoccupation invigorated him. Kept him from thinking about . . . *her*. More important things were at stake. His career. His country.

He stopped his Ford Expedition at the gated entrance to the underground parking garage. Manny Solis, one of the seventy-five FBI police officers who manned the Hoover Building's perimeter, leaned out of the guard's booth and peered at him while Jake showed his ID and badge. A CCTV camera above Manny's head swiveled over the SUV and came to rest on the driver. Jake waited while the head scan streamed to the security center and ran his face through its facial recognition software. He absently wondered if the software would be able to map his facial points and angles. His new mustache and short beard took up half of his face.

Manny shook his head and smiled. "Hey, Jake, almost didn't recognize you. You been gone awhile. You missed a coupla good games."

Jake got the joke. He'd joined Manny and his two sons the summer before at a Nationals game. That tedious experience had made him even more loyal to the Los Angeles Dodgers.

"Yeah, right. Crazy summer, Manny. All work, no play."

For a second, his thoughts turned to Meg Larsen, but he ignored the ache deep in his belly. Over, done with, ancient history. She'd never returned his hundred or so phone calls these past two months. Didn't matter if he'd indirectly caused her grandmother's suicide in June. He was doing his job and that was the logical, though not intended, end of his investigation. Her grandmother was an old Nazi spy wanted by MI-5 and Mossad for World War II crimes against humanity. They'd asked for FBI assistance and his boss had sent Jake. Still, he'd hurt Meg deeply, and it was clear she wasn't going to forgive him.

"Heard you were in Germany and England somewhere in June."

"Yeah. Wrapped up a two-week investigation." Jake signed in on Manny's computer tablet. The steel barrier didn't raise and the bollards didn't retract. Evidently Manny wanted some chat time. Or he was waiting for security to flash the green light. Jake would've enjoyed shooting the bull over baseball but he was due for a SIOC—Strategic Information Operations Center—meeting on the fifth floor. Hey, what was a minute for a friend and former Marine?

"Man, you look different." Manny scrutinized Jake's face.

"Looks like you're going deep undercover."

Jake smiled. The guy was smarter than he pretended to be at times. Jake reflexively raked his mustache and beard with his fingertips. Facial hair took some getting used to. He'd darkened his Irish-German complexion, too, with as many hours as he could get running around Quantico's outside track.

"New field assignment. Can't say any more than that."

"Will you be gone a long time?" The guy looked disappointed.

"Could be months." Jake shrugged. "We'll catch some games when I get back, okay? I'd rather watch a piss-poor football game than see the Nationals try to play baseball. Tell your boys I'll treat 'em to kraut dogs and a tub of popcorn."

"Sounds good. You take care, Jake." Manny patted Jake's forearm. "Watch your back out there."

"Always. Semper fi." Jake, a former SEAL and Navy officer, flipped Manny a half-salute, which Manny returned.

The steel bollards retracted and the arm raised. For the first time, a pang of uncertainty curled through him. What had he gotten himself into? By the time he pulled into a vacant space, though, his attitude had steeled.

Whatever. Duty calls.

The George Herbert Walker Bush Strategic Information Operations Center occupied forty-thousand square feet of offices on the fifth floor of the Hoover Building. The succession of offices and command centers held banks of computers, video monitors, and wall-sized LCD displays, fielded by agents of every age, size, shape, and racial ethnicity. More women dotted the scene, Jake noted. Had there been a hiring boom in the two months he'd been gone?

Women. No, don't go there.

The door to Operations Room G stood open. His Bureau

7

boss, Terry Thompson, Assistant Deputy Director of Investigations, did an exaggerated double-take before greeting him with a handshake and manly shoulder-bump. Nothing about Terry had changed except his hair. There was now a lot more salt than pepper on his thinning pate. And he was now on his third marriage, so overweight that he had no neck. His jowls sagged and dark circles under his eyes made him look raccoonish. The job. *It cost you your personal life, your health, your goddamned hair . . .*

Terry leaned over and whispered, "Hey, Bernstein, if you don't look like an Abdullah, I'll eat my tie. Still not Arab enough, so we'll make you a half-breed. Half-Lebanese, maybe half-Irish or Italian-American. How'd your classes go?"

Since Terry had gotten weekly reports from both Jake and the program's supervisor, he already knew. But that was Terry, breaking the ice of the moment with chatter. Jake smiled.

"Fine. If I were Abdullah and you Omar, I'd greet you with *Salaam alaikum* and you'd reply *Alaikum salaam.*"

The Muslim male's greeting—which he'd spoken at least a dozen times a day for the past two months—was the first Arabic he'd learned. So similar to the Hebrew, *Shalom aleichem,* and each time he'd mentally echoed the Hebrew greeting of peace be with you. His brave grandfather, Nate Bernstein, had fled Germany in the mid-thirties, gone to Hollywood, and joined the other German-Jewish expats working in the film industry. Jake's fluency in Berliner-dialect German was thanks to his grandfather, who'd insisted on lessons along with Hebrew School.

Even though Jake considered himself a secular Jew, his German-Jewish heritage ran deep inside, as deep as his love for his grandparents. Like a cool, fresh aquifer beneath a heated earth. If *Salaam alaikum* made him feel guilty, a traitor to his heritage, then saying the Shalom erased that guilt.

Always there. Reminding him of who he really was. Giving him a kind of peace.

Terry ushered him to a chair at a large oval conference table. A screen occupied most of the far wall, flashing now the SIOC logo. Beside the screen stood the chief of the FBI's Counterterrorism center—CTC—whom Jake recognized from his first briefing two months ago. The man nodded at Jake, apparently the last one to arrive. It was then, as ADD Terry Thompson made introductions around the table, that Jake acknowledged the four men across the table. All FBI agents who'd volunteered at the recruitment briefing two months ago, they'd taken the same immersion classes at Quantico. Preparing for what, they were about to find out.

Middle-Eastern-looking men, all in their twenties and thirties, with names like Tom, Patrick, Chris, and Zachary. Zack was the only other Jewish-American recruited for this assignment. Jake nodded at Zack, wondering how he felt when he was speaking Arabic. That was something they'd never spoken of while in the program.

The CTC chief, Harlan Peters—from a Georgia farming family—took charge as narrator of the Power Point presentation, his preamble a perfunctory overview and rationale.

"As you all know, since nine-eleven, the American intelligence community has relied on cell phone tracing, wiretapping, money tracking, interceptions of cyber data, and occasional INS alerts. Keeping our own watch lists current has become a full-time task. And that's in addition to sorting through mountains of decoded encrypted transcripts sent over by the NSA. To our credit, we've stopped hundreds of plots that the public has never heard about."

Murmurs swept the table, and the faces of the participants looked grim.

Peters's faraway look mirrored the horrors that could have rained down upon the American public had those very plots not been uncovered and nipped in the bud.

"Well, it's time again to beat the bushes out there and see what we can scare up. How many rocks in the pasture do we have to turn over to find the one or two deadly snakes bent on killing us? Maybe every damned one of them. We not only must do physical surveillance, but we must infiltrate and expose the jihadist cells that we suspect are currently lying low and plotting their next moves. On nine-eleven, the enemy showed us their sophisticated knowledge and appreciation of this country's security weaknesses. While we've plugged a few holes, we're still a free country. We encourage immigration and foreign visitors, and naturally that makes us vulnerable. As a result, we have to stay vigilant. The consensus of our sixteen intelligence agencies is that we need to take a proactive approach in ferreting out these sleeper jihadi cells."

Another slide flashed up. A map of the U.S. with small red circles over areas in five states — California, Texas, Florida, New York, and Michigan. All big population states, all with sizeable Muslim groups in urban, cosmopolitan areas. All with important, highly attended mosques.

Despite not being given specifics beforehand, Jake had known where this assignment was going to take him. Hence the language and culture classes and the changes in his and the other four men's appearances. He'd volunteered without hesitation.

One of his four classmates spoke up. "But we know that the nine-eleven jihadists stayed clear of mosques and fellow Muslims during their time in the U.S. They shaved, dressed in Western clothes, didn't draw attention to themselves. Some drank in bars and went clubbing. It was all part of their cover to blend in. Moussaoui's intel."

What he meant was what the intel community had learned after capturing the twentieth 9-11 intended hijacker, Zacharias Moussaoui, the one who'd been prevented from entering the U.S. at the last minute.

Peters nodded solemnly. "That was then, this is now. In spite of our success in eliminating the top echelon of Al Qaeda, various Muslim extremist groups have grown bolder—Hezbollah, Hamas, the Muslim Brotherhood, Lakfar, Ansar Al-Shari—in part due to the protections the civil rights laws of various Western countries afford them, in part due to their tendency to use intimidation and violence to accomplish their aims. The Center for American-Islamic Relations has become the Muslim civil rights watchdog in this country. But as much as our civil rights laws represent our strength as a people and government, they're also a crack in our armor. A crack that logically exists because we are a country that values freedom. A crack that you five agents"—Peters surveyed the five men—"we hope will help mend by infiltrating certain groups."

Another slide popped up, the red circles pulsating almost comically in intensity.

"The NSA alerted us months ago about the increase of cyber chatter emanating from the *imams* or clerics of five mosques in five American cities. The chatter, they're convinced, is part of a pattern that usually precedes something big. An event of some kind. In this case, all five mosques are expecting visiting *mullahs*—foreign Islamic clerics—all at the same time. Coincidence? We wonder."

The CTC chief looked at Jake, then in turn at the other recruited agents at the table. "Do you know the significance of the name Cordoba? And please forget political correctness here. Here we speak the truth as federal law enforcement officials."

Jake spoke first. "Cordoba, Spain was once the headquarters of the European Caliphate during the Middle Ages. The sheikhs and mullahs met in council there once or twice a year. There they plotted out their next conquest on the European continent and carried out Shar'ia Law. Rulings and punishments, like the stoning of adulterous women and the beheading of apostates. The subjugation of the Christians and Jews in their midst."

Another of the five chimed in. "Cordoba was thought to be a code name for Islam's ultimate goal for those who followed Muhammed's leadership. Their aim was the political and religious conversion of the world."

A fourth slide showed the same map and small red circles with names in bold-type black underneath. Five mosques in five states shared the name of Cordoba.

"These five mosques, according to NSA, have a recent history of intercepted communication links with the major Al Qaeda media site, *Shumukh al-Islam*. If they're good Muslims, why are they contacting this extremist propaganda media? Are some Islamic clerics encouraging American Muslims to go to this site? Like the mullah Al-Awlaki did to Major Hassan, the Fort Hood killer? Preaching hatred and jihad against the very country that has been their home and has given them shelter and freedom? They must know we're watching them. Is something about to happen that's so vital that they're willing to risk our taking a closer look?"

The three older men and one woman at the table, all assistant directors of four of the country's sixteen intel agencies, leaned forward in their seats, clearly captivated by the theatrics of the presentation.

Jake had to assume that the CTC chief and four directors had conceived and rubberstamped this operation. Ever since he'd learned that the New York mosque built near the Ground Zero site was named the Cordoba Center, he sensed . . . no, he'd *felt* certain that something was afoot. Especially since the four bombings in Europe that summer — the ones in Venice, Nice, Munich, and Madrid — had added to his growing sense of foreboding. That was one of the reasons he'd volunteered for this undercover assignment.

"The code name may be innocuous," Peters resumed. "And, for all we know, it may have evolved to mean pride in their religion, the glory of Islam—we don't know. Or, conversely, the truth may be lying in deceit. Like a venomous snake, it hides, waiting to strike. Daring us to turn over the rock."

Jake stared at the screen. Five circled names of mosques in five different states. His eyes darted to the area in California. The red circle centered on the San Francisco Bay Area. Silicon Valley, the tech center and venture capital of the country. More PhDs and brainiacs lived and worked there than anywhere else in the U.S.—that was, other than L.A., his hometown.

"Still, a lot of conjecture but no proof of conspiracies to commit terrorist acts," said the CTC chief. He proceeded to pass out folders, each one stamped *Classified*. "Agents, you'll be assigned to the state where you were raised or are most familiar with. Your mission is to go fishing. Let's hope you catch five big ones."

Jake was taken aback. A fishing expedition. This was the basis for their crash courses in Arabic and Islam? Nothing more than the name Cordoba? And some highly suspect coded cyber-chatter flowing to and from those five mosques?

Disappointed, he glanced over at Terry. His boss's flushed cheeks and embarrassed demeanor reflected his own concerns. What if this fishing expedition morphed into sting or entrapment operations which ended up making the five agents and the Bureau look like damned fools? Another round of *Bungling Bureau* newscasts would light up the American media like Fourth of July fireworks. The Bureau was still sensitive to having missed all the clues leading up to 9-11. Eleven years ago, Jake, having just graduated college, had joined the Navy in the hope of somehow undoing the harm caused by a deaf, dumb, and blind intelligence community.

About to turn thirty-three, he was still trying to undo that harm.

Terry made a gesture with his hands, as if to say *I wish they had more*. He leaned over and quipped, "At least you got California. You get to go home for a while."

Home. Mom, Pop, Gabriel, David.

A couple of old girlfriends from his randy UCLA days . . . *Who knows?*

Jake's cellphone vibrated. He stared at the screen. A text message. From Meg. When could she see him? It was important.

Just when he'd closed the book on her, she wanted to write a new chapter.

Damn. Women are impossible.

CHAPTER TWO

Meg combed out her long hair, let it cascade down her back. Jake would like it that way. Then she dressed carefully in light-blue cotton capris and a matching snug tank top. For the first time since her grandmother's death, she felt alive. Alive and brimming with hope.

Bubbles of excitement rose in her heart and mind. At long last, she'd see him. Apologize to him for her silence. His almost daily phone calls had gradually renewed her sense of hope — that maybe, just maybe, it was time to move on.

She inserted gold hoop earrings and looped Jake's chain with the amber pendant around her neck. She'd worn it every day since he'd given it to her. Ever since that day at the hospital in Hannover, Germany where her grandmother lay dying. Before she'd confessed everything to Jake and he'd recorded her story in her native German. That was all she'd learned from Jake. He'd promised her grandmother that Meg would never listen to that confession. Her Gran, whom she'd always known as Mary McCoy, an Irish immigrant to the U.S. after World War II, had revealed herself to be someone very different. A German and the notorious Nazi spy who was code-named Hummingbird.

At the time, in that hospital, Meg had thought the amber necklace was Jake's parting gift. A sweet, sentimental present, one she thought had meant he'd never see her again. Still, she'd worn it because, despite all the grief that had followed, she couldn't stop thinking about him. Bernstein — she pronounced it with a German accent.

Der Bernstein. German word for amber. Literally, "burn stone".

Her grandmother's suicide had sent her into an emotional tailspin. She blamed herself for taking Gran to Ireland in the first place and causing her grandmother's health crisis, even though Uncle John explained that MI5 would have continued to investigate her and eventually would have sought her extradition. Uncle John didn't blame her and neither did her own mother. They both told Meg that the experience in Ireland and Germany had freed Mary McCoy Snider of her burden of lies and had allowed her to be Clare Hillenbrand again, if only for a short while.

Sixty years' worth of lies and subterfuge had taken their toll on her grandmother's physical and mental health.

Giving Clare the opportunity to unburden herself of all the lies over the years had been a good thing, Uncle John had told her. Meg wasn't convinced about that, although the last thing Gran had told her that fateful night was *I want to stay in Hannover. Bury me with my German family.*

Gran's suicide had shaken her to the core. The shock of it still hadn't worn off. Gran had hidden her painkillers in the secret well underneath the jeweled Hummingbird pin. Half paralyzed from her stroke, she had still managed to open the compartment and get to them.

Nevertheless, Meg's mind agreed with her uncle, that Gran was indeed liberated. Meg's own emotions had taken longer to accept the fact.

Still, she hadn't been able to phone or email Jake. For two long months, she'd castigated herself and him for bringing about her grandmother's death. Then something snapped inside her which changed everything. A realization that it was time to move on. Gran would have wanted her to make a life for herself and find happiness.

As Uncle John said, she was young . . . and when you're young, anything is possible.

16

Meg's stomach fluttered with somersaulting butterflies, her head buzzed with a thousand bees. She practically skipped downstairs. In the spacious kitchen, she downed a glass of wine to calm her nerves.

Then she scanned her preparations on the kitchen table set for two. A salad of mixed greens with honey- and sesame-glazed chicken, water chestnuts, and slices of mandarins, all tossed with Thai peanut sauce. Her own creation. Two Porterhouse steaks, marinaded and tender, ready for the grill. A French baguette from her favorite bakery. Wine and beer. She'd even bought a couple of bottles of Guinness. Jake said the stout had grown on him. And dessert, a key lime pie she'd made from scratch, waited in the fridge.

Too excited to stand still, she roamed about the two-story, five-bedroom, six-bath house. Her grandmother's house was enormous, and now it was hers. Money had been left to her half-brother, Jack, and to Uncle John and his two sons—even her mother, though for years she and Gran had barely spoken. But Gran had wanted Meg to have the Texas house they'd shared off and on for so many years.

Now it was more like a mausoleum—too big and filled with too many memories of her childhood. And of a grandmother she barely knew but loved very much.

Meg didn't know how that was possible . . . to love someone deeply but not really know that person. But it was and she did. She shook her head. Time to make new memories.

The gate buzzer sounded. She raced over to the wall and pushed a button, opening the driveway gate. Suddenly she was struck with fear. What if Jake had only come to see how she was doing and nothing more?

His last message had been so cryptic. *I'll drop by on my way to L.A. Thursday night, around six-thirty.* She glanced at the kitchen clock. Six o'clock. He'd come straight from the airport. Meg took a deep breath.

Oh, piss on a brick!

17

Giving in to her bursting impatience, Meg ran to the front door. A yellow cab was parked along the curb at the bottom of the little knoll. She frowned.

A darkly tanned stranger with a black beard. Dressed in khakis and a Kelly-green polo shirt, his biceps bulged and his sinewy legs snugged his trousers as he strode up the driveway. He looked up and his eyes met hers. *Jake!* And he was no longer limping, she was happy to see. His thigh wound had healed.

She recalled in vivid detail the last time they'd made love. A quick, dry hump in that horrible little inn along the Ring of Kerry. He'd apologized to her. He'd told her he was courting her but doing a bad job of it.

Not so bad.

Lord, her eyes devoured him.

Wait a min—he didn't look happy. His sensuous mouth thinned ominously. His dark brows furrowed angrily. A dark brown forelock dangled carelessly over his forehead. He swept it back in a brusque manner.

"Jake, why is your taxi waiting?"

"Because this might be the shortest visit in history."

Her heart spiraled down.

"Why? I made dinner for us," she said. He wasn't even carrying a suitcase. "Aren't you staying tonight?"

Jake stopped in his tracks. His troubled, hurt expression metamorphized into total bewilderment. His mouth dropped open.

"Meg?" He braced his hands on his slim hips. "You never returned my calls."

Meg approached him, her eyes downcast. How could she explain something that she could barely understand herself?

"I know." She shrugged even while her hands slid down his chest to latch onto the waistband of his trousers. "I'm so sorry. After the family left—we had a memorial service for

Gran here in town, just family and friends. I had to grieve. Privately. I just moped around the house for over a month. Didn't answer the door. Didn't answer the phone. I guess I was punishing myself. And you, Jake. For what happened. I'm still grieving, just in a different way."

"Maybe I should go," he murmured huskily, not moving an inch. His eyes flickered down her tank top to her hands. There'd been a flare of recognition when he saw the amber pendant.

"No, stay. Please. You've changed your looks." She grinned up at the somewhat skeptical but slightly hopeful expression he now wore. She stroked his neatly trimmed beard. "Should I ask? Where y'all going this time?"

"L.A. For a short vacation. See my folks." He didn't move.

"Then off to somewhere exotic with that beard of yours?"

"Can't say."

She curled her fingers around his waistband and tugged him against her. Her breasts mashed against his hard chest, making her dizzy with lust. She detected a gleam in his eyes and a gradual curling at the sides of his lovely mouth.

"Meg. You put me through hell. No word from you for two months."

"I'm sorry." What more could she say? Her emotions were still raw. In time, maybe it would all make sense. All she knew was that something inside her was different.

His hands settled on her shoulders. "You sure you want to see me again? The way it all ended . . ."

She sighed. "You and your courtship of lies and undercover crap. Yes, I know. But somewhere along the way I came to know the real you. Somehow you won me over." She beamed brightly at his look of total astonishment. "Yeah, don't underestimate me, Jacob Bernstein. I know the real you now. I've never trusted another man as much as I trust you. So what do you say to that?"

He grinned as his arms slid down and encircled her waist. "I could say you're one crazy chick."

She laughed and swept an arm toward the house.

"Yeah, buster, I'm crazy all right. I'm fixin' to feed you, ya hear? C'mon, get your bag and shoo that cab away." She added teasingly, "Can you use your FBI badge to get me a ticket on your flight to L.A. tomorrow? I'd love to go out there with you and meet your family."

A ton of tension seemed to escape him then. His whole body relaxed and he smiled shrewdly. He leaned down to rub his lips against hers as his muscular arms tightened around her.

"Sorry, against Bureau protocol. I'd have to be on a case, and you'd have to be my star informant for me to bump a civilian off a flight."

She raised her hands, wrists together. "Can't you take me into custody? Charge me with—I don't know—some crime or other? Like conspiracy to capture a federal agent's heart?"

Rising on tiptoes, she nibbled the warm skin of his neck. He tasted so good. Smelled so good. Again, his woodsy cologne reeled her senses. Gave her a heady intoxication and evoked memories of that one night they'd spent together in Ireland. Smiling, she slid one of her hands lower to graze the fly of his pants. Yep, they were still hot for each other.

Two long months. How had they ever survived?

"Agent Bernstein, you're such a stickler for correctness," she teased, "Good thing you're not always so correct."

That got a chuckle out of him. He turned and whistled to the cab.

"Don't worry, I'll find a way to get you on that plane." He stepped away. "But wait, don't you start school next week . . . ?"

"Tell ya later. Things've changed around here."

Meg watched him hurry down, pay the cabbie, grab his

carry-on bag, then stride back up with renewed purpose and a lightness in his step. His eyes never left her.

Strange, how they'd met. Even stranger, how they'd fallen in love.

Meg wasn't lying. She knew the real Jake Bernstein. If her life depended on it, she wouldn't hesitate to put it in his hands. Again. He was a man she could trust completely. That kind was too sexy for words.

He reached her and, with one arm, pulled her to him. Instinctively, her arm patted his back. They'd always have each other's backs.

Together, they walked into her house.

Jake opened his eyes and couldn't believe his good fortune. Meg was sleeping, facing away from him. Her long blonde hair fanned out on her pillow, enticing him. He rolled onto his side and spooned her long, leggy body, breathing in the scent of her hair, her naked warmth. His right arm enclosing her, his hand explored her soft contours. He closed his eyes, feeling heady with longing. Possessing this woman's body was pleasurable enough, but how could he ever possibly know her mind? What made the real Meg Larsen tick? She was a complex woman.

He'd never met any woman quite like her. She was strong, yet vulnerable. Serious, yet funny. Loving, yet hard at times. Forthright, yet he suspected she hid a lot from him.

For that matter, he hid a lot from her. In his case, however, it was his job.

He was exhausted but in a pleasant, drained, happy way. They'd talked, made love, talked some more. Had the most incredible sex . . . passionate, hungry, no-holds-barred.

They'd said they loved each other. But was this really love? If not, it was a good facsimile. Good enough for him.

She squirmed, her ass digging into his crotch. He was ready to go at it again, but they had to get the talking over with first. Things were still unclear.

"Meg . . . baby . . . I need to ask you . . ." He felt her body tense up. "The next six months or maybe longer . . . well, I'll be in California on an undercover assignment."

"You're not going to Egypt?" she teased. "Darn. I was hoping to go undercover with you, help you spy on terrorists. Take in the pyramids while I'm at it."

He grinned. Meg had a way of making light of serious work so that even he had to see the irony in it.

"Wish it were that simple or that easy. Nope, the terrorists are now in-country. Never have to go far to find them. Anyway, I might be able to fly back once a month, maybe more often."

She rolled over onto her back and gazed at him. "Okay, Jakey boy, here's where it gets awkward. I didn't get a chance to tell you last night since we were so preoccupied." He kissed away her chiding smile. "Don't distract me now, I've got important news." Her hesitation threw him into a small panic.

"You're pregnant?"

Her blue eyes grew big. "Oh hell no. I told you before, back in Ireland, I've been on the pill for years." She stared at him and narrowed her eyes. "You trying to tell me something?"

Jake felt a twinge of disappointment and braced himself for bad news. "No. Go on, tell me your important news. Does it have to do with your teaching job?"

She smiled. "Well, yes. I'm taking a sabbatical, my first ever. A year off with no pay, but Gran left me enough money to keep everything going. The house is paid off, and I've got some savings, too. Anyway, I've decided to take German classes, get a minor in German so I can teach it. French is still popular but not as much as Spanish and German. Around here, there's a big German-American community. Speaking the language would come in handy."

Her words came rushing out, trickling to a stop with another big smile of hers. "So, whaddya think?"

"So great. Go back to school."

Her smile faded. "But that's it. This place is a mausoleum. I need to get away." When he said nothing, she scowled at him. "Like get away to California. I can take German classes there."

Jake's thoughts raced ahead. Having her close to him over the next several months would be great, fantastic, out-of-this world. But—and this was a huge *but*—what if the Bureau found out, which they would? What if she interfered somehow with his undercover role?

"Well, Jake Bernstein, don't look so disappointed. Uncle John invited me to come and stay with him and his family. In San Diego. I'm going to say yes. I've already applied to UC San Diego for those German classes." She turned her back to him. "Don't worry, Jake. Whatever you're doing in California, I won't bother you."

Her words relieved him. Good, San Diego was far enough away from Silicon Valley that she wouldn't get caught in the crosshairs . . . if it turned out he uncovered a sleeper jihadist cell and the assholes made him somehow. He leaned over her cold shoulder and kissed away her hurt.

"Sounds great, Meg, really. We'll be able to get together more often. Remember I promised you a real courtship? I'll make that happen."

Meg turned back to him, a warm smile creasing her lovely face. Her sapphire-blue eyes sparkled. God, she was beautiful.

"You mean that? You're not joking?"

"Damned straight. I promised you." Then he showed her how serious he was.

Chapter Three

The gallery of family photos captured Jake's attention. He paused to look at each one, cautiously, for he had two mugs of hot coffee in his hands. The long upstairs hallway showcased the Snider family's milestones. Birthdays, proms, her Uncle John's Little League trophies, Jack's AYSO soccer trophies, weddings, and graduations. At one end, the only photo from World War II bore the wedding portrait of Army Air Corps Airman John Snider and a very pretty, sleek blonde, Mary McCoy Snider, nee Claire Hillenbrand. Very successful Nazi mole. The other photos of the Sniders highlighted informal family gatherings.

Who would've thought . . .

One long row tracked Meg's life from pretty toddler in pink through confident college graduate. Jake studied these in particular, smiling all the while. The beautiful, little blonde girl had grown into a beautiful, confident woman. Other than the estrangement from her mother and the deaths of her grandparents, who'd raised her since the age of two, Meg appeared to have lived a princess's life, never lacking for anything.

"In case you think I was raised a spoiled brat," Meg began, leaning against the door jamb of her bedroom, "I wasn't. Gran and Gramps were very strict. Jack and I had chores. In high school, we had to work part-time or do community service. We bought our own used cars, paid for our own car insurance. And we worked while we were in college, too."

She approached, the end of her long ponytail wet. She

smelled of scented soap, citrus, and lavender. The short silky kimono she wore barely skimmed her slim, perfect thighs. Grinning, she inhaled the coffee he handed her.

"They loved us dearly, but they were unabashed, old-fashioned taskmasters. Y'know, the World War II generation was like that. They had it tough during the Depression, and then the war that had been fought on two fronts. They were very grateful to have survived, so they passed on strong work ethics and high standards. And they always quoted the Bible. To whom much is given, from them much is expected. That one." Her free hand flew to her mouth. "Oh, that's right. You might not've heard that one, being Jewish."

"My mother's Catholic-Irish, Meg. And yes, I've heard it before. There's a Hebrew saying that's similar. Jesus was a Jew, so where do you think that saying came from?"

They grinned at each other. She reached over and stroked his bare arm, enticing him back to her bedroom. "Well, I just meant they taught Jack and me not to be lazy."

Jake wondered about that. Was the grandmother's life after the war supposed to be her atonement for the atrocities she committed during it? That appeared to be the case, even though he knew she didn't regret what she had done and believed herself to be in the right. All the more reason why he was relieved that Meg's grandmother never went to trial. As a Jew, he knew how important atonement was.

Jake sipped his coffee, his interest in the Snider family wall flagging as soon as he spied Meg's creamy thighs. He let her lead him back to her room. Her mixture of scents preceded him like a fresh spring breeze.

A siren call. And I'm so there.

"Would you like to see my grandmother's room?" Meg flicked her dark blue eyes over his bare chest.

The intelligence analyst in him was tempted to take her up on her offer but he sensed she was testing him. Was he there as an agent or a man?

He shook his head. Their past—all two weeks' worth followed by two months of silence—was no longer his concern. If he wanted a future with this woman, he needed to show her he wanted to move forward with her. When she sat on a settee in front of the bedroom window, he joined her. They sat for a moment, silently sipping their coffee. He'd made his black, hers with a hearty dose of hazelnut-flavored creamer. Just as she'd requested.

"I'll be down to San Diego every weekend," he said. "Or as many weekends as I can manage." He gazed at her face, devoid of makeup. Her sleepy-eyed expression was sexy as hell. "If you're free . . ."

"Down? You mean, you'll be up in northern California? On an undercover assignment?"

"Yeah, somewhere in Nor Cal. All I can say is, I'll be down to see you every weekend if I can get away. I'll fly down and rent a car. The very devil couldn't keep me away."

Her smile dissolved into a frown. "Will there be women involved in this undercover assignment?" When he stared, she went on. "You said yourself you were sent to investigate my grandmother because the Bureau thought you had a knack for . . . how did you put it? Drawing out women. Was that a euphemism for seducing them?"

He looked down at the mug in his hands, grabbed at random from a kitchen shelf. It was hand-painted and signed by the child Meg once was. She was no longer a child. She was a damn, smart woman.

No more lies. Not if he could help it.

"More often the promise of seduction than the real thing. With you . . . well, that was unplanned and unauthorized. Not supposed to happen. If things hadn't turned out"—he saw a flicker of pain cross her face—"the way they did, I might've been fired. My job—my career with the FBI is important to me. What happened to you and me, Meg, wasn't part of the plan."

She touched his forearm. "I know. I don't resent you for what happened. What you did for us, Gran and me — well, I've accepted the way it all turned out. Only Uncle John and I know the truth. What Gran did during the war."

"Your mother? Do you think she knows?"

Meg's lovely face clouded over. "If she does, she's not saying. I think a long time ago she swore to keep Grandma's secret. That might've been what caused Mom's rebellion."

Eager to change the subject, he leaned over and nuzzled her temple. He detected lavender in her hair.

"So, Meg, are weekends good enough for you? I swear, you'll have my total attention two days a week."

She kissed his mouth, her coral-polished fingernails raking over one side of his beard. Her eyes probed him.

"Will you be in danger?"

"I doubt it. And there won't be any women involved, just crazy-ass men."

She actually smiled at that. Jake thought Meg was more relieved by the absence of women than the absence of danger from those crazy-ass men. Which was a lie. Danger came with any undercover assignment.

Good. She's jealous.

Another kiss. More raking and ruffling of his beard. He could tell the facial hair bothered her. Or maybe the whole Middle Eastern look made her uneasy. Good thing the beard wasn't a deal breaker. Some women liked them. Meg wasn't one of them.

"Jake," she began, her voice softening. "We don't know each other very well."

His gut tightened. Was this a brush-off? Or a back- off?

"Yeah, I know. Doesn't change how I feel about you."

"Same here." A small pause. "Here's the thing. I can't fly to California with you today. Too many things to do, gardener to call, neighbors to notify, some friends to call. But I can be ready to leave in twenty-four hours. *If* you're willing to drive with me out to California. I need my car out there."

Inwardly, Jake sighed with relief. "What — three days and nights together in a car? Think you can stand me that long?" A thought struck him. "What kind of car you drive?"

She shot him a puzzled look. "A Dodge Durango SUV. It's in the garage. Why?"

He snorted. "Figured you for a BMW convertible."

She pretended to punch his shoulder, let her hand linger there, warming his skin. "I'm Texas-born-and-raised, so don't mess with me."

"Three days of driving . . ."

"We can talk, share stuff about our lives."

"That should be a barrel of laughs," he said drily. "And nights?" His mind turned over the possibilities.

"Motels. I've got a Best Western card." She mirrored his teasing, lascivious look with one of her own, arched eyebrows and all. "King-size bed."

"How can I refuse?" He put down their mugs and reached for her.

Four days later, after Meg dropped him off at a San Diego rental car agency, Jake found himself doing barbecue duty in his parents' backyard in Torrance.

His brothers, Gabriel and David, along with their wives and kids, had arrived at noon that day. They'd spent the past five hours catching up on family news, hugs, and jokes.

Pop and the guys swapped football stats and career statuses. Gabe, three years younger than Jake's thirty-two years, was a biotech engineer for Amgen, one of the country's largest pharmaceutical corporations. David, a criminal defense attorney, worked with his wife in a big L.A. law firm. His father still taught history at USC and his mother's private art students kept her as busy as she wanted to be.

Grandpa Nate had died three years before from a massive coronary while having lunch with former colleagues from his Hollywood days. A year later, they lost Oma Bernstein. Two days a week, Jake's mother, Anna Lewis Bernstein, volunteered at the nursing home where Oma had spent her last few years lost in the mental fog of Alzheimer's. The painting lessons Anna taught the patients there were her way of giving thanks for the excellent care her mother-in-law had received at the nursing home.

Now his mother, still attractive and vivacious at sixty, sneaked up behind him and wrapped her arms around his waist.

"Tell me the real reason you showed up four days late. No lies, Jakey. There's something different about you. A kind of . . . glow." His mother's warm laugh filled him with undiluted joy. "Omigod, you're pregnant!"

He barked a short laugh. "Yeah, Mom, nice try. I just met a woman."

"Of course you did. You always do."

"No, this one's special. More than special."

"Not another Navy officer?"

Jake winced. His mother had never liked Barbara, his ex-wife. He'd married her while in the Navy, a short, two-year marriage doomed from the start. One of his biggest mistakes in life. Though there hadn't been many of those, thank God.

"Nope. Meg's a high school foreign language teacher from Texas. She's living in San Diego this year, studying German at UCSD. I'll be undercover in the San Francisco Bay Area, so I'll be down to see her as often as I can."

His mother slipped around to his side, her arm hugging his back. He noted the white roots at her part, the rest of her auburn hair styled curly and close to her head. She patted his back.

"When you feel the time is right, bring her over."

He nodded as he turned over a row of hamburger patties. It was way too early to push family on Meg. Or . . . maybe not.

"So you've found a normal girl . . . with a normal life."

He thought of Meg's Nazi-spy grandmother. "Normal is relative, Mom." He knew his mother worried about him when he went undercover, although not as much as when he'd served on SEAL Team Three and had been deployed abroad.

Anna sighed. "What is she like?"

Jake had to chuckle as he glanced at his father, playing with one of his little granddaughters on the patio swing. "Pop would call her a *shiksa* goddess." He brushed a liberal slathering of Pop's homemade BBQ sauce on the patties. "Tall, slim blonde. Smart, funny. Like me, she likes to run to stay in shape. Her name's Meg Larsen."

"How did you meet?"

Jake waved smoke away. "On a case. I investigated her grandmother."

His mother sighed heavily and frowned. "But she liked you despite that?"

"The grandmother was a former Nazi spy, guilty of war crimes, and MI-5 was about to charge her. She died before they could arrest her."

Anna groaned. "And this Meg Larsen still likes you?"

"Yeah. Go figure."

Yeah, Bernstein, you're one lucky dog.

His mother patted his hairy jaw and shook her head.

"Ah, my little warrior. So now you're going undercover to catch some Muslim terrorist. Yes, why else would you be looking like that?"

Jake smiled. *No fooling anyone.* "Somebody's gotta do it, Mom."

"Oh, Jakey, don't you long for a normal life? Maybe this

Meg wants a normal life with a man who has a . . . regular job."

He considered the idea for a moment. "Yeah, she probably does."

His thoughts flashed back to their first night on the road. Three days and nights traveling with Meg had proven how compatible they were. Somewhere in western New Mexico, she was undressing for bed, and he was curious about the white lace—bandeau, she'd called it—a bra-type thing she wore under her V-neck tee. He slipped it off her, up and over her raised arms, exposing her breasts. Playfully, she used the thing to encircle her hair as a kind of decorative hair band. The memory—one of many—flooded him with warmth. It would be almost two weeks before he saw her again.

His chest tightened. What if he lost her?

"Maybe I'm not cut out for normal," he told his mother. "Maybe I'll never be." Maybe four years with the SEALs had wrung it out of him.

In silent reply, his mother leaned her head on his shoulder as he towered over her. Her expression of sympathy evoked from him a rare pang of self-pity. He shook it off.

Not a good way to start an undercover assignment. With his free hand, he hugged his mother to his side, leaned over and kissed her forehead.

"Don't worry, Mom. I might make it to normal someday. Right now, normal can wait. Gotta scare up some badasses."

His mother sighed heavily but kissed him back.

"The only thing harder than being a soldier, I think," she muttered against his shoulder, "is loving one."

Chapter Four

Silicon Valley, Jake read from his briefing report, consisted of two counties. Santa Clara and San Mateo Counties had some of the highest concentrations of wealth in the country, and the share of wealthy households was growing, according to the latest census. Nearly fourteen percent of all households earned more than $200,000 a year, just below the sixteen percent of households in Manhattan who enjoyed such affluence. In Santa Clara County, the figure was almost thirty percent of households.

Wingtips, Hermes ties, and Lamborghinis were frowned upon, however, in Silicon Valley. Cycling, kiteboarding, and jeans and tees were preferred. Ostentation was rare among the high-tech nouveau tech-riche. The Venture Capital of the country, the valley fostered entrepreneurs the way Idaho grew potatoes. Today's young computer genius, tomorrow's billionaire. Young parvenus sprang up like dandelions.

He put down his report and drove into the Federal Building's underground garage in San Jose, pausing once to flash his FBI badge and give his name to the stranger on security detail. It dawned on him that two weeks ago, he was saying goodbye to Manny in D.C. and meeting with the counterterrorism task force.

A lot had happened in those two weeks.

Meg.

There was no time to dwell on her, their relationship, and where it was heading. Or whether or not it was going anywhere. Maybe Meg would be better off landing some young billionaire, hot off a new high-tech IPO. Certainly better off than with a feeb who made less than a low six-figure income and was now about to play the role of a disgruntled Muslim-American biotech engineer. Screw that. He'd rather stick an ice pick through his heart than give her up.

The FBI's San Jose field office was high in the Fed Building on Second Street. Its Special Agent in Charge, Frank Rodriguez, met him as the elevator doors pinged open. They'd been in contact for over a week, both by the Bureau's secure inter-office email system and by phone.

A tall, clean-shaven Hispanic in his early fifties, SAIC Rodriguez smiled, introduced himself, and shook Jake's hand. The man was stocky but muscular, looked like ex-military. His black hair was cropped short, and he had an easy-going manner about him.

"Man, if you don't look the part, Agent Bernstein. I expected a scruffier-looking dude, however. Y'know, down on his luck."

Rodriguez led him past the bullpen of cubicles where male and female agents glanced up from their computers and nodded perfunctory, curious greetings. An uneasy feeling wormed through Jake's insides. This was a mistake. He was too exposed. They should've met in a private location.

If he'd been thinking straight — instead of riding a euphoric cloud after his long visit with Meg — he would've insisted on it.

In one cubicle, a young male agent sat with a gray-haired man of about sixty who wore a ragged salt-and-pepper beard. Arabic school at Quantico kicked in. The hallmark of Salafists — the ultraconservative Islamists once aligned with Egypt's Muslim Brotherhood but even more radical and militant — was their long, ragged beards. The Salafists strongly supported the return of Shar'ia Law to Egypt and elsewhere in the Muslim world and appeared willing to do whatever was necessary to achieve it.

Both men looked up, the older man leveling black eyes on Jake, as if taking his measure. His gaze was speculative. Rodriguez paused at the open cubicle. "This is Fariq Al-Nasreen, our Arabic translator and private consultant on all Islamic community matters. Fariq keeps us informed on Al Jazeera as well, and radical Islamic news from abroad and within the U.S. We depend on him to sort things out for us."

Jake's internal alarms rang loud in his head as he realized what Rodriguez was about to do.

"This is Ag—"Rodriguez began, turning to Jake.

"*Salaam alaikum,*" Jake interrupted, placing his hand over his heart. A slight bow of his head followed.

Fariq's eyes snapped open as he stood and did the same. "*Alaikum salaam.*" A heartbeat later, they shook hands.

"I'm Samir Maalouf." Jake ignored the slightly surprised looks of Rodriguez and the young agent working with Fariq. Fortunately, they kept silent as Jake had submerged into cover and switched to Arabic. "I'm here to fill out some paperwork for a security clearance. I've just been hired at An-Vax in Hayward and my boss there told me to come here for this security clearance."

"*Habibi,*" — friend — "what is it you do for An-Vax?"

"I'm a microbiologist," Jake replied. "I was just hired by An-Vax. We're making vaccines against anthrax for the military."

An-Vax was a cutting-edge pharmaceutical on the East Bay, just north of San Jose and Milpitas. Jake's brother, Gabriel, had once worked there and could be relied upon for his expertise. This unique cover had been approved by the CTC task force chiefs in D.C. and his own boss, ADD Terry Thompson.

"Ah, very good," Fariq said in Arabic. "An educated Muslim brother."

"*Nam. Shokran.*" *Yes, thank you.* Jake was groveling a bit to his elder, knowing this show of excessive respect was expected. From what he could tell, Arabic was the man's first language. He spoke it with an accent that Jake wracked his brain to place. Arabic school at Quantico had brought in speakers from various Middle East countries. One country's Arabic was crisp, its vowels pronounced. Like British English to American English.

"Egyptian born?" Jake asked Fariq.

The man's bushy gray eyebrows arched in surprise. "For an American, that is an astute guess. How did you know?"

"My Lebanese-born father had a very close Egyptian friend. He spoke Arabic like you." Jake knew he was going out on a limb but decided to cultivate the man's confidence.

"Ah, so that is how you learned my mother tongue?"

"*Nam.* My father insisted. He was very traditional. My mother's Italian-American, but Father ruled."

Fariq beamed. "As it should be, wouldn't you say?" He waited for Jake's reply.

"Of course. As it should be. As the holy Qur'an states in chapter four, verse thirty-four, women are inferior to men and must be ruled by them. By the way, I'm looking for an *umma*"—a community of believers—"and would appreciate your recommendation for a local mosque."

"Ah, yes, *habibi.* I see you are devout, so I would advise you to visit the Cordoba mosque in San Miguel. Sheikh Hajizi recites the Surat at Friday Fajr." The Friday prayer meeting and recitation of the Qur'an verses was a requirement for devout Muslims.

"*Shokran.*" Jake looked at Rodriguez, smiled and switched back to English. "Sorry, just introducing ourselves. Muslim men like knowing each other's backgrounds."

"I see." Rodriguez gave Jake a look that reinforced his *I see.* The SAIC had almost made a colossal blunder. Exposing an undercover agent's real identity on his first day in the field would have gotten the man demoted and would have sent Jake back to D.C. Time and money wasted.

A round of *ma-a-salaam* followed between Fariq and *Samir* and then Jake headed with Rodriquez to his office. With the door closed, Jake wheeled on the man. His slow burn had him hissing through clenched teeth.

"Man, that was close! You almost broke my cover."

The SAIC cast his eyes on the floor, on the opposite wall, then back up to meet Jake's.

"Sorry, man. Stupid, careless . . ." His pride resurfaced. "But hey, no harm, no foul. You stepped in and covered yourself. Your Arabic sounds pretty darn good. Besides, Fariq's a good man. We had his translation work double-checked by an Arabic speaking agent in San Francisco the first six months on the job. We vetted him thoroughly."

Don't trust. Verify. The motto of today's FBI, anyway. After 9/11, the Bureau had finally awakened and wised up. Still, Jake wasn't about to concede ground. A Muslim cleric, a well-respected *imam* at one of the New Jersey mosques — well vetted, also — had the FBI buffaloed. While living off welfare and food stamps for him, his wives, and a household full of children, he preached hatred against America for years. He turned out to be the mastermind and recruiter for the first World Trade Center bombing in 1992.

Don't trust. Verify. And don't trust one damned Muslim.

"From now on, send copies of his translations to me. I'll send them on to D.C. if I can't do them justice. Let's triple-check his work, okay? It may be nothing, but this guy was feeling me out. In a harmless way, maybe, and I encouraged it, but I always listen to my guts."

Rodriguez nodded solemnly and indicated they should sit. "Coffee?"

Jake shook his head. His mind was still buzzing from the sudden rise of adrenaline. He'd sensed something about this

Fariq Al-Nasreen, but he wasn't sure what it was.

"I'm officially deep undercover as of today, Special Agent Rodriguez. No one else here must know me. You're to be my only contact. Not even that agent out there must know my true ID. As far as the whole bunch out there is concerned, I'm just a new Silicon Valley employee looking for security clearance."

Rodriguez looked a little nervous, as if he'd just realized that his career might be on the line if he screwed up.

"Understood. I'm here to supply you with anything you need, liaise with local law enforcement . . . when and if necessary. How will I contact you? Email?"

Jake shot him a wry grin. "There are more hackers in this valley than pancakes at IHOP. No, we'll do it Al-Qaeda style. Person to person. Once a week."

That evoked a frown from Rodriguez.

"A private venue of your choosing. You know the area."

A moment of deeper frowns passed while Rodriguez sipped from his mug of coffee. "My brother-in-law owns a bar —"

"I'm a devout Muslim who doesn't drink," Jake reminded the man. Only in San Diego would he let down his guard.

"Have you got a place to live?" the SAIC asked.

"An apartment in San Miguel. Across the street is a park called Central Park. There's a World War II memorial there, all in red brick."

Rodriguez blinked and nodded. "My great- grandfather's name is there, etched on one of the bricks." He shook his head in wonder. "I know that neighborhood very well, used to live around there. Okay, well, I work late on Wednesdays. I'll swing by there on my way home. Nine o'clock? The memorial?"

Jake stood, his heart rate having returned to normal. Based on the agent's wedding band and the framed photos on his desk, Rodriguez was a family man, eager to protect his job and government pension. Jake had no choice but to trust the man to be careful. Perhaps a mutual trust would develop between them as time went on. The guy was no slouch or he wouldn't have made it this far up the ranks.

"Sounds good. I'll do a nightly run in the park and time it about then."

Rodriguez stood also and extended his hand. Jake shook it.

"Hope you find what you're looking for." The SAIC smiled.

"We'll see. In a way, I hope there's nothing there to find," quipped Jake, taking his leave.

Walking back to the elevator, he passed the translator's cubicle. Fariq and the communications specialist were hunched over two computer monitors, taking notes. The Al Jazeera English website was streaming a video clip, announcing the latest suicide bombing in Afghanistan. Five American soldiers and four Afghans had been killed. Compliments of the Taliban's *mujahadeen*.

Will it never end?

Jake didn't stop but kept moving to the elevators. A second later, the hair on the back of his neck bristled. Like the hackles on a dog that got a whiff of danger.

Fariq Al-Nasreen. A Salafist? Or Muslim Brotherhood? Jake wondered why the man hadn't recommended the mosque in San Jose. Or why not the other handful of mosques between San Jose and San Francisco? He decided to run his name and description on several watch lists—NSA, State, INS, DOD, CIA, Interpol. See if anything shook out.

Paranoid? Maybe. But Jake had learned something from his years with the SEALs. Paranoia kept you alive.

And staying alive was something he was determined to do.

CHAPTER FIVE

October Third
Fort Worth, Texas

The Masjid Cordoba Center in Fort Worth was one of the largest mosques in Texas. The Friday Fajr prayer meeting drew about two hundred to its cavernous interior. Calligraphy of Qur'anic verses adorned the bare stuccoed walls, the only decoration within the mosque.

With great pleasure, Amad led the Fajr Prayer with a lengthy recitation. His deep baritone resonated as he stood on the pulpit and recited the *Surat Al Sajdah*, followed by the *Surah Al Insar*. With precision and eloquence, he intoned the ancient Arabic verses from the Qur'an, pausing at every stanza to scan the assembly of *ikhwan* — brothers of Islam. The men stood on the carpeted floor, their prayer rugs at their feet. The time for bowing and chanting would soon begin.

As visiting Qur'anic scholar, Amad could visit American mosques and speak with groups of Muslim men. His and Ali's British passports gave them easy entries to visitor visas, enabling them to travel at will. What saved time and made their fundraising and recruiting possible was identifying beforehand the true believers, which the mosque's *imam* was happy to do. Whether out of religious zeal, tacit support for *jihad*, or simple naivete, the imam's motives were not relevant. After such identification, these true believers would be honored by private seminars held by mullah Amad and his assistant, Ali.

Of course, to throw off the vigilance of the American intelligence agencies, Amad had to visit other less important mosques as well in smaller communities. Most *ummas* — Islamic communities — gave money, or at least pledged funds to organizations such as the Fund for Palestinian Orphans, a Hezbollah front, or FAIR, the Foundation for American Islamic Relations, in which a portion of the money found its circuitous way to Al-Qaeda on the Arabian Peninsula. Or UNRWA, a Hamas front. Amad suspected that a majority of the mosque worshippers had no idea that their hard-earned money was diverted to another cause. Or, if they did know, they appeared not to care.

No matter. As long as the steady flow of dollars continued, his efforts in fundraising would offset the steady flow of American currency to the Zionists, an accomplishment he was enormously proud of.

Ali, his much younger and beefier recruiter, was Pakistani-born, like Amad. Their parents had immigrated to Great Britain as healthcare workers, finding jobs in the British national healthcare system. Though his father had wanted Amad to become a doctor, he'd chosen a different path, the holy path of Allah's Messenger. As a practicing *imam* in the tough working-class Muslim neighborhood of Manchester, Ali had become his first recruit ten years before. They'd been busy ever since, traveling the world and exhorting followers to follow in their footsteps. Recruiting martyrs for *jihad*, or holy war.

An outgoing, affable man, Ali usually found the most compliant and eager holy warriors in *madrassas* and in countries occupied by the enemy, American armies of death.

Posing as his assistant during this visit to the United States, Ali found his new assignment in America much more challenging. Most of the Muslims they encountered were immigrants, their backgrounds and philosophies so diverse—Shias and Sunnis, secular and religious fanatics all mixed together—that these immigrants were unpredictable. However, Ali had honed his skills to a fine art.

Three hours later, in the anteroom to Sheikh Mehdi's office, Amad and Ali sat together on a couch and faced four young men on an opposite couch. Ali had met the teenagers secretly for several weeks, his time spent listening to their collective troubles and shaping their malleable young minds toward adopting a *jihadi* solution to their unhappiness. He'd stressed the verses in the Qur'an that promised a paradise of virgins and rivers of milk and honey for the most devout of Muhammed's warriors. They'd listened, Ali reported, the zeal glowing in their faces.

At Ali's prompt, the four teenagers placed hands over their hearts, their dark eyes shining with passion. Each one spoke the pledge of total obedience and in turn Ali kissed each one's cheeks. Amad, touching the tops of their heads, blessed each one as he cited an ancient Arabic blessing of praise for their loyalty to the Prophet. None of the boys could understand the ancient language, just as few if any of the two-hundred or so men that evening could understand the Qur'anic verses Amad had recited. Even Sheikh Mehdi's mastery of the Qur'an was spotty. Interestingly but not surprisingly, the sheikh had declined to come to this meeting.

Plausible deniability, eh, Amad thought disdainfully. What the Americans called a *don't ask, don't tell* philosophy. Such scared little mice, these American Muslims.

No matter.

"The Americans love Pepsi-Cola and swimming pools, but we love death," crowed Ali, his still round, youthful cheeks inspiring trust. The four boys' eyes grew large. "To quote Qur'an chapter fourteen, verse three — *Those who love the life of this world more than the hereafter, who hinder men from the path of Allah and seek therein something crooked, they are astray by a long distance.* So you see, my little brothers, when you slay the enemy, you attain the honor of martyrdom. I quote again — *Those who slay and are slain for Allah, for theirs in return is the garden of Paradise* . . . Qur'an chapter nine, verse one-hundred-eleven."

Amad broke in to intone further, *"Know that Paradise is under the shades of swords* — meaning jihad, my young brothers — *And say not of those who are slain in the way of Allah, that they are dead. Nay, they are living, though ye perceive it not.* Qur'an chapter two, verse one-hundred-fifty-four."

The leader of the boys, the tallest and most courageous of the four, spoke up. "Blowing myself up is the only chance I've got to have sex with seventy-two virgins in the Garden of Paradise? And my parents will bless me and love me more if I become a holy martyr?"

Both Ali and Amad nodded. The boy looked at his friends. "We have no life here. Let's do it. Let's become jihadis."

Another boy smiled. "Allah's holy war. We'll be holy warriors."

"Yes!" Ali exclaimed, beaming, "Allah's holy warriors! Who will enter the Garden of Paradise and be greeted by beautiful virgins."

The other two remained silent but, stared down by the first two, finally agreed.

Amad gave a silent prayer. To control a man's mind and behavior — that held the potential for a global revolution. Albeit a gradual one, Amad had to concede to himself. True devotees had no choice but to win over one man at a time, one madrassa and mosque at a time, one country at a time.

The Prophet Muhammed's triple choice — a command that he issued to every realm he conquered — was *Convert, subjugate or kill.* "Embrace Islam and you will be safe," Muhammed had warned them all. The rulers of the seventh-century Byzantium Empire did not, and they fell like dominoes to the Caliph, Umar. And so did half of Europe. In time, many converted to avoid subjugation or beheading.

"Allah be praised!" He gave each young man his most sincere and beatific smile.

The four teenagers all nodded solemnly, their eyes big with wonder and fear.

Ali stood and so did the boys. He gave the leader of the foursome a flash drive. "You will keep this in a secret place. No one must see this but you four young men." They looked impressed to be called young men. He then handed the boy a prepaid untraceable cell phone. "This is for you only, Khalid. I shall call you on November first and give you further instructions. After tonight, you cannot change your mind or the Prophet and Allah Himself will hold you in the same contempt as a filthy apostate. And you know the punishment for apostates."

Death by beheading. The same as the punishment for infidels who refused to convert or be subjugated. Such had it been since the days of Muhammed himself and during the long ruling Caliphate of Europe.

The boy pocketed the cell phone and flash drive in his jeans as he glanced at the others. His friends stared and appeared to admire his courage and devotion. More prayers followed, then Ali and Amad hugged them and kissed their cheeks.

After the four teenagers left the room, Amad turned to Ali and shook his head. In hushed tones, they spoke the Arabic dialect of Peshawar, their home province.

"Truly, my brother, is this the best we can do? They shall wet their pants in fear of your call."

Ali scowled. "I did the best I could. These boys are angry and miserable. They say they hate this country, they hate Americans. Their peers call them terrorists and bully them. Their parents are so busy working, they have no time for them. They carry the misery of orphans and they want revenge."

Revenge.

Amad's thoughts harked to his brother. His heart stabbed at the memory. Mostafa was the most brilliant among his siblings, graduated at the top of his class in nuclear science. He'd no sooner begun work at the Iranian nuclear facility at Qum than two assassins on a motorcycle drove up beside his car and attached a magnetic bomb to the driver's door. The explosion blew Mostafa's head off his body. The bomb was the hallmark of Mossad, the spy agency of the Zionist regime. Such state-sponsored terrorism was only possible through the support of the Americans. His face grew hot at the thought and he had to mop the sweat off his brow with his sleeve.

"If the fires of Allah's Holy War do not inspire them, the fire of revenge will," Amad hissed, studying the calendar on the wall.

Will there be enough time to arrange it all? Yes, Inshallah. God willing.

The other three teams of recruiters and facilitators were having better luck than he and Ali. If not, they would have to import several groups or locate the sleeper cells sent over years before. They needed men, not boys. America had indulged them, made them soft. He'd already received word from the others. Detroit, Michigan, New York City, New York, Miami, Florida. Plans were progressing according to the timetable set up by Amad and the other mullahs at their last strategy meeting in London.

"So we proceed to California as planned?" Ali asked.

"Yes." Amad's fist socked the palm of his other hand. "We shall hit the technology heart of the Great Satan. The Cordoba mosque has approved our visit and arranged lodging for us. We'll come back as often as necessary in order to secure what we need. Before we leave tomorrow, I shall contact the Houston cell and have them move up here. They can continue to recruit followers while we're in California. We have less than two months to arrange everything."

Ali's stubbled chin lifted with the pride of such a challenge. "Very good. So, the date has not changed?"

"No, we shall adhere to the timetable. Allah be praised, we

shall hit the heart of the Americans on one of their happiest days."

The two men exchanged nods and smiles.

CHAPTER SIX

Silicon Valley
October Tenth

Suburban tedium would have described the next two weeks. In Jake's mind, this was a necessary component of undercover work, like *in country* military deployment. Long periods of boredom punctuated by minutes or hours of terror. In this case, relieved by his daily calls to Meg on a burner phone.

Nearly every day he'd driven in his long-term rental, a two-year-old Ford Explorer, to An-Vax in Hayward. Standard counter-surveillance impelled him to vary his route. One day he took the most direct route, driving the Bayshore Freeway east to the junction of Eight-eighty, then north to Hayward. The next day, he followed the Bayshore west to the Dumbarton Bridge, then crossed the southern tip of the San Francisco Bay to the eastern side to head north up Eight-eighty to the An-Vax exit.

The An-Vax facility was housed in a square four-story steel and black-glass building with a large inner enclosed courtyard. One mile from Jake's freeway exit, he had no trouble finding the place.

A tanned, sandy-haired man about his age greeted him in the lobby after buzzing him inside the front entrance. Security was intense. CTC cameras perched everywhere. In the tile-floored lobby alone, Jake counted five well-armed security guards, one stationed inside every door.

His sandy-haired host, Todd Walinski, appeared nearer to

forty at closer inspection. A workout buff, his biceps rivaled Jake's. Within five minutes, Jake learned the guy's brain outstripped even his brawn. Todd had been appointed as Jake's *cover* supervisor and would maintain the agent's cover if anyone came or called to inquire. For now, and for appearance's sake, Todd treated Jake like a new hire in the Validation Department of An-Vax. Todd swiped his card key under a scanner before they rode the elevator to the second floor.

"This is QC, Quality Control, and VR, Validation Reporting. GXP, or Good Compliance of our lab and manufacturing process. Our reports are classified, highly scientific data collections ultimately meant for the FDA's and DOD's scrutiny, but they provide us quality, validation, and production checks. They cover lab protocol, analysis and testing, Q and V of every aspect of the manufacturing process."

Todd waved him over to a bank of open cubes, leading him inside one of them. Gray fabric covered the walls, and the floor was gray tiled. Dull and bland, Jake decided.

"Fairly nondescript but people decorate and personalize their own cubicles. You can do that, too"—he checked the small notebook that he took out of his sports jacket pocket— "so go for it, do what you like to the walls, your desk. Let's see, I'm supposed to call you Samir." He broke into a sly grin and lowered his voice. "Never done this before, helping an undercover FBI agent. Kinda exciting. Will it be dangerous? I mean, will someone try and break in and blow up our labs?"

"No, don't think that'll happen. Maybe nothing will come of this, but I needed a cover. Having bio-tech skills might be a lure for certain people. My brother, Gabriel Bernstein, used to work here." Thanks to Gabe, Jake had grown familiar with all the dizzying abbreviations.

Todd's grin stretched into a wide smile. "Oh yeah, Gabe. I was just hired when he was here. He helped train me in QC and VR before he moved on to Amgen in L.A. Tell him hi for me."

Jake nodded. He'd learned from his brother what QC and VR meant. Both steps were important in the biotech process before applying to the FDA, or Food and Drug Administration.

Todd resumed his orientation of the facilities. "If the others in QC or VR should ask, you've been hired on a part-time basis with flexible scheduling, so you don't have to sit here all day trying to look busy. If anyone calls, however, they'll channel the calls to me, your official supervisor, and I'll verify your full-time employment. We can also forward calls to the cell number you gave us."

Jake nodded and surveyed his cubicle. Typical office equipment cluttered the desk and adjacent countertop. Computers, fax machine, printer, inter-office telephone, FDA and company manuals a foot thick. On the floor around his cubicle, occasional signs of the Periodic Table of Elements brightened the gray walls in addition to graphics of atomic molecules, cellular biology, and the DNA double-helix. No mistaking that scientists worked here. But he suspected the real work took place in the labs upstairs.

A young woman in sweater and jeans walked by. She smiled and slapped palms with Todd. After giving Jake an appraising look, she kept walking.

"C'mon, the fun stuff's on the upper floors," said Todd. "Where the labs and production lines are."

Jake followed him, frowning. He knew the company made anthrax vaccine for the military and other government agencies, including the FBI, CIA, and NSA. There had been talk at HQ in D.C. that they'd all start taking the vaccine. Just in case.

"Won't I need to wear some kind of HazMat suit?"

Todd laughed as he swiped his card key before entering the elevator. "Don't worry, we're not letting you close enough. Can't risk it. You're not properly trained and this isn't Hollywood. You'll see."

Intrigued, Jake took the man's word for it. When they stepped onto the third-floor landing, a steel door barred their way. Through glass security windows, Jake could see a warren of lab rooms, all set off from each other by glass walls and steel doors. All visible but inaccessible. There were security scanners at every lab door. Unless you had Todd's card key, thumbprint, and retina, you weren't getting past that steel door.

"You need special BL-3 gowning to get beyond this point, Jake—uh, Samir. Booties, mask, gloves, the works. This is a Bio Safety Level Three facility lab. Level Four is one floor up. Only Heffa labs up there."

"What's that? Heffa?" Jake asked. He saw giant, stainless-steel tubes and what looked like large, silver-metal crock pots. From the ceiling hung huge ventilation pipes.

"Stands for High Efficiency Air, a kind of filtered air. The air quality is so high up there, at any given minute there are fewer than one-hundred particulates of bacteria per zero-point-five micron. Only hooded containers are used, and the gowning is double thick." Todd had lost Jake with the scientific verbiage but he continued listening, anyway. "Although the lab guys deal with dead anthrax bacteria, anyone can die from exposure to more than one-hundred micrometers of the dead stuff. That's how powerful and deadly that stuff is."

"Dead bacteria? It's still lethal?"

Todd nodded grimly. "Oh yeah. I could explain why but you'd need a microbiology degree to understand."

Holy shit. Jake unconsciously backed away. Instinctively, irrationally, he wanted to run as far from this place as humanly possible.

"Never mind, I believe you."

"Anthrax is one of the deadliest bacteria known to man," Todd stated matter-of-factly, "Which is why, Agent Bernstein, we can't let you go in."

Jake put up his hands, palms outward. "Hey, okay by me. Just say, if anyone calls, that I have full clearance to the labs."

"You're hunting for bioterrorists?"

Jake smiled. "Possibly." With relief, they re-entered the elevator.

"Al-Qaeda? Is that why—" Todd left his question unfinished as his eyes combed over Jake's dark beard.

Not fooling anyone. Jake rubbed his knuckles over his short, trimmed beard. Would a real *jihadist* in a sleeper cell even wear one? Probably not. They'd be told to blend in, not stand out. Look like anyone's ethnic minority.

The beard's gotta go. A heartbeat later, *No, I start out a devout Muslim and just a scientist.*

He said nothing as they rode down to the lobby. Todd extended his hand and they shook. Jake liked this no-nonsense scientist.

"Whatever you need, let me know," said the biotech engineer.

"Thanks, Todd. I have your card. And the card keys you gave me for the ground and second floors."

"I'm here Monday through Friday, eight to five. Whenever you feel like showing up, man, it's cool. HR has your cover name. They'll route any calls for you to me."

"Appreciate it." Jake turned to leave but thought of something else. The parking lot for employees was gated and located behind the building. The entire property, in fact, was surrounded by an electrified cyclone fence. "If I wanted to leave here and not be spotted by someone in the street out front, is there a back street entrance or exit?"

"Exit only, yeah. You go past the exit gate in back and right for a few blocks to the Eight-eighty on-ramp."

"Gotcha."

Even better.

A convenience which proved helpful when, on the

Tuesday of his second week, Jake noticed the dark green car one length behind his rental on the Eight-eighty freeway. It got off the ramp behind him about fifty yards and parked in the access street as Jake continued around to An-Vax's back parking lot.

No coincidence there.

By day three, he'd identified it as a Toyota Camry. The sedan trailed him from his apartment building in San Miguel to An-Vax in Hayward, a distance of about thirty miles. When he checked two hours later, it was gone. Having the back exit would prove useful if he was followed again. He could leave after an hour or two and exit out the back. Whoever was following him wouldn't know he'd left early.

Wednesday night, Jake shut off the TV in his sparsely furnished two-bedroom apartment. Restless and bored out of his skull, he slipped into sweatpants and running shoes. He grabbed his carabiner lock containing house and car keys and stuffed his burner cell phone into his pants pocket. No gun or badge. Those were hidden away, along with his secure laptop with encryption software and other gear, in a special container behind the apartment's refrigerator. If anyone tossed his place, they'd find an English version of the Qur'an, an Arabic-English dictionary, his prayer rug and beads, assorted photos of his Lebanese-American father, who used to live in Florida but was now dead. And photos of his divorced and remarried Italian-American mother in Tampa. Not much else. No girlfriends or best pals, Samir Maalouf was a loner.

The cool breeze woke him up and he pumped his legs faster. A memory of Meg running alongside of him surfaced. They'd run all over downtown Cardiff, Wales, each one throwing glances at the other, trying not to smile at the sheer pleasure of exercising their bodies. He'd been mesmerized by the sweat spots on her shirt and pants, the way her sweaty neck wet the tendrils pulled loose from her long blonde ponytail. Found himself oddly aroused by her expression of euphoria. It was then he knew he was hooked.

His panting subsided into an even breathing rhythm as he began his second lap around the block-long park. The halogen streetlamps were dimly lit but there was ample light to mark his way. Two other men shuffled around the grassy portion of the park, avoiding the full perimeter path that Jake had taken. With his thumb, he flicked on his watch light and checked the time. After his second lap, he stopped at the World War II memorial.

Frank Rodriguez sat on one of the benches encircling the round, ground-level area of etched bricks, each one bearing the name of a war veteran. In the center of the circle was a solar cell-fueled torchlight, lit now in the darkness. The SAIC wore a dark warmup suit and smoked a cigarette.

"I quit last year," he groused, staring into the night, "Damned if I didn't pick it up again."

Without preamble, Jake bent over another bench to retie his laces. While doing so, he brought Rodriguez up to speed regarding his cover job.

"I'm being followed. Dark green Toyota sedan." He gave Rodriguez the license plate number. "Followed me three times to An-Vax. Only three people know where I supposedly work. You, your communications specialist, and Fariq Al-Nasreen. I went to Fajr prayer meeting last Friday at the Cordoba mosque in San Miguel, came home right afterward. Fariq was at the mosque that night although I didn't speak to him or anyone else. Someone must've followed me after Fajr that night and found out where I live. Interesting development, wouldn't you say?"

The SAIC swore under his breath.

"Not my guy. Not Fariq. He drives a Cadillac SUV. Comes from money, owns apartment buildings, a couple of strip malls. Rich landlord."

"And he does translation work for the FBI?"

"Community service. He came to us with good referrals from the Chamber of Commerce." Rodriguez just shrugged, said nothing more but stood and ground out his cigarette in the dirt under a bush. After the man was gone, Jake went over and picked up the sealed yellow envelope he'd left behind.

Fariq's translation work.

Great.

What was there to gripe about? Hadn't he asked for it? At least now, he'd no longer be bored during the week. To stay abreast, he was reviewing the Arabic he'd learned at Quantico while driving to and from An-Vax, trying to look like a busy but single and lonely biotech scientist.

Jake slid the envelope under his T-shirt. Something to do until Friday Fajr. Then off to see Meg on Saturday.

Suddenly inspired, he whipped out his burner cell and punched in her number. The call went straight to voice mail.

It was nine PM, Wednesday. Where the hell was Meg?

Switching mindsets, he schooled his thoughts to the job at hand. The bait was set, and someone was interested. He'd keep doing what he was doing and see what happened. Maybe some crazy jihadi assholes would chomp on the bait.

His two lives. All the more reason to keep them separate. Keep Meg safe.

Keep himself from going wacko.

CHAPTER SEVEN

Amad watched silently and smiled with mutual deference as Fariq al-Nasreen, the current treasurer of the San Miguel Cordoba mosque, greeted him, the visiting imam from England, and his assistant, Ali, with such a display of humility and respect that even the mosque's imam looked surprised. The Cordoba cleric, Mahmoud Hijazi, excused himself and left his office to arrange for tea.

While the cleric was gone, Fariq invited Amad and Ali to sit. Comfortable upholstered wing chairs were grouped in a semi-circle facing a fireplace whose hearth roared with flaming logs.

"California, and yet it is so cold," Amad said pleasantly as he sat in the chair closest to the fire. His face and hands warmed instantly.

Fariq appeared nervous. Had this American *ikhran* heard the rumors on *Al-Shumukh*—-although no names were given on the online website of Al-Qaeda—of Amad's and Ali's exploits in Europe that summer? There had been allusions to the Al-Qaeda branch that would soon seek glorious martyrdom in the United States, but details, of course, were always omitted. Or was their brother, Fariq, just anxious to please? His obsequious behavior, while not unexpected, annoyed Amad. It seemed out of place for a rich Egyptian-American immigrant.

"A cold spell's coming through the Bay Area. There's talk of rain," said Fariq. "The eyes in the sky and those on the ground suspect a storm is about to hit. No one knows where or when."

Fariq's coded message was not lost on Amad, nor on Ali.

"Let's hope not. But, *habibi*, this is not news. This is the on-going state of affairs for those who carry the sword of Allah. I assume you have found quarters for us to stay in while we're here."

"Yes, of course," said Fariq. "I would have offered my house, but my son and his family have just moved back in during the upcoming year for graduate school. Your quarters at the rental house, I think you will find suitable. It has just become available, so we can move you from the hotel. The house has a garage for your rental car. Or for storage. You'll have more privacy there."

Fariq left unsaid what he probably assumed was unnecessary. Amad and Ali expected a shipment by truck in two or three weeks. Just in time for their preparations to begin.

Amad glanced back at the door to the kitchen area. Since they couldn't be certain that Imam Mahmoud Hijazi was not a confidential informant for local law enforcement, he and Ali had to be very careful and cautious.

"You, Fariq, my friend, came highly recommended. Have you found any prospects for the work that Ali and I require?"

"Two, perhaps, but I can't be sure. They work for me, but they may not help you. You'll have to interview them, feel them out." Fariq did not look optimistic as he said this.

Amad smiled. "Feel them out. What a quaint American expression."

Ali nodded. "Just like we felt out the Somali youths in Minnesota three years ago. Nearly twenty of them flew to Somalia and joined our holy cause. And you have maybe two." He gazed at Amad and shook his head. "This does not look promising, my sheikh. What about the committed we sent over two years ago? There were two separate cells, four men each. They haven't checked in for several months."

Mindful of Fariq's sudden stare, Amad told Ali, "We'll discuss those later. Not here."

Ali realized his mistake and shut up. Fariq cast his eyes downward, then onto the fire. A half-minute passed in silence.

"There is another one," Fariq finally said. "An educated American of mixed heritage. He's a newcomer to the mosque, a single man who's just moved here to the valley for a job. A devout Muslim, I believe. Most importantly, though, he works for An-Vax."

"What is that?" Amad asked, growing impatient with this man's ineffectiveness. He was very little help even though one of the officers in the Egyptian Muslim Brotherhood had recommended him.

"A bio-tech company on the East Bay. I looked them up. They make anthrax vaccine for the American military. He has special security clearance."

Anthrax. There was no one in Amad's operation who could handle the bacteria safely and turn it into a bioweapon. His men knew explosives, especially Ali, but not bioweapons. Still, he wondered about the possibility.

Amad frowned. "So, this man has access to these ghastly bacteria. What makes you think he would be capable of dispersing it? I understand it's extremely lethal. Also, would he be willing to help us?"

"I checked," said Fariq. "I called the company and pretended to be interested in a job in their labs. They hire microbiologists with experience in what they call biosafety protocols. This man, this Samir Maalouf, is a microbiologist with the right kind of training. He would know how to handle the bacteria, maybe even how to disseminate it. Would he be willing? I don't know. Maybe."

"What makes you think so?" Ali asked, his mild tone of voice masking what Amad knew was the heat of his true passion for their holy war.

Fariq shrugged. "This Samir looks very unhappy. And he prays with intensity. It's worth a shot."

"Worth a shot," Ali remarked ironically. "I have more confidence in weapons I know how to shoot."

"Perhaps." Amad tossed the two men a warning look. He could hear the mosque's imam returning with their tea. "Introduce us tomorrow after Fajr prayer."

Fariq said quickly and quietly, "He comes after work to the six-thirty service." He looked up as Sheikh Mahmoud Hijazi burst into the room, carrying a tray laden with cups and a teapot. "Ah, wonderful!"

"Mahmoud," added Amad. "We were just discussing this cold spell. How inviting, a cup of hot, sweet tea. On such a day."

"Allah be praised, it is our finest, Sheikh Amad. Imported from our brothers in Indonesia."

They bowed their heads as Sheikh Mahmoud led them in a prayer of thanks, leaving Amad free to think.

The American day of Thanksgiving was in six weeks. There was much to do before then. As the Cordoba mosque's foreign guests, he and Ali would help with the sermons and Qur'anic seminars at the mosque. Between duties, they'd shuttle back to the Dallas-Fort Worth area and perform their tasks at the mosque there. Their hidden agendas were just that—hidden—for they had to assume that at each mosque they visited there were police informants. His and Ali's identities were clean. Neither had so much as a traffic citation. They were on no country's watch or No-fly lists. Both imams in San Miguel and in Fort Worth, unaware of his and Ali's connections to Al-Qaeda, were grateful for the extra help and had accepted their offers almost immediately.

On Thanksgiving Day, Americans watched their football games as devotedly as true believers of Islam chanted the

Qur'anic holy verses. While the foolish Americans faced their beloved gridirons, the true believers faced the holy city of Mecca.

After the imam concluded the prayer, the four men turned to their cups of tea. Amad sipped his tea and smiled to himself. The Dallas Cowboys' stadium would be packed on that day. He wondered where football would be played in the San Francisco Bay Area. He asked this very question of Sheikh Mahmoud.

"American football? I didn't know you were a fan, dear sheikh." The cleric frowned as he thought, then gave up, went to the door and asked one of the men in the kitchen. When he returned, he was smiling. "The San Francisco Bay Area Forty-Niners will be playing at Levi stadium in Santa Clara. That is now their home stadium. It's fairly new, very large and colorful. Right in the heart of Silicon Valley. Would you like me to find you and Ali tickets for the game?"

Exchanging a wry glance with Ali, Amad shook his head. "No, thank you, Sheikh Mahmoud. We'll be content to watch it on the television."

Jake hunched over his prayer rug and touched his forehead to its nubby surface. The visiting British mullah chanted the Surah with so much zeal that his velvety baritone shook with vibrato intensity. His booming voice bounced off the walls, but Jake blocked him out with his own set of thoughts and prayers.

Although his father was a secular Jew, out of respect for Gramps, he'd made Jake and his brothers go to Hebrew school and attain Bar Mitzvah. Become a good, righteous man. Jake's father had no idea how much would stick to the boys' psyches. With Gabe and David, it was something you had to do to make your family happy, get a blast of a party thrown in your honor, and, best of all, get lots of bitchin' gifts.

The Hebrew recitations from the Torah hadn't stuck with them, Jake knew. His brothers hated the Hebrew, especially the difficult, guttural phonemes, whereas Jake had loved it all. He was a natural linguist and had mastered German by age twelve — thanks to Gramps — and Modern Hebrew by fourteen, thanks to Pop's insistence on Hebrew school.

Though Jake could now maneuver in Arabic with ease, all that the language implied — the enemies of Israel and America — spoiled his full enjoyment of it. Despite this, he could discern the sound similarities between Arabic and Hebrew. After all, they were both Semitic languages and both had origins in the same area of the Middle East. Both the Muslims and Jews were descendants of Abraham, the patriarch of monotheism. Under the line of Abraham's son, Ishmael, Mohammad had descended, while the prophets Jacob, Moses, Solomon, David, and Jesus followed the other son, Isaac.

Two different branches from the same tree. And yet so different now in their modern-day manifestations.

The twenty verses of the Qur'an that the Arabic instructor at Quantico had forced them to memorize in the ancient Arabic, Jake now listened to as Imam Amad spoke them. The cadence of the Arabic was almost hypnotic.

The rest of the Qur'an he'd read in the English translation, including Muhammad's Haddith, the commentaries attached to the Qur'an. These commentaries explained that God, or Allah, had given Muhammad permission to take any woman he wanted and plunder and pillage any caravan, village, or army that stood in his way. While in his trances, the prophet Muhammad claimed that God had spoken to him through the angel Gabriel and had given him the Surah, the Qur'anic verses. The word of Allah. In the early seventh century, this claim to divine inspiration was probably accepted by some, rejected by others.

Other commentaries explained that anyone who would not pledge allegiance to Muhammed as Allah's True Messenger, and who would not adhere to Islamic Laws, would be dealt with accordingly. Therefore Muhammed had exhorted his followers to show mercy but, when facing stubborn resistance, to convert, subjugate, or kill those who did not follow his way, the *True Path* of Islam.

Convert, subjugate or kill.

That command gave Jake chills.

What Allah's Messenger and his followers did succeed in doing, Jake knew, was unify all the disparate tribes of Arabia. That they accomplished all of this through force and sheer terror, he could understand. By early seventh-century standards, the sultans and caliphs who followed Muhammed's Islam were probably no better or no worse than the Teutonic hordes of Europe or the Holy Roman Empire's zealous armies.

As far as Jake could observe, the worshipers at this mosque seemed enlightened and tolerant of Americans although some were foreign-born immigrants. But he was no fool. Looks often deceived, and so did civil manners and etiquette. The men around him had nodded and some had shaken his hand and introduced themselves, recognizing a newcomer to their mosque. He appreciated their courtesy and hospitality. He had to remind himself that he wasn't hunting law-abiding Muslims. He was lying in wait for monsters who subverted the Islamic faith and twisted the Qur'anic verses for their own evil, violent purposes.

Islamic terrorists.

All this passed through Jake's mind as he went through the motions and mutterings of Fajr prayers. Inside, he was hearing himself recite the Torah in Hebrew, his old Bar Mitzvah memorizations. And hearing Gramps exhort him in his heavy German accent, "Go get dose sons-a-bitches, Yaakov, my dear mitzvah boy." My dear, righteous boy.

Gramps, Gramps. If you could see me now, what would you

think? His German-Jewish grandfather had narrowly escaped the death camps when he immigrated to the U.S. in 1934. An acclaimed film editor in Berlin, Nathan Bernstein had found a community of fellow Jewish refugees in Hollywood. They'd found work, food, and shelter for him and his young wife.

Yaakov, my boy, vat are you doing in dis place?

When prayers concluded, he stood with the other hundred or so men. Most of them spoke English with a variety of Middle Eastern accents. Some were native English speakers, like himself. Jake nodded and smiled to the ones who did the same to him and chatted with a few. Slowly, he wended his way through the milling crowd of men toward the main doors.

Fariq appeared beside him.

"Salaam alaikum, Samir."

"Alaikum salaam," Jake said. "Nice to see you again, Mr. Nasreen."

"Please, call me Fariq." Dressed in casual slacks and long-sleeved shirt, the older man nevertheless looked tense. He indicated the visiting British mullah standing next to Sheikh Mahmoud Hijazi in a reception line that led to the all-purpose hall. Tables had been set for refreshments after the prayer service. "Would you like to meet the mullah and join us for tea?"

Jake had spent the last two days poring over Fariq's translations from Arabic into English, especially the news and commentaries of *Al-Shumukh*, the online propaganda machine of Al-Qaeda. As far as Jake could tell, the translations were accurate, but he sent copies on to FBI Headquarters in D.C. anyway. The NSA and others in the Counter Terrorism intelligence community could assess the accuracy and search for imbedded or coded messages that the local FBI field office had perhaps overlooked.

"I'd be happy to," Jake began, already inching his way to a group of men near the reception line. "But I can't stay long. I've got a plane to catch."

"Oh, where to?" Fariq steered him to the front of the line.

"L.A. To see a good friend of mine from college."

"The sheikh will be our guest for two months, Allah be praised, but his time is limited." Fariq turned to the British imam and introduced Jake to him and to the taller, husky man standing next to him. Ali Waleed Mohammed.

Jake inclined his head and shook the British imam's proffered hand. The middle-aged man was of medium height, slightly built but with a strong grip. His head was bald but his facial hair was iron gray. What drew Jake's gaze were his eyes, a pale shade of green. His expression appeared kindly and patient but speculative. His assistant, Ali, was the wolf to Sheikh Amad's sheep, all dark, furrowed brows and the black, intense eyes of a zealot.

"I'm honored, Sheikh Amad." Jake nodded to Ali but didn't shake his hand. Nor was it offered. Nevertheless, Fariq looked pleased as he addressed the British cleric.

"This is the man, the bio-tech scientist I was telling you about. Like you, Sheikh, an educated man. The sheikh earned a doctorate in mechanical engineering at Cambridge," he added for Jake's benefit and for anyone within earshot.

"I see." Jake smiled. "Well, I hope to speak to you again before you leave. My hours at work are flexible, so I'm often available during the day."

The British cleric scanned the crowd of men waiting to speak to him and then leaned toward Fariq. "I'll leave it to you to arrange." To Jake, he said in parting, "So pleased to meet you, Samir. We'll speak another time."

Jake took his leave and wended his way toward the exit doors. When he stepped outside, he took a deep breath. He should've stayed longer, he supposed. It was his job to cozy up to these men. There was something about the British mullah's assistant . . .

Mustn't appear too eager.

He checked his watch. There were hourly flights down to

San Diego from San Jose. What if . . . ?

He got in his car, started the engine and peeled out of the parking lot. Several others were right behind him, anxious to not waste an entire Friday night. The weekend had begun.

He'd surprise Meg by showing up that night.

CHAPTER EIGHT

When Jake's taxi pulled up to the curb, he double-checked the address Meg had given him. Finding the commute to campus from Coronado Island, where her Uncle John the Navy captain lived, an hour long, Meg had moved closer to UC San Diego. The apartment building he now stood in front of, though within blocks of the UC campus, appeared below the upper middle-class housing Meg was probably accustomed to. Typical shabby student housing, a U-shaped building contained an inner courtyard and exterior staircases. Still, she'd probably figured convenience outweighed aesthetics and her stay here was short-term, anyway. One semester or two.

Short-term plans versus long-term ones was a topic they'd have to discuss at some point. Just not yet.

He paid the cabby, hoisted his weekend sports bag over his shoulder, and approached the tiled staircase on the right. The apartment upstairs nearest the landing had just disgorged about a dozen students. Eleven o'clock was early for a Friday night party to be ending.

Then he saw Meg. She was hugging an older man, who apparently belonged to this outgoing group. The bespectacled, fortyish guy passed him on the stairs, still flushed and smiling. Jake drew wary glances from the guys and appraising stares from the girls as he made his way up.

Meg was waving the last stragglers off when she spied Jake. "*Auf wiedersehen, Freunde*—Jake!"

Her round-eyed look made him sorry he'd pulled a

surprise. For the first time, he considered the possibility that Meg might not appreciate his showing up unannounced.

Dammit, Bernstein. You blew it.

Seconds later, Meg recovered and rushed into his arms. Gratefully, he closed his eyes, breathed in her various scents, felt her breasts crush against his chest. He dropped his bag, wrapped his arms around her and found her lips. He kissed her soundly. God, she felt so good.

"You're not angry?"

"No! Heavens, no! Just surprised. You said to pick you up at the airport tomorrow morning. No, I was just saying good-bye to the German Club. I volunteered to host our get-to-gether—Come in and see my humble abode."

Meg led him inside and spun around in her excitement.

"Oh, Jake, the place is a mess. I've gone backward in time to my college days, so I've slacked off on housework. Gran would be shocked."

Jake stared at her outfit, a kind of white sweater-tunic over snug, black leggings, set off with a wide black belt. Her blond hair was swept up and hung in a long ponytail and she wore little makeup. Her tanned face held a healthy glow, as if she were spending more time in the sun.

She looked happy. Carefree. Young.

"I'm glad you're making friends," he said dispiritedly, wondering how long it'd take before she tired of waiting for him to show up at her door. Something in his voice gave him away. She seized his arm and steered him to her sofa.

"Jake, these kids seem so much younger than me. I'm just trying to meet people and practice the German I'm learning."

"Meg, you're only twenty-six," he reminded her. "Who's the older guy? He looked like a smitten schoolboy."

As soon as they sat, Meg jumped up and began gathering glasses and bottles of beer. The bowl of pretzels on her coffee table was nearly empty. She whisked that up, too.

"Oh, you exaggerate. Prof Heinz is our advisor. He's from

Munich—München, I mean. Here on an exchange program for professorships. He teaches German History and Language. The German History class in English, thank God."

Jake's heart sank. Just a matter of time and Herr Heinz would be teaching Meg other things.

Her smile faded as disappointment eclipsed her once happy expression. She moved toward the kitchen, picking up and straightening as she went. Jake cursed himself. His jealousy was about to ruin their reunion. He slapped his thighs and stood up.

"Let me help you."

She glanced over at him. "Okay, you can bring me all the beer bottles. Dump 'em in the trash."

He did so, then came up behind her at the sink and wrapped his arms around her. Not about to apologize, he could at least change the subject.

"How're your classes? You having fun with German?" Unable to stop touching her, he nuzzled her temple, the back of her head. She relaxed in his arms and sighed. A good sign. Maybe she'd forgiven him for being such an ass.

"They're fun and hard, both. Challenging. I miss my colleagues in Dallas, my friends at home. Most of all, I miss you."

"I'll be here every weekend. I promise."

He knew he was promising the impossible. If someone took the bait and upped the ante, he might have to put in weekend time. Make himself available to the bastards 24/7.

She leaned back against him. "I'm volunteering at a local school. Kids of illegals and recent immigrants from Mexico who aren't literate in Spanish. I teach them to read and write in Spanish so their literacy skills will transfer to their English learning in school. It's a good thing, makes me feel involved, y'know. There're a lot of Spanish-speaking immigrants here, many more than I've seen even in the Dallas area."

He murmured something unintelligible into her hair

before caressing her cheek with his own. She spun around in his arms and they kissed.

"You hungry?"

"Just for you," he admitted. With a smile, she drew him back to the sofa and straddled his lap. Her lips ground against his and their tongues played tag. He lost track of time while reveling in a fog of lust and pleasure.

He forgot his insecurities as they showed each other how much absence made the heart grow fonder. Absence had certainly spiked their passion. His self-imposed celibacy these past two weeks fueled a hunger for her that surprised him. Like a starving man at a feast, he couldn't stop himself. He had to have her. *Now.*

Two hours later, sated for a while, they lay on her bed, having made love on the kitchen floor, on her sofa, and a few other places of which he had only a faint memory. The haze of lust wearing off, Jake realized his need for this woman had become as powerful as an opiate addiction.

The thought both scared him and elated him.

Finally! He was in love. Madly in love.

Fuck!

She cuddled up against him, her head on his bare chest. "What do you think of my place?"

Uh-oh. Trick question.

"Nice." Jake looked around the bedroom. The bedside lamp illuminated the tiny room. Her favorite print of Van Gogh's *Irises* hung on the wall facing the bed. She'd carried it in her Dodge Durango all the way from Texas, said it reminded her of nature's beauty, and she loved the colors — purple, violet, periwinkle, and all shades of green. Okay, he was on the right track.

"You brought in the colors from the painting," he remarked confidently, "In your drapes, bedspread, and sheets. Even the towels in the bathroom. Looks great."

She fondled his belly. "You're so observant. I'm sure that's one of the reasons you make such a good agent."

Oh, yeah. Atta boy! "You have good taste."

She chuckled. "In men, you mean?"

"You could do better than me, Meg. I'm no great catch." His thoughts turned glum and the German professor sprang to mind. "Still, I probably earn more than Herr Heinz."

She shook her head but snuggled in closer. *"Ich liebe dich."*

He knew what that meant. When women said that, they expected the same in return. *"Auch, ich."* Me, also. Ditto. *Not very romantic, Bernstein. "Ich liebe dich sehr."*

He hadn't said that to a woman since his marriage. Was he ready to commit? They'd already agreed to exclusivity but . . . A commitment of eternal love and fealty? After his last disastrous relationship ended so badly? He had a hateful ex-wife as proof.

Still, he liked this version of the military term, CQC — close-quarters-contact. He missed it. Wished they could do this every night. Maybe then he'd be able to shake off the feeling of doom and gloom. The feeling that evil was overtaking the world.

After a long moment, she spoke again. "How's your undercover work going?"

"Slowly." He couldn't talk about it without compromising her safety, so he changed the subject. "You don't mind this building, all the raucous students?"

"No. It's a little noisy at night. But they're mostly grad students, like me."

"Taking a big load of classes?"

"Hmm, yes. I'm taking German One and Two concurrently. Y'know, to speed up my accumulation of units to earn my teaching minor. By the end of the winter quarter, the end of March, I might have enough units to satisfy credential requirements. I could go back to Texas . . . or stay here and teach. Uncle John wants me to stay in California. I'd be closer to him and his family. And Jack."

Jack was her half-brother, an attorney in San Francisco. It was what she said before that stuck in his throat. Stay in California? And him in D.C.? Hell!

"That reminds me. Uncle John's having a barbecue tomorrow, and he specifically asked me to bring you. He likes you."

The last time Jake saw Captain John Snider was in a German hospital in Hannover. The man had thanked him for keeping the whole investigation of his mother's Nazi past under wraps. Had it become public, his Navy career might've suffered, maybe even been destroyed. An unjust outcome for such a loyal patriot.

"We Navy men gotta stick together," Jake replied. "And yes, I'd really like that." His left hand stroked her head while the fingers of his right hand ran through the ponytail that splayed across his chest. Frustration built inside and threatened to spill over. "Meg, this job might conclude in a couple of months, maybe even sooner if nothing comes of it. After that, I go back to FBI Headquarters in D.C. We'll end up living on opposite coasts. That's FUBAR."

"Fubar? Is that German?"

He chuckled deep in his throat. "No, it's a military term. FUBAR means fucked-up-beyond-all-recognition."

She looked up at his face and playfully raked her fingernail over his grizzled cheek. "Yes, that would be FUBAR."

"So, what can we do about it?"

He couldn't believe what he was saying. Wasn't he the one pushing her now? Maybe pushing himself, too? Things were going too fast, happening too quickly. And here he was, smack in the middle of the most difficult undercover assignment of his career. He'd already made her promises he knew he couldn't fulfill.

"I don't know," she whispered, as though keeping her

emotions in check, "If I go back to Dallas, it's not going to be any better."

He lay there, silent, thinking, his thoughts churning into froth. No solution presented itself. Rather, several did but he wasn't ready for them.

"What's going on, Jake? You don't seem ... I don't know ... very happy. Is the job getting to you?"

That was Meg. She had an uncanny ability to cut to the chase.

"Maybe. The boredom, the waiting, the phony religious devotion." The sudden insight struck him. "The whole thing, it's twisting my guts." *My soul.*

Meg raised up on her elbow and propped her head upon her palm. Light brown eyebrows furrowed in the lamplight but her sapphire-blue eyes lasered into him.

"You mean you don't like pretending to be something you're not? But isn't that your job?"

He stared at her expression. She'd never judge but her opinion and esteem meant the world to him.

"Maybe I was a bad choice for this assignment," he explained, "The Arabic came easy enough ... but I'm a Jew. Not a devout Jew, but it's in my blood, my genes. That's what my grandfather told me once. He was right. It's a deep part of me. Saying the prayers of the enemy—it makes me sick. Soul sick."

Her eyes softened in sympathy. "It's your job, Jake, the one you chose because you feel you're making a difference. Y'know, maybe it's the lies instead. Remember, you told me once, the bitterest truth is better than the sweetest lie. That helped me face what I learned about my grandmother."

All the lies ...

"You said," she went on, "that sometimes to get at the truth, you had to become a bodyguard of lies. You had to wear the lies like a cloak so that you could discover the truth that someone has tried so hard to hide. That's what you're doing. You're wearing a cloak so that you can uncover an evil plan." She shot him a wry smile. "Oh, don't look so surprised. I know what you're doing. You're trying to uncover a terrorist plot. How's it going?"

"Slowly." They'd come full circle, it seemed, but at least she was cheering him on. There was a lot at stake, she was saying, and the possible safety of countless numbers of people was worth the discomfiting deception. God knew he needed the pep talk.

Later, as Meg slept, Jake got up, slipped on his pair of black briefs and went to her small L-shaped utilitarian kitchen. Meg, the gourmet cook. He wondered if she longed for her well-stocked kitchen and the other amenities in her Dallas home. It was obvious she was a little homesick. All the more reason to fly down every weekend, he told himself.

He filled a glass with ice and water from the fridge. Love-making was dehydrating, he mused to himself, but damn. Worth every ounce of sweat.

And then some.

They'd left the prospect of future separations on the table for the time being. *Wait and see*, he reminded himself for the hundredth time. They were both in a temporary state. It was enough for now to know they were in love.

As he drank from his glass, he wandered over to the picture window facing the street. Meg's apartment was situated in the outermost corner of the right-side rectangular arm of the U-shaped complex.

Jake drew the drapes closed but, as he did, he scanned the street in front of the apartment complex and the street that ran perpendicular. Parked cars and SUVs cluttered all the curbs in the vicinity, but one yellow cab stood out. It wasn't the taxi Jake had taken from the airport—he'd memorized the number—but a similar one. A long line of yellow cabs had waited in their designated queue at the San Diego International Airport outside of the Arrivals terminal.

Strange. Too damned strange.

Students don't sit in taxis on a Friday night. Could be a pickup.

He used the bathroom, then returned to the window. The taxi remained, emitting exhaust. Someone was paying a hefty fee to keep the cabbie's meter running so long. Then Jake noticed a movement, a blur of a face. The rear window of the cab faced the apartment complex, the cab one building away from the corner streetlamp. Someone was in the back seat of that cab, but Jake couldn't discern the person's features. Something nagged him.

He placed the glass on the kitchen counter and searched for the jeans he'd worn earlier. In their haste to undress, he and Meg had flung their clothes about helter-skelter. Once he found them, he hastily shrugged them on and yanked on his loafers. Forget the socks and shirt.

Taking two steps at a time, he leaped down the exterior staircase and sprinted across the grassy area in front of the sidewalk. He vaulted over a small hedge, lost a loafer but kept on going. He kicked off the other shoe and crossed the street, sprinting in his bare feet.

Tires squealed as the taxi peeled away from the curb. By the time Jake ran up to the spot where it was parked, the cab was a block distant and turning a corner. He braked himself and stood there, catching his breath. All he'd seen from the back seat was the blur of a man's face. Hell, it could've been anybody. He looked up at the small, twelve-unit apartment building, dark except for two apartments from which he could hear music and voices. Had he just scared off a cabbie whose customer was sharing a ride to the airport?

Shaking his head and wishing he'd stayed in Meg's bed, Jake went to both apartments. Standing in his bare feet, wearing only jeans, he felt slightly foolish. A pretty girl answered the door of the first apartment. Was anyone waiting for a cab? No, but he was welcome to join their little sleepover. The five other young women gathered around the door, sizing him up and cracking jokes about the new Chippendale dude. They began digging into their purses to pay for a strip dance.

Laughing, he extricated himself and trudged upstairs to the second apartment. The big guy, looking like a potential first-draft pick of a linebacker, told him in no uncertain terms to bug off. No one there needed a taxi.

Jake walked back to Meg's place, collecting his shoes as he did. Had he been followed from the mosque to the airport? If so, why would anyone go to all the trouble and expense? Fariq was the only one who knew he had headed for the airport. Or maybe it was a simple coincidence. Some passenger was lost and consulting a map or notes to figure out where he needed to go.

And paranoia was wearing him down.

So why take off like that? Why not wait around and see what the guy running up to him wanted?

Coincidence? Not likely. Someone had followed him.

Sonofabitch!

CHAPTER NINE

M eg heard the front door open and close. Immediately, she jolted fully awake and reached over for Jake. Finding his side of the bed vacant, she got up and pulled on her favorite kimono robe.

Her pounding heart subsided. Since she always kept the stove light on at night, his dark figure by the front door reassured her but nevertheless perplexed her. He was standing there, examining the door jamb, running his hands around the windowsills.

"You checking out my security at three am?"

Apparently he'd already heard her rustle about, so he continued what he was doing. Whatever that was. Ignoring her. She sighed. He was on super-focus mode.

She decided to make an attempt at reason. "You see the deadbolt, the chain latch? Each window has a rod and lock. So what spooked you?"

He slowly swiveled around, his arms crossed over his bare chest. Biceps flexed and his pecs heaved, reminding Meg of his gorgeous build, his slim but muscular stature. At six-two and mostly muscle, he was a man who could take care of himself. Occasional military terms crept into his language, harking back to his days in the Navy. With SEAL Team Three, he'd seen combat action in the Second Gulf war and in Iraq. Then he'd abruptly quit, he'd explained, after four years.

When she'd probed further, he revealed that one of their ops in Iraq had turned ugly and bad. The team of twelve lost two men and civilians were killed. All due to bad intel, he'd said. Still, it was a drastic thing to quit like that, she thought, which supposedly was why he'd joined the FBI Intelligence Division and become an analyst. Good intel was everything, he'd told her. It saved lives and got the job done.

"I might've been followed here."

She absorbed that bombshell, staying silent as she processed that bit of information. Coming from a military family — the grandfather who'd raised her was a career Air Force officer and her uncle was a Navy captain — Meg took the news calmly.

"Are you sure?"

"A cab from the airport was out in front. Might've followed me from there."

"You're not just being super paranoid?" She backpedaled when she considered that he might not appreciate that assessment. "Understandable, I mean, being undercover. If you were followed, that's a problem, isn't it? Might be difficult to explain, Jake. A Muslim man dating a non-Muslim woman." She frowned as another possibility struck her. "Should I be concerned? For my safety?"

In a flash, his arms enveloped her. "Not if I can help it. I'll figure something out. That's why they hired me. I'm flexible. Adaptable."

"Which means what?"

His arm around her back, he steered her into the bedroom. She knew what he was doing, trying to distract her and change the subject. She knew why. He'd stop seeing her while the undercover operation continued. So afraid of women blowing their stacks, he was going to try to soften the bad news.

Typical male.

Her annoyance spilled over and she shook herself loose. Flicking on the bedside lamp, she opened one of the nightstand drawers and pulled out her Lady Smith & Wesson. The black-metallic gun was a thirty-eight caliber, snub-nosed revolver that Grandpa Snider had given her when she turned sixteen. He'd taken her to the shooting range on base once a month until she turned eighteen and went off to college. Grandma had joined them a couple of times and had proven herself a better shot than her and Gramps combined. Nearly four months ago, Meg had learned why that was.

"It's loaded at all times, and don't think I don't know how to shoot it." She stormed over to the small closet, which held one-tenth of her Texas wardrobe, flung open the door and seized the stock end of a canvas cloth gun sheath. "Here's my Mossberg twelve-gauge bolt-action shotgun. I always keep it loaded. If anybody tries to break in, they're going to leave with a head full of birdshot."

She returned the shotgun to its location just inside the doorframe. When she turned around, she cocked one hip and propped fists at her waist. Jake was smiling, but it was a troubled smile that marred his handsome features. He scratched his bearded chin.

"You've made your point. You also kick-box and do karate chops?"

"No, but I run fast. As you well know."

His scowl softened when she alluded to their time together in Wales and Ireland, taking five-mile runs around the town.

"Yeah, but I'd feel better if I put in a security alarm and you let me pay for it. It's my fault, I was too focused on coming here, on seeing you . . ."

"So?" Her challenge was a test.

"So nothing. I got careless. That won't happen again." His eyes slid away as if he were calculating how he could avoid involving her in his undercover operation. Maybe he couldn't. Maybe she was now as much involved in this case as he was. How did she feel about that? Not friggin' good.

More crap to worry about besides her German classes. And how Jake was faring in Northern California.

A ripple of fear coursed through her. Her bravado of a moment ago was just that—-bravado. A flash of memory. Four months ago, a pair of Celtic Wolves had jumped her at the Irish Stud Farm, had chloroformed her and tossed her in a private jet bound for Germany. Unwittingly, she'd gotten involved in another of Jake's undercover schemes. That case had exposed a whole lifetime of lies—her grandmother's. Gran's stroke and then her suicide were the horrible results.

Her Uncle John lived nearby. His wife and two sons were now teenagers. How would they feel, being indirectly swept up in all of this?

In all of what? She didn't even know what Jake was doing in northern California, except maybe trying to pass as a Muslim. Or where exactly he was doing it.

Her gaze bore into Jake until he finally returned her stare.

"Okay, here you're relatively safe. But on campus? Walking around, shopping, going about your business? Meg, what I've learned is that anybody, anywhere, can be taken down. If the perps are motivated enough, no one is safe. These perps—they're of the cold, calculating, highly motivated variety. Crazy-ass fanatics on a holy crusade against Americans. They're not going to let anybody stop them. And here I've stupidly put you in harm's way. Damn, I can't let you get dragged into this op. It's too dangerous."

Through a watery film, she watched him cross over to the bed and sit down. He placed his elbows on his knees and hunched over. His fists covered his mouth while his eyes raked the floor.

"It's better if I don't come down and see—" His voice caught and he paused to clear his throat, "—don't come down for a while. Just until this op's over." He leaned back and dug into both front pockets of his jeans. Both hands cupped cell phones. "Look at my life right now. I've got an untraceable, disposable cell for making calls to you and my family, and another one as the Muslim man, Samir. A man who might have something to hide. Samir is cagey, staying under the radar. But he's a loner and vulnerable to persuasion. That's how I'm playing him."

His dark eyes swung up and locked with hers. "As Samir, you're a loose end from my old life. My boss at Headquarters doesn't even know you're here in SoCal so he thinks I'm making fake calls to old college buddies, old girlfriends, setting up a cover life. He'd have my badge if he knew I was flying down to see you. Involving and endangering a civilian. Shit, I can't even see my folks, my brothers and their families. Endangering them is unthinkable, not to mention blowing my cover. When you're undercover, you can't lead a normal life. Seeing you, I'm being a selfish bastard, trying to live in both worlds. Can't happen. Shouldn't happen."

Again, his voice hitched. He held up the cell phone from his left pocket and looked up, his deep-set brown eyes dark and hooded, almost haunted. "Here's the other one, my other world. A secure cell with satellite transmission and encryption capabilities. For calls to Headquarters. I call in a report every night. I'm on the job twenty-four-seven. At least, I'm supposed to be. I live in the shadows, Meg."

She couldn't speak. Her brain had glommed onto some of his words. She was a loose end. He was endangering a civilian. He was a selfish bastard. He was trying to live in both worlds and it couldn't happen. It was impossible, dangerous.

The rims of his eyes were red. Jake looked so miserable. She'd never seen him so distressed.

She felt a tear spill over and roll down one cheek. Irritated by her own show of weakness, she knuckled it away. She couldn't let him lose his job over her. Finding a terrorist and stopping him before people were killed trumped their seeing each other. Well, okay, just barely, if she was honest with herself. Her throat clogged, a lump rose and she swallowed it down. She tried to speak anyway. What came out was barely a whisper.

"I understand, Jake. I-I do."

Defeated, she slumped next to him on the bed. Their thighs rubbed together and her shoulder touched his naked upper arm. Startled by his sudden movement, she watched him toss both cell phones down on the carpet, as though they disgusted him. His life disgusted him.

He didn't look at her. "I'm going to lose you, aren't I?"

She said nothing. What could she say? She had no idea what the future held for either one of them.

The bitterest truth is better than the sweetest lie.

Jake's motto. Hers now, too.

The rest of their weekend stretched before them, and now she was sickened by the thought of spending it alone. Without him.

She raised her head. He was staring at her . . . Then, all at once, he was on top of her, opening her robe, kissing her all over, unzipping his pants. And she was clutching at his back, his waist, helping him shed his jeans, his briefs.

Hungry kisses covered her and hard, rough caresses bruised her flesh. She paid him back with angry, desperate ones of her own. Soon they were rocking, he inside her and she gripping him with strong legs, not letting him go. He growled when she climaxed and bit his neck. While he arched his back, she watched his face. He was a stranger, his new bearded look concealing half his face, and yet he was the one man she trusted with her life. She knew he'd do the right thing. That was the strangest thing of all. How she knew this, she wasn't sure, but her trust in him was absolute.

Her lust for him was absolute.

Was it enough, though? Her loneliness had gotten her into trouble before. She'd chosen the wrong men to keep her company — handsome, self-serving devils who'd wanted only one thing from her. Well, two. Sex and a pretty girl to hang on their arms.

Jake was different. But his work was causing them grief.

They lay in each other's arms, unwilling to break apart their conjoined bodies. She listened to his breathing as it slowed. What was she going to do with this man? At this point, did she even have a choice?

"Meg . . . baby, will you—"

"Ssh, don't talk."

"No, have to." He sighed against her hair. "Wait for me? Until this op's done?"

What? Where was he going with this?

How long? Weeks? Months? Years? Hell, she wasn't getting any younger. She wanted to return . . . someday soon . . . to her teaching job, her life. Marry someday, have a family. All the normal things other women did.

Was all that even possible with a man like Jake?

If it wasn't, she knew what she'd have to do. The outcome was suddenly and painfully clear to her.

He levered himself on his elbows above her. "Guess that's a no."

"I was wondering . . . how long? Can't do years. Weeks, months, maybe."

She couldn't believe it. A crooked smile quirked up his mustache on one side. He'd put her through the hell of a breakup minutes ago and now he was smiling?

"Weeks. I'm gonna wrap this up as fast as I can. *If* I can. Then . . ." His dark eyes traveled around her face, as though he were taking a mental picture of her. "After this is over . . . Meg, where you go, I go. Texas, here, I don't care. I'll make it happen. Quit the FBI if I have to."

Huh? "So . . . we're not breaking up?"

"Hell, no. I can't give you up. This job's driving me crazy. Every time I bend over in that mosque and mutter the *dhikr*— the remembrance of God prayer—I feel sick. I thought I could

80

handle it, but now . . ."

Jake shook his head slowly, his eyes crinkled with worry. "The thought of you dragged into this scares me shitless. I just need to play it smart. Just take a breather until this job's done. If I'm asked, I'll spin it. You're an old girlfriend and I'm seeing you for the last time 'cause I'm a devout Muslim and I'm re-dedicating myself to Allah, blah, blah, blah." He lowered his face and kissed her shoulder. "Can you wait for me? Don't go hook up with Herr *Scheisse-gesicht*?"

Mr. Shit-face? She almost smiled at his jealous insult of Professor Heinz. The about-face took her longer to process than it had Jake, obviously. Could she wait for him and not date anyone else while she waited? In other words, spend a lot of weekends alone in a new place where she had no friends? Uncle John would be deployed soon, her Aunt Gloria worked, and the two boys were busy with school and sports. Her half-brother, Jack, lived in San Francisco and had his own life.

Honestly, she had no idea if she was capable of waiting. Her track record with men was sketchy at best. Was Jacob Bernstein the one who would finally seal the deal and make a home with her? Make a normal life with her? Become her new family?

"Meg? Can you wait for me?" he repeated, this time more softly.

"Yes," she said finally. That was what he wanted to hear. And what she wanted to believe.

Chapter Ten

It was nearly eleven o'clock Sunday evening when Jake trudged up his apartment stairs. He unlocked the deadbolt and entered. As he swung open the door, the hair on the back of his neck bristled. Something was off. His trained military instincts kicked in. Maybe a lingering scent in the air.

He flicked on the kitchen and hallway lights. Dropping his weekend sports bag silently and slowly in the entryway, he slid along the wall, his back one with it. Unarmed, he went into the classic CQC defensive posture, or Close Quarters Combat, ready to deflect an attack with his arms or legs. In that posture, he made his way to the living room, around to the small, galley kitchen, back into the entryway and hall. The bedroom door was slightly ajar. He'd left it open at forty-five degrees, as he always did when undercover. If someone was stupid enough to remain hidden inside his bedroom, that person would soon need a new set of front teeth.

The light was off, which was how he'd left it. Three . . . two . . . one! One hand flipped on the light switch as he bolted through the doorway, slamming the door against the wall and doing a half roll across the carpet. A moment later, he felt foolish and had to chuckle as he arose to his feet. The intruders were no longer there. Nevertheless, he finished his survey of the rest of the apartment, scanning the closet and bathroom adjacent to his bedroom. The furnishings were sparse, the décor all but absent, in keeping with Samir the scientist's isolation.

In fact, it was a depressing place with none of the sports-collectible pictures he'd carefully hung in his condo back in Georgetown. There were none of his framed photos of his family, and his SEAL brothers in camo, in wet-suits, in full dress uniform. None of his books or CDs, none of his favorite DVDs or his forty-five-inch-wide television with stand-alone woofers. No home gym or handpicked tools such as those in his condo's attached garage. He was a fish out of water in one sense, just like Meg. Separated from all that was familiar and dear to them.

No wonder they were both floundering and desperate for each other's company. They'd left everything behind except their growing feelings for each other. At least, he hoped her feelings for him were mutual. He couldn't believe he'd actually promised to leave the FBI for her. Yet he had. Now with a cooler head, he realized that had been an act of desperation. He wasn't sure he'd ever be able to follow through on that promise. Or even if he'd marry a woman who would demand that kind of sacrifice of him.

The next time he saw her, he'd tell her the truth. The job came with him, like it or not. If she couldn't handle it, then they'd call it a day.

Well, fuck that!

He stopped his own train of thought. Here he was, dwelling on Meg and their impasse of a relationship when he should be concentrating on the case. What the hell was he doing?

A loud knock drew him to the front door. He looked through the peephole and recognized the older woman from next door. What was her name?

"Hi Samir." His neighbor was a heavy-set woman in her sixties, he estimated, with soft, blond curls framing a still pretty face. She had vibrant blue eyes and a ready, friendly smile. Whenever she saw him around the condo complex, she greeted him by name.

"Hello." He racked his mind for her name. Linda Brown!

"I just got home, Linda, from visiting friends in San Diego. Did you notice anyone at my door?"

She nodded, then said nothing. He studied her while waiting for her to open up. She was wearing her usual outfit, jeans and some kind of cotton-knit top. Always careful not to impose, she often brought him baked goods such as bran muffins, coffee cake, cookies, and once even a fruit pie. Like his older female neighbor in Georgetown, their kindness was appreciated. And he never turned down an offer of home baked goods. This time, she held out a plate of brownies.

"Thanks, Linda, I love brownies. Uh, would you care to come in?"

"No, I can't. One of my favorite crime dramas is on TV. But I wanted to tell you there was a man who came to your door. I was on my way out last night and in a hurry. He acted like he had a key and was having trouble with it. I stopped and looked at him. I thought it strange since I knew you weren't home." She shrugged her shoulders. "But, y'know, he could've been a friend of yours for all I knew."

So, that was confirmed. A man had broken in, using lock-pick tools no doubt. Someone experienced in B and E, so it wouldn't take long to do the job. He was expecting a closer look from someone, just not this soon.

"He wasn't. He broke in but nothing was taken. What did he look like?"

Her hand flew to her mouth. "O my God, I knew it. I should've called the cops. Samir, I'm so sorry."

He patted her shoulder. Her plate of brownies smelled great. They'd go well with a tall glass of cold milk. Another thought intruded. He realized he had no *halal* food—meat cooked according to Sharia law and tradition—in his fridge although he'd passed a few Middle Eastern markets on his way to the mosque. No *hummus*, *shawarma*, or *biryani*, no lamb *kebabs* or Egyptian salad, which would've been available at those markets. Whoever had checked him out would've noticed that and wondered. A devout Muslim man would be buying that kind of *halal* takeout from the deli counter at such markets.

Comfort food for a Muslim man with a Lebanese-American background. Stupid slip-up.

"No problem. You couldn't have known. Did you notice what he looked like?"

Her hand came down and she frowned in concentration. "Well, a lot like you. Young, dark hair and beard, only shorter. Much shorter. He wore a black leather jacket and a blue baseball cap if that's any help."

He nodded and smiled, wanting to assuage her alarm. "An acquaintance from the mosque. I didn't give him permission to use my place. If you see him again, feel free to call the cops. That'll teach him."

Linda Brown seemed reluctant to leave, but after more reassurance from him that she needn't be frightened, she did. He said goodnight and thanks again, deadbolted his door and strode to the kitchen. He spent the next hour searching the cabinets, under the table and chairs, moving furniture in the living room and bedroom, and examining the drapes and rods, the bedroom closet, the bathroom, his television and speakers, every corner of every wall.

Finally, satisfied that the guy hadn't bugged the place or left any cameras — wireless or otherwise — Jake went back to the kitchen. After sliding special plastic casters under the feet of his refrigerator, he'd been able to move the fridge away from the wall quickly and quietly, in a matter of seconds. You couldn't see the casters unless you were looking for them. He grabbed hold of the fridge and pulled it away from the wall.

Relief flooded him. The molded plastic container with all of his FBI spy craft gear was still in its place. Appearances were often deceiving but in this case Jake was certain the fridge and the hidden container hadn't been moved. The dust on the floor hadn't been disturbed since the last time he'd slid out the appliance.

Fariq. He'd sent someone to follow him to the airport, catch the same plane. So why hadn't he noticed? Simple. He'd been distracted, so full of anticipation in seeing Meg again. The guy had caught a cab right after Jake and had sat in that cab outside of Meg's apartment. Later, he or one of Fariq's other minions had checked out his apartment. Why the intense interest? With time, money, and risk involved?

Something was afoot. Maybe time was short. He suspected he was going to find out very soon.

Two weeks into this op and things were finally moving.

A part of him—the Boy Scout part, he had to admit—was deeply saddened. Fariq was a naturalized American citizen. Sad to think a fellow American might be involved in a plot to take down his own countrymen.

Still, not too surprising. He'd learned that deep cover moles often became citizens of the very country they aimed to sabotage. Nothing new there.

All the more reason to spin Meg out of the equation.

The cynical part—the FBI analyst whose eyes were open to all kinds of nasty, deadly plots, homegrown and foreign—smirked inwardly.

Bring it on, assholes!

The second floor of An-Vax was deserted of Quality Control and Validation experts except for Todd Walinski. Jake sipped from his Starbucks drink—three shots, venti vanilla latte—while Todd explained.

"Most are off today because tomorrow's a twenty-four-hour marathon of oven testing."

"Oven testing?" Again, Jake felt like a fish out of water. He'd seen the enormous stainless steel ovens on the third and fourth floors and knew they baked and converted the anthrax vaccine into powder form before being compressed by sterilized machines into tablets.

"Once a month we have to calibrate and notate the ovens at various temperatures to make sure they're FDA approved. This takes a twenty-four-hour testing cycle that we all have to witness and verify. You'll be involved in this, too, so that the others don't think something's fishy with you. Right now, they think you've been hired—or rather, Samir Maalouf has been hired to double-check my reports. I need to keep you as separate from the others as much as possible. Once they find out you can't talk the talk, your cover will be, how do you say, blown?"

Jake nodded. "They know I'm part-time, right? I'll be out of the building more often from now on, but plan on me showing up in the mornings. You cool with that?"

"Sure. Guess things are heating up on your end." Todd led him to his office and they sat down. Jake pulled out a notebook and pen. "You said you had a lot of questions regarding security, Samir—uh, I mean, Agent Bernstein."

Jake smiled, understanding the man's confusion. "Yeah, but please in here, always call me Samir. That way, there won't be a slip up. First of all, can a bioweapon be made from the dead anthrax bacteria you use upstairs to make this vaccine?"

Todd turned serious. "No. What we're actually using are the protein markers that exist on the outer cell wall of the anthrax bacterium. To produce the vaccine, we have to develop an antibody that links up with that particular protein marker. To isolate that protein marker, you have to use a live anthrax bacterium. That kind of high-level lab work isn't done here. It's done elsewhere and the protein markers are shipped here. We insert those isolated proteins into dead bacteria so we can grow them for production purposes."

Todd paused as if recalling Jake's original question. Jake's eyes were crossing from the complexity of it all. He appreciated his brother Gabe's work even more. Also, Todd's decision to keep him from talking to the other scientists. They'd know in two minutes that Jake was not one of them.

Todd shot him a wry grin. "So no. Bio-weapons can't be made from these proteins. If you're exposed to them, you could get good and sick, but to use them as part of a large-scale weapon? No, not possible."

Not understanding the subtle distinctions, Jake nevertheless continued. "My targets won't know that, of course. Would it be out of the realm of possibility to think that live bacteria would be used here in this facility in order to grow and produce this vaccine?"

"No, most people don't understand what all's involved in making these vaccines. This facility is about as secure as it gets, but only the CDC and certain private and highly government-controlled facilities have Level Five labs where there might be repositories of live anthrax. It's very rare to find it, thank God. Those anthrax deaths you heard about a few years ago, those spores were sent by a Level Five scientist who had his own agenda. Obviously."

"One of the Headquarters' teams worked that case." Jake consulted his notes, trying to get back on track. "So, let me get this straight. There is no live bacteria on stock here."

Todd shook his head and smiled. "No way, Jose."

Jake processed that. "Okay, but if there was a Level Five Lab here, would someone with my validation job here have access to it? Y'know, to turn it into powder form?"

"For use as a terrorist bioweapon?" Todd apparently knew where Jake was going with this line of questioning. When Jake nodded, he went on. "You'd have to grow lots of it, of course, if you're planning to spray it in a crowd. You could convert it to powder or aerosol form for large dispersal but that would be suicide. You wouldn't need so much, in fact very little, if you're targeting a few people or a group in an enclosed environment. Keep in mind, live anthrax is tenacious. It survives in elevated temperatures, a cold environment, water, pure or filtered air. Its spores are some of the deadliest substances you'll find on this planet. Do we store it here? Hell no."

"Well, that's a relief," said Jake. On the one hand, good news. On the other, he—Samir—would have to do a great job faking it. "So this vaccine you're making is for the military?"

"It's a huge U.S. government contract. We're contracted to produce seventy-five million doses at a cost of eight hundred-million plus dollars. The vaccine will be given in three injections over a six-month period and offer a protection of two to three years. It's a very expensive stockpile, since bio-anthrax has a shelf life of about three years. Four million out of sixty million doses expire every year. Does the cost justify the risk? That's not for me to say. The Pentagon seems to think so."

A few more questions and Jake let Todd get back to his work. Jake sat at the secure company computer for another hour, caught up on his email—including encrypted messages from an anonymous sender to both his brothers, his pal Eric in D.C., and a brief one to Meg. In his email message to her, he reminisced about their weekend. On Saturday, they had run down to Torrey Pines Park, following the trail to the beach and crossing the pedestrian bridge over to Del Mar. The cool ocean air had braced up his equilibrium and restored his sense of well-being. His sense of normalcy. Meg had clearly felt it, too.

On Coronado Island, they'd attended her Uncle John's barbeque. Meeting the captain's family had further lifted both his and Meg's moods. Captain Snider and his wife seemed to have a close relationship, and their two sons appeared to be happy, winsome teenagers, typical in their joking and rough-housing. When they'd learned Jake was once a SEAL operative, they'd bombarded him with questions. After dinner, he'd had to prove his hand-to-hand combat skills by taking them on, one at a time, in a kind of mock-martial arts exhibition. He'd faced their amateurish Tae Kwon Do assaults with explanations for how to counter each attack move, gently and in slow motion. He'd left with a renewed feeling of optimism. The Snider family had showed Jake that there might be a way to both serve your country and live a normal life.

He logged off the secure email service, then sat there wondering how soon he could press the issue with Fariq. As if by telepathy, his An-Vax office phone rang. He answered it, pausing a moment to remind himself that all incoming calls for his cover name, Samir Maalouf, would be routed to this phone.

"Samir Maalouf."

"Samir, friend, we need to talk. Can you meet me for dinner? There's an Afghan restaurant on the El Camino in Santa Clara, near Lawrence Expressway. Delicious kebabs, gyros, salads. Oddly enough, it's called Kabul."

So Fariq was willing to joke with him but still had doubts about him. Not surprising, Jake realized, given what Fariq had learned from his minions that weekend. His friend, Samir, had a non-Muslim girlfriend and never ate *halal* food. But then, Jake had plenty of his own doubts about Fariq too. As Samir, could he trust a Muslim man who worked for the local FBI field office? Or was he a double agent? Spying on the FBI while pretending to help them?

"Sure, Fariq, I'd like that. How about six-thirty? I stay a little later than the others so I can pray alone."

"Fine. See you there, my friend. Kabul, on the El Camino Real in Santa Clara."

90

CHAPTER ELEVEN

At six-thirty sharp, Jake pulled into the small parking lot in front of a strip mall. At one corner, perched on the front facade of the restaurant, was the sign, *Kabul*. The name was surrounded by Arabic writing, some of which Jake couldn't decipher since Arabic school had focused on the phonetic learning of the language — the audio-lingual approach. The written language would take years to master.

The restaurant didn't look like much on the outside, but the interior was pleasant with white-clothed tables, subdued lighting, and framed Qur'anic verses, or *surah*, in typical, flowery, cursive Arabic script. Some of the verses looked familiar, since he and the other four agents had memorized both the cursive writing and the spoken word of the *Surah*.

At first glance, he couldn't see Fariq, but when he gave his name to the *hijab*-wearing hostess, he was led to the rear of the restaurant to a table set off in a private alcove. Adjacent and seated at a square table, two large, muscular men had just finished their meal and were having tea. As soon as they saw Jake, they straightened in their chairs and shot him openly hostile looks.

So Fariq had come with his minions, possibly bodyguards. Not the one who'd broken into his apartment, though. These guys were too beefy and didn't fit Linda's description. So who the hell *was* this man? A local Muslim mafioso who just happened to work for the San Jose FBI field office and who had people followed all the way to San Diego? The middle-aged man's innocuous appearance, the sparse beard, thinning gray hair, and wire-rimmed spectacles, belied his true role among the local Muslims. Fariq was a man with money and power.

Fariq stood, all decked out in suit and tie, and greeted him with the usual "Salaam alaikum", to which Jake, as Samir, wearing more casual attire—jeans, white polo shirt with the UCLA logo, and sports jacket—replied with the usual "Alaikum salaam." When his host indicated a seat, Jake sat across the table but, as he did, he glanced over at the two husky men and nodded. *Hey, pals, I see you and I'm not worried.*

He tried his best to assume instead a solemn, respectful demeanor. Fariq smiled slightly, offered a few suggestions from the menu along with polite conversation. Jake noticed the Lebanese dish, *hashweh*, on the menu and remarked about it.

"My father taught me how to cook it. The roast chicken is stuffed with rice, lamb, and spices. I just need to find a *halal* grocery store. Can you recommend one, Fariq?"

The older man's bushy salt-and-pepper eyebrows shot up. "You haven't found one yet?"

"I've been too busy with work." Jake shrugged. "But I'm certainly going to order it tonight. This is a real treat."

Fariq told him the names of several Middle Eastern grocers, butchers, and restaurants in San Miguel and San Jose. They ordered when the male server, who couldn't grovel enough, approached their table. Then the older man changed the subject from food to what was really on his mind. He asked Samir about his work at An-Vax, and Jake did the best he could to recall the scientific gobbledygook the biotech engineer, Todd, had dished out to him that morning about calibrating and testing the ovens. Blessed with an excellent memory, Jake made the jargon sound convincing, as though he really knew what he was talking about. He even included a discussion about the military contracts and the vast number of doses prepared at the An-Vax site. Fariq looked suitably impressed.

The conversation took a more interesting turn when Fariq began questioning him about the anthrax vaccine itself and the production process. Again, Jake, as Samir, repeated most of Todd's explanations about the bacteria, omitting the fact that the An-Vax facility kept a stockpile of the bacteria's protein markers, not the live bacteria itself.

Important omission, he felt. A vital fact that no one would know except the high-level lab personnel.

"Naturally we use all of the biosafety, Level Five lab precautions when handling the stuff. It's always kept in sterile, sealed stainless-steel tubes, and we wear our double-thick hazmat suits whenever we're in the lab."

Specially sealed Level Five suits, Jake implied, were necessary when working with live anthrax bacteria.

Their dinners appeared. They ate in relative silence, commenting occasionally about the flavors of their respective dishes. Fariq was having *biryani*, a rice and lamb kebab. Jake found the halal-spiced and cooked chicken delicious, liked the cilantro-based dressing on his salad, and meanwhile searched his memory for the various Middle Eastern dishes he'd sampled at the FBI's Arabic School. As he wiped his mouth, he looked over the dessert menu.

"Good, they've got *halva*. I love the stuff. Dad taught my mother how to make it and we had it a lot when I was young. Before they divorced and went their separate ways."

Halve was a Lebanese dessert, a kind of cake made from sesame paste and chopped pistachios, that went well with hot sweet tea or sweet coffee. Being half Lebanese, Samir should have been familiar with the dish.

Jake's words must have struck a chord with Fariq. The man smiled broadly, showing a gold tooth in place of his upper left canine.

"Excellent, you must have it. Their sweet tea is good here, too. I'll have the *rusk* with pistachio ice cream."

After they gave their dessert orders to the obsequious server, Fariq glanced over at his two musclemen, gave a slight nod and then turned back to Jake with a totally different expression. He looked like a Muslim father about to scold a son who'd strayed off Islam's *straight and true path.*

"It's time to talk about you and what you're doing here."

Shit! He's made me. But how?

Jake remained silent. But not for long. He sensed what was coming and decided to go on the offensive.

"You sent someone to follow me, didn't you?" He kept his tone of voice mild and calm, unwilling to alarm the two bodyguards. Fariq's nod confirmed it.

"What I do with my free time is none of your business, Fariq, and I'm offended by your intrusion into my private life, however well-meaning that might be."

Surprisingly, Fariq was not put out. He splayed his hands, palms up, in an insincere gesture of apology. His dark eyes hard and flinty, he lowered his voice and leaned across the table.

"I know you Americans regard your privacy and various freedoms as sacred. But I do have my reasons. We are looking at you as a prospective participant in our cause, and so I've taken the liberty to evaluate your usefulness. And qualifications as a true Muslim of honor and purity. Of course, you know that your relationship with that woman, that *kafir*, is forbidden." He sat back when Jake bristled at his choice of words.

That unclean woman, that infidel.

Jake's mind forked into two trains of thought. One, he was outraged and would have liked nothing less than to give the old coot a swift uppercut to his jaw. The second, as Samir, he knew he had to tone down his anger and accept his elder's criticism, just as a secular Jew might accept with humility his rabbi's reminders to stay on the road to righteousness. Stay kosher.

"She's an old girlfriend from college," Jake explained. "She wants nothing to do with Muslims. She told me so this weekend and we broke it off. So that's that."

Fariq's smirk glinted gold. "Really? It took two days for her to decide that? You didn't return until Sunday night." Jake shrugged but looked down at his plate. Emboldened by Samir's silence, Fariq continued. "And you seem unconcerned about observing halal. You keep to yourself—"

"I just moved here from Florida, Fariq," Jake interrupted. "I don't know anyone except the people at work. They try not to show it, but I know they feel uncomfortable around a Muslim. Y'know, they're nice enough but they walk around on eggshells. That's why I started going to Fajr prayers on Fridays. I feel a sense of community at the mosque." He paused and sat back in his chair. "As far as the woman goes, I'm human, after all. So I called an ex-girlfriend from college, who's down there working on an advanced degree. We hooked up but it didn't work out." He allowed himself a sly grin. "The sex is good and we like each other. But she knows there's no future."

Fariq's dark eyes flickered over the younger man's face. "I quite understand, my young friend. You're a handsome man with needs and you must attract women like a magnet. Temptation with a kafir is, how you'd say, a slippery slope into the infidel's world, the world of Satan. Your life for the moment lacks purpose and direction, does it not?"

As Samir, Jake was going to play it cool. If he appeared too eager, a cagey old fart like Fariq would smell a trap.

"I don't know. After my father's death, I decided it was time to start fresh. My mother remarried years ago, now she lives in Georgia. She never converted, which was why she and my father divorced."

Samir's family life was broken, and Jake tried hard to look and sound the part of a drifting, lonely man.

"I've had a private investigator check your background, Samir." Again, he offered a tacit, insincere apology with splayed fingers. "You spent four years in the Army, mainly serving as a translator for military intelligence. It didn't take and you left to go back to the university. Scientific work seems to fulfill you more than anything else. Even more than Islam?"

"Draw your own conclusions, Fariq. I'm devout but in my own way. I'm what you might call a maverick."

Jake allowed Samir a sarcastic smile. He'd forgiven Fariq's interference and said nothing about someone rifling his apartment. Samir Hussein Maalouf's life history had been carefully manufactured by the FBI's Tech Division, although the military and college segments closely paralleled Jake's own life.

"Your father gave you a very noble middle name. The name of the Prophet's grandson. Hussein. He must have loved you very much."

Jake bowed his head, as though the mention of his father's love pierced him deeply, and said nothing.

"I read the report about your father's untimely death." Fariq shook his head. "How tragic, my son. To leave his country and culture behind and come to America, only to be shot and killed by a pair of stupid, racist rednecks who assumed the worst about him. A drive-by shooting, the newspaper article said. They shot him and left him in the street like a dog."

Jake remained silent. He sipped his tea, tensing his jaw and focusing on some distant sight. The FBI techs had thought this tragedy might be the convincing emotional trigger to Samir Maalouf's seduction into jihad. There had to be something that would push an educated Muslim American like Samir over the cliff. They were right. Nine-eleven did it for Jake Bernstein. As soon as he graduated UCLA, he joined the Navy.

Evidently, Fariq concluded Samir's father's senseless murder would also be a sufficient trigger. But for another purpose.

"Do you, Samir," Fariq went on, "ever think about revenge? About avenging your father's death?"

Okay, here it comes.

He lifted his gaze to Fariq's face and looked directly into the man's glittering eyes.

"Every day. But then I say some prayers and the rage subsides."

Jake broke eye contact, realizing he was speaking about himself. The truth of it jarred him. He and Samir weren't that different. Extremely motivated, but on opposing sides. He assumed the FBI techs knew that and created his undercover curriculum vitae accordingly.

"Every day. Yes, I can understand that. I can understand it very well. Perhaps what you need are certain prayers from the Qur'an that will enlighten you to the righteousness and justifications of jihad. The rightness of a holy war against those who have harmed us and our brothers. There are certain passages in the *Haditha* that justify jihad against infidels."

The words *righteousness* and *holy war* sparked a light within Jake and he let it shine within Samir as a flame of enlightenment. He allowed his eyes to burn with it.

"Prayers? What do you mean, certain prayers? Certain passages?"

"The mullah is more qualified than I to speak of them. You must meet the visiting mullah from England. He will help you understand that taking up the sword of Allah is a true and just path, according to the Qur'an. You must hear what Imam Amad has to say. His words will inspire you."

I'll bet.

Jake nodded glumly. "All right, I'll meet with him. Just tell him I'm not blowing myself up for anything or anybody."

Fariq's eyes flared and he leaned forward.

"Keep your voice down. Of course he wouldn't ask that of you. A man with your talents can be useful in other ways. So,

Samir, do I have your consent to arrange a private meeting with the mullah? And will you pledge to keep this meeting and what the mullah has to say confidential? Within the Muslim brotherhood?"

"Of course. I wouldn't rat on my Muslim brothers, Fariq. I'm not a good Muslim, in your view, but that's one thing I don't do. I'm not a rat. To honor my father, I try to be a good Muslim."

"And a good Muslim man can also be an angry one. With justifiable cause."

Across the table, the older man suddenly grabbed his forearm and held it, viselike. Fariq was surprisingly strong for a man his age. A glance over at the next table reassured the men there, evidently, for they appeared to visibly relax. Fariq smiled and nodded, first at the two men and then at Samir. When he stood up, so did Jake, out of respect. They shook hands and then hugged and kissed each other in the Muslim way. Once on each cheek.

"Samir, my son, you will find what you seek, Allah be praised. I'm certain of this. I will call you soon about the meeting. It will be discreet and away from the mosque. There is always the threat at the mosque of police informants. People whom we believe are FBI plants."

Jake frowned appropriately and nodded again his consent but decided to be a little bold.

"But, Fariq, you work for them, the FBI. I saw you that day."

The older man smiled. "Now, why do you think that is so?" When Jake said nothing, Fariq shot him a cunning look before paying the bill in cash. After the man and his entourage left, Jake sat back down and finished his tea.

If anyone looked closely at his expression, they would assume the man sitting there was newly content. Even happy.

All Jake was really thinking was, *Okay. Game on.*

Chapter Twelve

M eg left the classroom with a young woman whom she'd learned on the first evening of Spanish Renaissance Literature was from New Orleans. They'd heard each other's accents, and sensing a common interest other than their shared Southern heritage, began to pal around on Tuesday and Thursday evenings. She and Sharon had met for dinner at a nearby Italian restaurant, then drove over to the campus in Sharon's car for their evening class. Her new friend lived a couple of miles away and so always drove to school.

"Y'all want a ride home?" Sharon asked Meg.

"No, I'll walk. It's only three blocks, and the weather's nice." Meg glanced at the sky. The night was cool, but the sky was void of clouds, the usual state of San Diego autumn weather, she was learning. The constant perfect temperature, between 65 and 85 degrees, was getting monotonous, and she found herself craving a good ol' Dallas thunderstorm, complete with lightning flashes and crashing booms. The kind that kept you awake all night but made you grateful for your warm bed. On the plus side, she was getting accustomed to walking around in jeans and a cotton-knit top. Oh, and sneakers or sandals.

God, what a life. Could she get used to living here full-time? Living near family and with the ocean so close? With such perfect weather and everyone bearing suntans all year round? Only, she decided, if Jake lived here, too. They could get a place by the ocean . . .

Meg chatted a bit with Sharon, then waved goodbye. Not

as lonely as she was a month ago, she was beginning to relax and enjoy the SoCal scene, as Jake called it. Her German language classes were somewhat challenging, especially the German history course she took Monday, Wednesday, and Friday mornings. German verb conjugations and pronoun declensions were a royal pain in the butt.

And there was a complication. She hated to admit that Jake's jealousy was justified. Professor Heinz had clearly taken a special interest in her, a turn of events that made her feel uncomfortable as well as threatened her status in the class. If she continued to decline his invitations for dinner, he might turn vindictive and —

Her thoughts were interrupted by the young man beside her. He'd come abreast of her strides down the sidewalk and had fallen into step with her before she recognized him.

"Oh hi, Alejandro," she said, then switched to fluent Spanish. They'd spoken a few times in the central court patio of their apartment building, and she'd learned he was from Spain via Mexico City. A foreign exchange student studying engineering and English. He was far from fluent in English, so most of the time when they ran into each other, they'd drift quickly into Spanish. "Do you have a night class, too?"

"*Si*, CAD drafting for mechanical engineering." He'd slung a backpack over one shoulder and was easily keeping pace with her fast stride.

His head came to her shoulder, but he didn't seem to mind the height difference. Why should he, after all? Not a bad-looking guy, he hadn't shown any interest in her other than as a friend. Which was just fine with her. Keeping Prof Heinz at arm's length was enough trouble.

They mostly talked about the mild weather for mid-October, her tutoring in the San Diego Unified Latino Literacy program. Which gave her an idea.

"Your roommates, they're all Spanish speaking, aren't

they?" She'd seen three other guys all about the same age in the same apartment as Alejandro's, and he'd told her once they were all here in California on student visas.

"Si, Jesus is Mexican. Roberto and Marco are Spaniards. We met up the first week at the housing office. They're taking classes in town at San Diego Community College. Until their English improves."

"I wonder if they'd be interested in helping with the Literacy program. That's working with K through twelfth-grade students with poor English skills. Immigrant kids. Mostly translating the English books they're assigned into Spanish, helping them with English and Spanish comprehension by asking questions, vocabulary work, correcting their writing assignments, that kind of thing. A lot of kids in San Diego are children of Mexican nationals and they speak only Spanish at home. If your friends have any free time, they could help out. Their English might be good enough. Probably is, if they're taking classes at SDCC."

Alejandro held open the wrought-iron gate to their apartment complex. It was never locked, so she never understood why the complex was fenced and gated to begin with. What was the point? She suspected students had complained to the owner and he'd given in to their demands.

"Here, give them this flyer—or better yet, I'll talk to them and explain about the program."

He took the flyer, one of several she carried at the request of the program supervisor. The woman had encouraged Meg to recruit other UC San Diego students to volunteer with the Latino Literacy program.

"No, not tonight." His stance, withdrawing quickly over to his side of the complex, baffled her. "Another time. They're in Drafting class tonight. I can't disturb them."

He was gone before she could say another word. Odd behavior, she thought. As though Alejandro was discouraging them from socializing.

Mentally shrugging, Meg went up the stairs to her apartment, unlocked the door and hurriedly punched in the keycode to turn off the alarm. She'd surrendered to Jake's insistence on a security system and even allowed him to pay for it. If it eased his conscience, so be it.

Something continued to niggle at the back of her mind as she brewed a Keurig cup of tea. She had Cervantes' Don Quixote to slog through—did the man ever write a short book, she wondered wearily. Cervantes' Spanish was Old World and difficult to translate into the modern Spanish she'd learned to use and teach. Still, it was a way to advance her knowledge of Spanish history and literature. If she taught Honors Spanish the following year, that would come in handy.

Succumbing to paranoia—thanks to Jake—she pored through the Fall Catalogue of classes. No CAD Drafting offered on Tuesday and Thursday evenings. Not anywhere on campus.

Odd. Why would Alejandro lie about such a thing? Was he lying in wait for her to come out of her class and didn't want it to look obvious? Was he waiting for her to split off from Sharon so he could talk to her alone? Why? He certainly didn't act like a man with a hidden crush.

Bizarre. She sipped the hot tea and thought again of Jake. What was he doing? Would he be able to get away and come down to see her that weekend? With no further hesitation, she impulsively punched in his latest cell phone number. He'd told her that he bought a new, untraceable, prepaid cell phone every two weeks. When she'd asked him why, he said he had to keep his calls to her a secret. Meaning, she supposed, that he hadn't informed his superiors of his relationship with a woman involved in a former FBI investigation. She wondered about that, too.

Meg let it ring until it went to voice mail. She left a brief message as all thoughts of Alejandro and his roommates fled her mind. So where was Jake? Ten-thirty on a Tuesday night. What was *he* up to?

Was he having a secret meeting with jihadis with sharp-as-razors box-cutters in their back pockets? Was he lying somewhere in a pool of blood? Decapitated? God, no! She was watching too many crime dramas on TV. That didn't happen to FBI agents . . . did it?

Then she remembered Jake's close call with the Celtic Wolves, how they'd fired at him while chasing both Meg and Jake on their motorcycles. How the stallion at the Irish Stud Farm had nearly stomped Jake to death. How those neo-Nazis had held them at gunpoint—

She swore under her breath and punched his number again.

Alejandro unlocked the door and entered the apartment. The mini blinds were shut tight and the only light in the small living room came from an end table lamp. Three men knelt upon the carpet, shoeless, their foreheads touching the floor. They were facing east toward the holy city of Mecca and muttering low to themselves.

Only one of them glanced up. Roberto was his alias, his real name Khalid. He knew little Spanish, which was why Alejandro had to prevent that tall, blonde woman from speaking to them. More than a couple of sentences and she would know they were impostors.

On a special mission, they'd flown from the Libya training camp to Morocco, then to Ceuta, a Spanish territory in North Africa. Then on to Mexico with their new Spanish passports. Six months ago, the three men in Alejandro's cell were in training at a Libyan paramilitary camp financed by the wealthy supporters of Al Qaeda. Now they were supposed to be community college students in San Diego, looking the part of middle-class Spaniards. He shook his head. Staying here in San Diego was a flawed idea. Sure, they looked Hispanic, but only Alejandro was fluent in Spanish.

"Aren't you going to pray?" Khalid asked in Arabic.

Alejandro, a Moroccan who'd spent half his life working in the south of Spain, shrugged one shoulder. He held aloft one of the newspapers he'd bought on campus that evening. He tossed his copy of the San Diego Tribune down on the carpet.

"Open it to the classified ads. Under Used Cars. You'll see."

Their prayers forgotten, the three men gathered around the open newspaper. Khalid's forefinger ran down one particular column. His finger stopped and he read the precise wording of the simple English advertisement.

"*Allahu akbar! Allahu akbar!*" he exclaimed loudly before Alejandro hushed him up.

"Turn the TV on," their leader commanded, "to mask our voices. We've been called, Allah be praised. The sheikh has called us. Finally."

Khalid raised dark, sinister eyes to the cell leader, his expression writhing with disgust. "Finally. I hate these people, these Satan sun-worshippers. I can't even bear to look at them, these spoiled children."

"Yes, finally. Two months of waiting here in this strange land and we are finally called. The greatness of Allah's blessings is upon us," Alejandro said.

He gazed at the three young men for whom he was directly responsible and studied their faces and bodies for possible signs of defection. He might put them through one last test before they left. For this, the tall blonde across the way might be useful.

"Now we must discuss the plan. As the sheikh advised, we must stay until the end of the month. On Halloween night, when there will be a lot of commotion and many people in the streets, we shall pack up our belongings, leave and go north."

The other three men made no comments. Their expressions told him that they were mentally taking it all in—the venue change, their new destination, and their upcoming roles in the Great Plan that lay ahead.

"Cordoba," Alejandro said, his breath catching. The once greatest of the Spanish Islamic caliphates, where his own ancestors held reign over the lowly Christians and Sephardic Jews in their midst and all was great in the world.

"Cordoba," the three men echoed.

"*Allahu akbar.*" Alejandro raised his eyes to the ceiling, his voice quivering with emotion.

"*Allahu akbar,*" the three chorused.

Then, all together, they bowed low, their foreheads touching the carpet, and gave thanks and praise to Allah.

CHAPTER THIRTEEN

At nine o'clock, the usual time Jake reported in, he went out onto his balcony. The night air was cold and the ocean breezes spilling over the coastal mountains to his west stirred the branches in the nearby redwood tree. As he punched in the secure series of numbers on his Bureau-issued cellular phone, he gazed out across the street at the park. From his vantage point, he could survey the southernmost end of the park, including the World War II memorial. SAC Frank Rodriguez hadn't yet shown up. Then Jake mentally smacked his forehead. It was only Tuesday. Funny how he'd begun to look forward to those clandestine Wednesday night meetings. That was how lonely Jake was. At least, now he had something concrete to report to both the CTC chief and his boss back at Headquarters. And a slew of questions for Rodriguez. All about Fariq and their great vetting process. The guy was a damned Islamist recruiter and they were allowing him to work for them. Were they nuts?

Speaking extemporaneously, Jake left a verbal report on the encryption machine, which would immediately decrypt the message on the other end by a Bureau decoding computer. Then his words would be transcribed, printed, and copied by another computer. A Bureau-liaison staffer would send the copies to the appropriate federal officers. In hours, he'd expect a reply and instructions to either proceed or halt. The latest developments were insufficient to produce a search warrant, of course, but would be enough to initiate a preliminary investigation of Fariq Al-Nasreem.

He'd go into the meeting with the mullah with a wire or hidden camera. For that, he'd need Rodriguez's help. What the cleric and his assistant said at that meeting would determine how much further the CTC would or could go without stepping on individual rights or religious freedom.

Although religious freedom was a right held dear by any American, it also served as a shield from prosecution for those who sometimes abused that freedom. That was what their lawyers would claim, anyway, in court. One American Islamic organization was already suing the New York Police Department for infringement of individual rights and harassing a holy place of worship, just because the PD was keeping an eye on individuals at those mosques who were on government watch lists.

If you have nothing to hide, why should you care?

Back at CTC, ICE — Immigration and Customs Enforcement — would be ordered to run extensive background checks on the two visitors from Great Britain, more thorough than the ones required to issue them temporary visas. The Brits would help by digging into the mullah's life, his reputation in the Muslim community of East London in which he sermonized, including his latest travels, and so on. At least, Jake hoped the extra scrutiny would take place. That wasn't his call. He was just a foot soldier, after all.

When Jake clicked off, he stared for a long moment at the swaying tree branches through which the breeze sighed, as if speaking to him. *Proceed with extreme caution.*

Too late for that, he thought. If he made the wrong judgment call now, his career would be on the line. Headquarters was watching, he knew. His boss, Terry, wanted to promote him. He'd told him so just before Jake volunteered for this assignment. If he succeeded in exposing a sleeper cell or a terrorist plot, they'd claim him a hero and boot him upstairs. Or maybe give him a SAC post (Special Agent in Charge) in a field office. If he failed or fucked up in any way, it was desk duty in Intel for the next thirty years. Which was what he'd started out liking, but then . . . along came the excitement of field work and undercover assignments. And Meg.

He was about to switch cell phones and dial her when a knock sounded at his door. A glance over at his neighbor's balcony just feet away told him that Linda Brown was home. Lights could be seen through the sheer curtains behind the drapes. It could be her again. Maybe with another plate of brownies.

Sure enough. Standing before him and holding out a plate of goodies, this time chocolate-chip cookies, it looked like. Linda was beaming.

"Boy, Linda, you're going to make me fat." He took the plate gladly and set it on the kitchen counter. "Hold on. I'll transfer the cookies to something else and you can take your plate back."

She'd followed him into his galley kitchen, just steps from the entryway. "No, Samir, keep the plate. There's something for you underneath. I was asked to give it to you." She looked over at the fridge pulled out at an angle from the wall. Happily, she said nothing about it.

Puzzled by her words, he held up the plate. Taped underneath was a white envelope. "What's this? Who gave it to you?"

"A man who said he was Frank Rodriguez."

Jake covered his surprise as well as he could. "When did he give you this?"

"Today. When I came home from the grocery store, he was sitting in his car at the curb. He knew I was your next-door neighbor."

He brightened at her opening. "Yes, I told him your great baking was going to make me fat. I probably described you. And to burn off these calories, I've gotta go running"—he looked at his watch—"like soon."

Still wearing his work clothes, he didn't want her to think he was brushing her off by hinting at having to change. "Linda, you've been so nice, so generous. I want to buy you dinner one evening but this week is a little crazy. Can I come by and set up dinner for next week? As soon as my schedule at work opens up?"

She looked delighted and said for him to come by anytime. When she left, he noticed a bounce in her step. For that, he was glad. Nice lady. But what the hell was Rodriguez doing, involving such a nice lady in their cloak-and-dagger routine?

When he tore open the envelope, he found out. "Miss Brown works for us. She's Special Support."

A little shocked, Jake read on.

"Miss Brown helped us solve a local corporate espionage case last year and we kept her on. Be extra kind to her. She's good at courier work and counter surveillance. If you need to get a message to me, go through her. You're under surveillance, and not just by Fariq's man. Two others, a Muslim-looking man and a scarf-wearing woman, have been on your tail ever since this morning. Be careful. They either suspect you're a fed or they're checking you out. It's too risky for us to meet on Wednesday nights. Make sure your apartment and rental car aren't bugged. Use her cell phone to call me with updates. Good luck, compadre."

Using kitchen matches, he set fire to the note and let the curled-up paper turn to ashes in his sink, all the while pondering his next move.

And wondering why he hadn't picked up on the extra tail. They were good, too damned good for amateurs. Decisively, he pulled out his untraceable cell phone and punched in Rodriguez's private number, the one he'd given Jake that first day at the FBI field office. He'd hoped that face-to-face contact would build a sense of trust and camaraderie between them.

Obviously that wasn't going to work.

When Rodriguez picked up, Jake launched into his list of needs.

"Look, man, I need a round-the-clock tail on Fariq starting tonight, and also one on this British cleric, Amad, and his side-kick, Ali. They're planning something, I know it, and they've got me in mind for it. Or at least some part of it. As far as I know, Amad and Ali are staying at a Residence Inn near the mosque, but they'll be moving soon. I overheard some talk at the mosque about this. Make sure the surveillance teams you send out understand the priority of keeping them in sight at all times."

Rodriguez began to protest the logistics of forming teams this hour of the night, but Jake cut him off.

"That couple, I think they work for the cleric. I've re-quested that ICE and the CTC dig into his background. Look, I dangled the bait and they're about to bite. This is top prior-ity. We can't let them disappear in the wind, so put your best details on them, Frank." He was about to add the fact that they knew how to get to his girlfriend in San Diego but de-cided against it. He'd just have to convince Fariq that his re-lationship with Meg was just a lapse of judgment and it wouldn't happen again.

He had to break off contact with her. Which meant, he had to conclude this deal quickly, the sooner the better.

When the SAC finally conceded the need, Jake added one more thing, "Oh, and forget the notes back and forth with Linda. Takes too long. Things are going to start cracking fast. They always do with undercover work. I need people close by to back me up. I want a surveillance van with muscle and techies aboard. I might not have much time between contact and meeting. Are you with me?"

Jake rang off as soon as Rodriguez gave the okay.

You better, pal. If this goes down and I'm put to some hairy-ass test, you and your guys better back me up.

Feeling reassured, he shed the work clothes and donned his running outfit, throwing a sweatshirt over his T-shirt. The hood partially hid his face, allowing him to scan the area surreptitiously while running.

Before Jake left his apartment, though, he took out his waist holster, chambered a round into his Glock, then holstered the pistol. It snapped onto the waistband of his sweatpants on the side but was concealed under his baggy sweatshirt. Tucking the encryption cell phone in the plastic case, he locked it up and duct-taped the case to the back of the refrigerator. Slid back within the surrounding cabinetry, the fridge stuck out an extra half a foot. But you wouldn't notice it if you weren't looking for it.

With his Glock and holster in place, Jake was ready to take on this cat-and-mouse game.

During his third loop on the park's perimeter dirt path, he finally saw them. The couple was in a car in a parking lot at the far northern end of the park beside the main administration building. They were pretending to be deep in discussion, but sheepish looks around them made Jake almost laugh out loud. At the southern end of the park, next to the World War II memorial, Fariq's man pretended to run through a series of exercises on the Par course. A scientist-civilian like Samir would assume the man lived nearby and was doing what Jake was doing, trying to keep fit.

The cool air was now turning cold, a hint of winter touching his face. His heated body barely registered the change in temperature. As far as he could tell, the two teams on his tail posed no threat. Not at the moment, anyway. They were checking him out, although Jake had no doubt that he'd eventually be tested in some way. At some point, he'd have to prove his loyalty and devotion to their holy war.

The prepaid cell phone he'd pocketed vibrated against his thigh. He looked at the number but didn't answer it. Meg. He didn't want to be distracted or give anything away while under surveillance. He'd wait until he got back to his apartment. Meg and his family were the only ones who had this current number. Inevitably, memories of this past weekend with her flooded his insides with pure pleasure. Arousal. Deep aches.

After one more loop around the park, ignoring the lovers in the parked car at the north end and the Par Course fanatic at the south end, Jake called it quits. He hoped like hell the show of his fitness regimen had bored them to death. Thirty minutes later, after stashing his Glock under the companion pillow on his king-size bed, he took a hot shower. Then he called Meg.

"What's new?" he asked.

"Nothing much. I went on a run down to Torrey Pines, then had dinner with Sharon before our night class. Spanish Renaissance lit. My strange neighbor walked me home . . ."

"Why is he strange?" He tensed up at the possibility of a new rival. Immediately wondered when he was going to see her again. Impossible, not until this was over. But he couldn't tell her that.

"Oh, it's nothing. He's not so strange but his roommates are. They're Hispanics, but what's strange is, I've never heard them speak Spanish. They stay together, rarely go out. Not typical Spaniards, who tend to be social animals. I know, I've been to Spain several times. Any excuse for a fiesta or social gathering. Fun-loving people. These guys are the antithesis of that. Even Alejandro keeps to himself." Her sigh transmitted across the wire. "It's nothing. I'm just bored and overly curious, I guess, living here in this place. Like that old movie, *Rear Window*, where the guy in the wheelchair watches his neighbors through binoculars."

She laughed and he joined her. "Good to hear you laugh, Meg." He meant it, too. Her happiness was vital to him, he realized. As much as her safety.

They talked for almost an hour about this and that before her chatting slowed to a pause. He could hear her breathing turn into heavy sighs, which meant she was about to get emotional, maybe even maudlin. When he couldn't be there to comfort or reassure her, or distract her with sex, her emotions usually spilled over. Made him feel frustrated and guilty that he had to keep this distance from her.

"I miss you, Jake. Are you being careful?"

"Yes, trying to. Me, too."

"What do you mean, me too?" Her tone took on a hard edge. Jake knew what she wanted him to say. Why were such simple little words so hard for him to say?

"I mean, Meg . . ." It took him a couple of starts and stops before he was able to finish. "I miss you, too. More than I can say. Words cannot express how I feel, Meg. I've never been good at saying how I feel. I'd rather show you than tell you."

That produced a wistful chuckle. "So when can you show me again how you feel?"

The wheels were already turning. God, he was so weak. When it came to her, he was as soft as a marshmallow. He shouldn't risk it. Still, he had to make it happen.

"Soon, I promise."

The lie stuck in his throat, clogged him up long after they hung up.

Chapter Fourteen

Two weeks passed with no further developments. Jake was about to conclude that something he'd said or done had spooked the mullah and his sidekick, Ali. Headquarters, or rather his boss, Terry, and the CTC chief, had placed a discreet wiretap on the mullah's and Ali's cell phones. But nothing smacking of criminal intent had shown up. Other than a few calls to London and Dallas, to the mosque administrators in both cities, nothing suspicious had emerged. It was the same situation, Terry had reported, in the other Cordoba cities in the U.S. Visiting mullahs from a variety of foreign countries and their entourages were conducting seminars and preaching at Friday prayer services, but nothing seemed out of place. Even the cyber chatter had diminished, according to the NSA listeners.

The calm before the firestorm, Jake wondered with growing disquiet. Or simply nothing to begin with? False alarms?

After a face-to-face meeting, if a terrorist plot was revealed and details came to light, Jake would ask for search warrants, including a thorough dissection of other electronic devices the mullah and his assistant used. With Amad's engineering background, Jake suspected he carried a laptop with him at the very least. Digging into that laptop was crucial. But for now, lacking a legal reason, their hands were tied. At the moment, the local FBI surveillance revealed that Amad and Ali were bunking down at a San Miguel Residence Inn on the El Camino Real.

Meanwhile, Jake dutifully logged into the An-Vax facility

every morning at eight AM, parked in the employees' back parking lot hidden from the street, and swiped his card and passed the iris scanner into the elevator which whisked him up to the second-floor offices. After a couple of hours, working on his government issued laptop—appearing to validate Todd Walinski's QC reports—he would slip out the back parking lot and take a different, circuitous route to a nearby gym. Running on the treadmill and lifting weights resulted in honing his abs, biceps, and quads to their most muscular in years.

During his breaks at the gym, he'd check in with Meg and his family on his burner cell phone. So far, he'd broken off two weekend dates with Meg, hearing the disappointment and tension in her voice each time. The frustration in himself was building. She'd invited him down for Halloween weekend— the holiday falling on a Saturday that year. The German Club's advisor—*Herr Scheisse-gesicht*, Mr. Shithead, to Jake— was hosting a party and everyone was supposed to dress up like a famous German or Austrian. Meg suggested their going as Captain Von Trapp and his singing wife.

Knowing he'd never make the event—did he even want to?—Jake nevertheless joked about going as Schwarzenegger and Meg as Marlene Dietrich, the WW II movie star. He nearly tossed out the idea of her going as her grandmother, the famous Nazi spy, Hummingbird, but caught himself in time. The ironic truth about her grandmother was still too painful for her to appreciate, he knew. At any rate, the Halloween party was the kind of thing normal people looked forward to, but it was definitely not his thing. Certainly not in the middle of an undercover assignment.

Pressure came from his mother, too. Thanksgiving was around the corner, and Jake's family was hoping he would come and bring his *new girlfriend*. He'd given his mother a tentative yes since—jeez, he hoped, anyway—this damned assignment would wrap up by then, one way or another.

Social planning with Meg was an exercise in futility because he couldn't risk another lapse of self-control. As sure as the night followed the day, Amad and Ali were watching him. The same couple sat in the parking lot across the street every evening while he jogged around the park. At the mosque on Fridays, he felt his hackles rise and knew Ali's dark eyes were lasering through him. The guy had military or paramilitary training, Jake could tell, just by the man's posture and watchfulness. Reasonable, since most bodyguards were ex-military. But there was something about the two of them, Jake sensed. Something he couldn't yet define. Ali's eyes were always alert as men gathered around the mullah after prayer service, watching their hands, their upper bodies.

The man's eyes reminded him of a training video he'd watched at Quantico, a CIA secret rendition session with a Hezbollah recruit from southern Lebanon, who'd been caught driving a truck loaded with Semtex, charges, and detonators across the border from Syria. Even incarcerated, the hapless man's eyes roved and hunted like Ali's.

There was Fariq, too. His man also watched Jake, although he'd cut back his surveillance to just the weekends. The same green sedan followed him home from the mosque two Fridays in a row, and Jake spotted the same vehicle around the apartment complex for several days afterward. Rodriguez had run a vehicle license check, revealing the car was one of several in Fariq's fleet. The man was an employee of Fariq's, had no priors, and was a naturalized citizen, born and raised in Egypt like Fariq, and introduced by him as a distant cousin. The young man had no connections to the Muslim Brotherhood, which surprised Jake. He was convinced that Fariq and his pals were all covert Muslim Brotherhood supporters, if not actual foreign operatives. But he had no proof. Yet.

They were all basically asking Jake the same questions. Are

you really the devoted Muslim man you claim to be? Or do you run to the kafir woman every chance you get? Are you an FBI confidential informant? An undercover cop?

Jake had overheard the men at the mosque talk about new-comers in such a way, very suspicious and on guard. There was even a flyer on the mosque's bulletin board: *If the FBI contacts you, contact us first. You have the right not to speak to them.* So, Jake wondered, if they had nothing to hide, why be so suspicious?

Until his dinner meeting with Fariq, reports back to FBI Headquarters and the CTC task force had been brief — No movement. His request for round-the-clock surveillance of the British mullah and his assistant had been blocked. According to Terry, the request had been kicked upstairs, then kicked back down again. Someone with power in D.C. was afraid of a lawsuit by the same American Islamic organization that was suing the New York P.D. Someone in D.C. with no balls, Jake figured, and maybe a palace full of wealthy Saudi friends, many of whom financed that organization's very lawsuits.

So Jake finally turned to Rodriguez. The local field office had two teams tailing Fariq but no teams on Amad and Ali.

"Not good enough," Jake told him during one phone call, his frustration spilling over. Their communication had become frequent, so now they were calling each other on weekday mornings, Jake using his burner cell phone at An-Vax to report in to the San Jose SAC. "I think the mullah and his pal are the key players, not Fariq. He's second string. Fariq observes and suggests the person to approach, but it's the mullah who's calling the shots. Ali's his muscle. I'd bet my Georgetown condo on it."

"Okay, man, I'll see what I can do. I'm in a tough spot right now since we're short-handed. The assistant SAC, Mike Cho Jordan, is swamped trying to get replacements. He's a good man, but three agents quit on us this month alone. Left to do private security for high-tech billionaires and make big bucks.

One joined the DEA, said our field office was dullsville. He's an ex-Ranger, an adrenaline junkie. He thinks he'll get more action chasing the drug cartels. Actually, he's probably right."

Jake thought of Linda Brown. "Two of our most effective surveillance teams in D.C. consisted of older women. They called themselves the invisible ones. Linda seems like she wants to do more, so if she's up to it, it's worth a try."

"We'll see, Jake. Linda's just a temp with the Special Support Group, not an agent. But she's had surveillance training."

"I realize that. With your permission, I'll get some photos to her" — the ones he took in the mosque with the hidden, miniature camera. "There was some talk I overheard about moving Amad and Ali to another place. We need to keep track of their whereabouts outside the mosque."

"Okay, I'll call Linda now and ask her if she's willing."

Jake kept his voice even, but his insides seethed. He shouldn't have to beg for this kind of support, but under the circumstances, he was lucky to get this much.

"Good. Thanks, Frank."

Linda Brown pinned the hijab tightly under her chin and followed the other covered-up women to the women's prayer room. Individually, they stored their shoes on hallway racks outside the double doors and then filed in. Small children of both sexes accompanied their mothers, older boys went into the men's prayer room. Once settled on the carpet, the women watched through glass walls while the men in the front prayer room took their places on the carpeted floor.

The visiting mullah began to speak, his British accent sounding educated to Linda's ears. The middle-aged cleric was beginning the sermon by evidently quoting in Arabic from the Qur'an. Then he launched into a translation and explanation of the chapter and verse in his lilting English. At that point, Linda tuned out and just focused on observing the people around her.

Older men and women sat in chairs while most of the others sat, squatted, or kneeled on the carpet. The congregation was quiet and respectful as the mullah spoke.

When other women glanced over at the newcomer in their midst, Linda merely nodded and smiled, as though she went to Muslim prayer service every week. Not the least bit nervous, she already had a cover story set up in case someone asked. She used to be married to a Muslim man, had converted, then after divorcing him, had returned to her Christian faith. Now she was exploring the idea of reconverting. Sounded plausible enough to her, anyway.

She'd immediately recognized the middle-aged British mullah and his assistant, thanks to Jake's photos. A couple of the photos were close-ups, which didn't help in this particular case because she was at least fifty feet away. But the middle-range shots of the two men were very helpful. Today they wore the same garb as they wore in their photos. The mullah, Amad, wore a white tunic over loose, white pants and a white skullcap on his head. She forgot what Jake had called it in Arabic.

His assistant, Ali, wore the same dark brown suit and unusual tie—wide stripes of black, red, and green. The Western attire both surprised her and relieved her. The younger, taller man looked like so many of the others in the men's prayer room, with the exception of, as Jake called it, his Palestinian-flag tie. A code for where his sympathies lay. There was no question in her mind who these two men were.

After the mullah's sermon, something about the importance of total obedience to the will of Allah, everyone— man, woman and child—bent over in prayer. Linda copied the women around her, laboriously lowering herself to her hands and knees. Chrissakes! Her stiff, creaky body told her she wasn't getting any younger. Had she known groveling on the floor was part of the deal — Oh well. She touched her forehead to the carpet, as the others were doing, hoping all the while the damned rug had been cleaned lately. Her low mumbles blended in with the muffled prayers of the women and girls around her. She mentally went through her grocery shopping list — milk, bread, mumble, mumble. Eggs, yogurt, a bottle of glucosamine for her joints, mumble, mumble.

There was no music or singing, no statues to pray to, no photos or images of either Allah or the prophet Muhammad. No incense or candles. Nothing to look at except white walls and raised rear ends of the women near her and the male butts on the other side of the glass.

Ten minutes later, the service was over and everyone stood.

Linda noticed Jake stand up on the far side of the men's prayer room. My, he was such a tall, good-looking guy. That sleek dark hair and broad shoulders lent him such masculine appeal. If she were only thirty — no, forty years younger. The heads of the younger women in the room pivoted as he walked to the pulpit and shook the mullah's hand. Other men stood and then blocked her view, so she stiffly rose and headed for the exit.

Rather than linger to socialize afterward in the hallway, social hall, or cafeteria, Linda retrieved her shoes and hurried to her car in the vast parking lot behind the mosque. Still wearing her hijab, she pretended to be waiting for a friend to come out and join her.

Half an hour later, the mullah, his assistant, and a young couple emerged from the back exit of the Cordoba Center. The taller man, Ali, took his place behind the steering wheel of a white Toyota sedan. Already dark at five-thirty, the parking lot was brightly lit with halogen lamps. Afraid they might have noticed her entering alone, Linda crouched down until the sedan pulled out of the lot.

Quickly, she whipped off her hijab and put on a black wig with an attached red-felt cloche styled hat. Big, tinted glasses and red lipstick completed the new disguise. Her car, a nondescript, black mid-size sports coupe, fell into line three cars behind Ali's.

This assignment was a little nerve-racking, Linda decided, but also fun. Helping the local FBI two years ago as a CI, she'd kept watch on a visiting Chinese engineer suspected of corporate espionage at her former employer, Random Electronics. The operation had been so successful that as soon as she retired, she decided covert operations were a heck of a lot more fun than what she'd been doing. Basic FBI training in surveillance and counter-surveillance had helped, of course. Nevertheless, her heart pounded as she maintained a steady tail as far as the El Camino Real, where traffic thickened and slowed.

But instead of swerving off into the Residence Inn, Ali's white sedan continued on for another couple of miles before taking a left onto an expressway that connected the town of Sunnyvale to the posh bedroom community of Saratoga. Linda fell farther behind but managed to keep the white car and its red taillights in view as the thoroughfare narrowed and branched off into two distinct roads.

Following the white sedan along a two-lane, residential street, Linda drove more slowly, pulling back behind another vehicle, this one a jacked-up pickup truck. She took off the tinted glasses and rubbed her eyes as fatigue set in. Despite the cold outside, perspiration trickled down her face. She kept her cell phone handy just in case she had to make a quick call to Frank Rodriguez for help.

The white car turned right onto a street in an upper-class neighborhood where the lots were a half-acre or larger. Linda knew the area and, not panicking, drove past the street, took another right and then stopped. The white car didn't drive past on a cross street, so she doubled back around and took the street it had originally turned onto. Spying the red tail-lights on a side street, she pulled over to the curb, then backed up to keep the white car in sight.

Linda plucked off her black wig and cloche, fluffing up her short, bleached-blond hair, transforming herself again. In the trunk of her sports coupe, she'd stashed a lightweight, fold-up stroller. She grabbed it and stuffed an old Cabbage-Patch Kid into its seat. The doll was wrapped up to its little pug nose in a blanket and looked almost real. She then straightened out the wheels and set off on a short walk down the side street. Two houses away, Ali stood outside while the garage door lowered behind the white sedan.

With her fur-lined, jacket hood pulled up, Grandma walked past nonchalantly with her baby grandchild. She kept her face averted until the lights went on and the man disappeared inside the house. Pretending to adjust the stroller harness, she noted the address then fast-walked around the court back to her car. After tossing the stroller and fake baby into her trunk, Linda got inside and called Jake's burner phone, then reported in to Rodriguez. Both thanked her and said she'd done well.

Sighing with contentment, Linda made her way back toward the heavy traffic. After her success, she needed a reward—not that Jake's gushing gratitude wasn't enough. He'd promised her a dinner at P.F. Chang's and she intended to collect on that promise. Meanwhile, though, she'd treat herself to a Baskin-Robbins ice cream cone. She steered into the shopping mall where she knew she'd find one.

All in an evening's work. She'd earned her modest paycheck in addition to that Chinese dinner. While she licked her strawberry-and-cheesecake ice cream, she smiled and plotted her next round of disguises.

Three days later, while at An-Vax, Jake got the call. A distinctly British-accented baritone voice, after the *Salaam alaikum* greetings, told him pointedly to be at his apartment-complex curb that night. Ten o'clock sharp. He was going for a ride.

By eight o'clock, he'd gone over his instructions with Rodriguez. He'd be unarmed and not wired. He wanted no interference, just ultra-discreet surveillance. They'd located the mullah's new residence in the Saratoga hills — on a short-term lease, the field office's tech agent had discovered — and Rodriguez had arranged twenty-four-seven covert surveillance. The neighbor across the street, a retired executive, had taken a spontaneous journey abroad and rented out his house to a childless couple in their thirties.

Jake knew this "ride" with Amad and Ali was a test of his loyalty and obedience. He'd learned in Arabic school that potential jihadists were always subjected to a test. It was his intention to pass that test and emerge unscathed.

Jake moved out the fridge and unlocked the case. The tech guys at Headquarters had prepared Samir's cell phone for such an event. It was programmed with Samir's history of calls from his time in Florida, a directory of names, all staged, to within days of that moment. Fake calls had been logged with a few false names of Samir's former Florida friends and several real locations that he would have called, such as barbershops and restaurants. A fake history of correspondences and communications, along with fake texting.

He pocketed Samir's cell phone within the deep front pocket of his gray sweatpants. Besides that, he wore a black T-shirt and hooded, black sweatshirt. Looking around on his body, he found everything in place. The watch he wore had a wireless GPS locator and one-way transmitter imbedded. The techies had the back engraved with an Arabic inscription from Samir's father. The inscription was a verse from the Qur'an, to discourage destruction. If anything happened to that watch, Jake would be without any communication with his support team. Without it, he had only his wits.

And the knowledge that this step in the vetting process was a vital and dangerous one.

CHAPTER FIFTEEN

At nine-thirty PM, Jake heard a knock and Linda's frantic voice. He opened his apartment door and immediately noted her frazzled expression.

"Frank Rodriguez has been in a car crash. He was on his way to supervise the surveillance van in Saratoga—" She burst in, swallowing some air, her hand crossed over her heart.

Jake encouraged her to sit down and catch her breath. In a few moments, she continued. "They took Frank to the hospital. A DUI hit him. His car was T-boned on the driver's side. Frank's got a couple of broken bones and a concussion. Mike—that's his assistant, Mike Cho Jordan—is now acting Special Agent in Charge. He just called to alert me so I could tell you. He didn't have your burner phone number and Frank wasn't coherent enough to give it to him. Anyway, the van's on its way here. They're tailing the white Toyota right now but they might have to pull over—"

"To let Car Two take primary position?" Jake interjected. There were usually at least two cars in a moving tail, the second taking over while the first fell back.

"That's why Mike called me. There is no Car Two. The van was it. Mike wants me to leapfrog with the van after you're picked up and to use my cellphone to stay in touch. See, I don't have a car radio linked up to FBI frequency. But Jake, I've done this once in training, so I think I can do it. I've got to use my own car and make do. Only problem, I have no gun training. I mean, they gave me a class and I did some target shooting using their pistols but . . ." She shrugged, but her bugged out eyes revealed her true fear. And a smidgen of excitement. "Is it going to get violent? Will I have to use my gun?"

For a moment, Jake took it all in. He was sorry for Frank's rotten luck but damn, this was such bad timing. Linda's question hung in the air but it was one he couldn't answer. Instead, he asked, "How many agents in the van?" If worst came to worst, four armed agents would come in handy.

"Just two. The techie and the driver."

Jake swore under his breath. Two armed agents against four possibly armed unsubs, including Ali and the cleric. Jake wouldn't be armed but he'd earned the equivalent of a black belt in karate during his SEAL training and could take care of himself. Assuming he wasn't unconscious or shackled, that is.

Linda frowned. "What are you thinking? Are you going to call it off? This meeting with them?"

He shook his head slowly and clasped her upper arms in an attempt to calm her down. "Look, you have an advantage. You know they're coming here, so you're prepared to tail them. I doubt they'll be taking me back to their Saratoga house. Too risky with neighbors close by. They'll be taking me somewhere else, somewhere remote, away from crowds. If they don't take my watch"—Jake held it up for Linda to see—"and if I have a chance to talk alone, I'll talk to the tracking team through this transmitter. Here's the frequency." He wrote it down on a slip of paper and gave it to her. "Just note the place and give this to the techie. Make sure they understand it's a transmitter, not transceiver. Like a GPS tracker. It doesn't receive audibles. Let the tech van and this new SAC take over. The main thing is, they must give me room to maneuver. I've got to pass this test of theirs. But if things go sideways, this Mike Jordan knows what to do."

Call in the sheriff's Tac Squad, if he has any competence. Apprehend the assholes and wring the truth out of 'em.

He thought a second. *And send condolences to my family. And Meg.*

Linda whipped up her hand. "Oh my God, I forgot. Mike Jordan's on hold. He didn't have your phone number, so he called me."

"Last minute change of plans," Jake quipped sarcastically. "Always fun." He took her cell phone and spoke to the now acting Special Agent in Charge, Mike Cho Jordan. A memory of their first and only meeting surfaced. A young guy, appearing bi-racial, half Asian, had met him that first day at the San Jose field office. Introduced himself as Michael Cho Jordan. Looked smart, eager, and physically buff.

Jake and Mike spoke for several minutes, then rang off. There was no time to doubt. Only time to hope the people around him would follow his lead.

At ten o'clock sharp, the white Toyota pulled up to the curb near Jake's apartment building. A minute before, he'd noticed Fariq's man in the park but, as he stepped to the curb, the man had vanished.

The woman in the hijab was driving, and the cleric, Amad, was in the front passenger seat. In the back, the young man and Ali. The young skinny bearded man opened the door and got out. They exchanged *Salaam alaikum* greetings cordially, as if they were headed off to a local high school football game. Jake squeezed in between the two men in the back seat, nodded to Ali to his left, and exchanged a greeting with Amad.

"Do not be afraid, Samir, my son. We have come to talk, that is all," said the mullah. His Western dress—a winter jacket, sweater, and slacks—drew Jake's attention. He could've passed for an older American male in need of a barber.

"I understand, Sheikh Amad," he said mildly.

"We are people of peace who have been forced to take drastic action to defend ourselves," Amad continued. "So, with that mission in mind, let us speak the *Shahada*."

When the mullah began and the others joined in, Jake also spoke the profession of faith in Arabic. This profession of faith began all meetings of devout Muslims.

"There is no God but Allah, and Muhammad, peace and blessings be upon him, is the Messenger of Allah."

No sooner had they concluded than Ali's arm rose as though he were going to wrap it around Jake's shoulder.

In a sudden reflexive move, Jake jerked to his right side and bumped the shoulder of the young man. The metallic taser in Ali's hand reflected a streak of streetlight and flashed. The two prongs hit Jake's chest, tore two holes in his sweatshirt and tee shirt. The volt of electricity seared through him like a hot, jagged knife. Pain rippled through tissue and hit bone. For a split second, he smelled his own burnt flesh. His head swam. His vision tunneled. His stomach revolted.

Before Jake blacked out, a single oath tore from his throat. "Sonofa-"

Eleven o'clock and Jake still hadn't called. Meg tossed her German language textbook on the coffee table and snatched up her cell phone. She rang his latest burner phone number for the third time. It wasn't like Jake to forego an evening call. Not that she was an expert, but in her experience, she'd learned that most men were creatures of habit. In some ways, Jake was a buttoned-up kind of guy, probably due to his military training. He liked routine, liked a set way of doing things. And one of his routines was calling her every evening between ten and eleven. His calls uplifted both of them.

He couldn't say much about his undercover work, so she had to read between the lines, note his inflection of voice, a nuance of excitement or boredom, his pauses and silences. Most of the time, he spoke about his hobbies in D.C. His condo renovations, which he was doing, himself. His best buddy, Eric, the investment banker, and their football pools. Lately, Jake told her of his plans to spend time with her after this op was over. Introduce her to his family. Take off during her Christmas break and go skiing at Bear Mountain or Lake Tahoe.

His promised courtship, however, was turning out to be the opposite of what he'd led her to expect. Sure, she was disappointed. Except for that one weekend a month ago, there'd been no moonlit strolls, no romantic candlelit dinners, no shopping together. She hadn't even shown him around the UC San Diego campus or taken him for a jog along the towering eucalyptus trees. Tomorrow night was Halloween, and he hadn't yet gotten back to her about his plans for the weekend. Would he show up late that night? Tomorrow morning? Would he go with her to the German Club's Halloween party? Two nights ago, he'd evaded her questions about their costumes. What did that mean?

She knew. He either didn't want to go to that party or he wasn't planning to come. His undercover work demanded his focus, she suspected, and he didn't want to let her down. Still, he would have called and not left her hanging. So what went wrong?

Her heart raced. Exasperation and worry drove her to her front door. She'd swum earlier that day in the complex's heated pool and had hung her body towel over the upstairs railing. The dark red-and-blue terrycloth material was still damp to the touch. Time to bring it in and hang it over the shower.

Alejandro's door opened. From her second-floor vantage point across the square courtyard, she could observe them — all four of the men — carrying suitcases and boxes out of their furnished apartment. Instinctively, she crouched down behind the body towel, not sure why she wanted to remain hidden. There'd been something strange about Alejandro's behavior the evening before as he walked her home from her night class. He'd been chatty and friendly as he usually was, but this time he asked her personal questions. What was she doing that weekend? Did she expect anyone over Friday night? Was she going out or staying in? Were friends coming over? He'd seen her boyfriend that one weekend. Was he coming over?

Meg said she was going to a party Saturday evening, that her boyfriend might be coming down from northern California. Realizing too late that she was revealing too much, she backtracked and tried to shrug off all her plans. As usual, he clammed up whenever she asked him about his roommates. Alejandro said they might have to go away for the weekend and do some work for a friend of theirs. She hadn't probed further.

She peeked around the edge of the oversized towel. They were loading up their SUV with all of their suitcases. One of the guys dropped the box he was carrying and swore aloud. Another guy laughed and said something back to him.

That wasn't Spanish. She'd heard Arabic spoken in the south of Spain on several of her trips abroad, couldn't understand it, but recognized it when she heard it.

Her mind raced. The 9-11 hijackers had come over on student visas, had passed themselves off as hardworking, Westernized students. She knew from her travels that Spain had problems with Moroccans coming over to study or work. Some had radicalized and joined the jihadist movement. The Atocha train station explosion in Madrid in 2009 was the bloody handiwork of such radicalized Moroccans.

These guys with Alejandro didn't behave like regular students, although Alejandro was nice enough. But what did that matter? The 9-11 jihadis were reported to have been polite, shy but friendly. They didn't bring attention to themselves by engaging in criminal activities and they made a point of blending in, even going to bars and drinking. What did Jake call it in Arabic? *Taqiyya*? Displaying one intention while harboring another. The classic feint of Islamic extremists.

Meg shook herself mentally. Christ! Dating Jake was making her paranoid. She was seeing fanatical jihadists everywhere, even in her apartment complex. How crazy-ass was that?

She stood and, while bunching up the towel, called out to Alejandro.

Locking his apartment door, he looked up and frowned. "We're leaving for the weekend," he called up to her.

She wondered about that. It didn't appear that they were coming back, they'd carted away so much. "For that job you were talking about?"

"Yes."

"Looks like you guys're moving out. What happened?"

Alejandro stared at the key in his hand for a long moment, then walked across the courtyard. He stood beneath her railing and gazed up at her. His posture had changed, as though he had a rod up his back, and his eyes swept the entire courtyard before settling back on her. Every apartment was lit, but students had settled in for the evening. The patio and pool area was deserted, the sky thick with rainclouds. Humid air made her skin feel prickly but it was Alejandro's behavior that sent crawling sensations up the nape of her neck.

"No, we're not moving out. Just putting some things into storage. I'm wondering if you could pick up some mail for me. I'm expecting a very important package. I'll come up and give you my key. When the package comes, you can put it inside the apartment. So it doesn't get stolen while we're gone." He looked up at the overcast sky. "Or get ruined by rain."

"Sure, I'll do that. Just toss up the key, Alejandro." She

leaned over the railing and held out her arms. She glanced over at their SUV parked at the curb in front. The three other men were watching Alejandro and talking among themselves.

She didn't like the nasty smirks on their faces.

"No, I must give you the key and write something down for you." A tone in his voice alarmed her. They were about to take off with all of their possessions and Alejandro wanted to come into her apartment, something he'd avoided doing for over two months. What kind of parting gift did he have in mind? Why was he acting so furtive?

"No, stay there, Alejandro." Her voice was firm but he was already moving up the stairs, a determined hunch to his shoulders. She might be crazy — and if someone saw the way she was acting, he'd be certain of it — but she didn't care. She grabbed the towel, stepped into her apartment and locked the door. Knob, deadbolt, alarm on. Checked the windows near the landing. All the rods were in place.

Then she ran to her bedroom and grabbed her revolver. She spun the barrel to make sure it was loaded. The insistent pounding on her door, followed by Alejandro's voice, shocked her. Now he was pleading in Spanish, apologizing for frightening her, cajoling her, begging her to let him in.

She replied firmly in English. "Leave the key outside. I'll get it as soon as I see your car drive away. I mean it, Alejandro. I don't know what the hell you and your buddies are doing, but if you barge inside, I'm shooting first and asking questions later. I'm holding a loaded gun. You hear me?"

A half-minute passed before she heard his footsteps on the staircase outside her living room window. She went over to the window and watched Alejandro climb into the SUV with the others. His three pals didn't look happy with him, as though he'd messed up. Had he nearly jeopardized their plans with some last-minute mayhem?

When the car pulled away, only then did Meg rush to her front door. Turned off the alarm, unlocked and opened it. There was no key on the landing.

So much for his important package.

The adrenaline rush banking off, Meg began to tremble. The revolver shook in her hand. God, what was that all about? Was she going bonkers, pulling her gun on some foreign student like that?

Except that Alejandro and his pals weren't foreign students. At least, that wasn't all they were.

Another lesson reinforced, taught to her by her grandmother, alias the Nazi spy, Hummingbird. *Always trust your instincts.*

CHAPTER SIXTEEN

Jake floated up to a semiconscious state within five minutes, but he kept his eyes closed and remained limp—which wasn't hard to do, since he found it impossible to move or open his eyes. Not all of his muscles were working yet, but his hearing was back. He sagged across the young man's body, listening to the men on both sides of him argue in Arabic. While unconscious and thanks to the volts of electricity, his bladder had emptied, so he'd wet not only himself but the two men in back. They weren't happy about that.

He suppressed a smile. *Tough shit, you assholes.* They'd already yanked his arms back and shackled his wrists and ankles with plasticuffs. A hood covered his head and hung loosely around the base of his neck. He ignored the dull throbs of pain in his chest and tried to concentrate on their rapid, angry Arabic. While he couldn't translate it all, he picked up enough to know they were taking him to a storage facility somewhere in the San Bruno hills.

He recalled the map he'd studied of the San Francisco Bay Area. San Bruno, north of Redwood City. About fifteen miles south of San Francisco and twenty-five miles north of San Miguel.

Levi's Stadium, home to the Forty-Niners, was within ten miles of his apartment and hugged the edge of the South Bay. San Francisco International Airport was about forty miles north, off the Bayshore Freeway. Also, a major biotech firm, Genentech, had its headquarters in San Bruno. The old Moffett Field hangars, now used by NASA, were nearby. Jake considered those four possible targets and wondered if the other four undercover agents in Dallas, Miami, Chicago, and New York City had uncovered similar storage units in target-sensitive areas.

So what was in this storage facility? He hoped that Linda Brown and the FBI tech van had been able to keep the tail all the way from his apartment. This development was a crucial break in the case.

What followed in their conversation, with Amad interrupting often, was a heated debate about Samir's loyalty to Islam. Fariq had assured them that he was loyal and obedient, had given up the kafir woman and had rededicated himself to the straight and narrow path of Islam. Ali argued against trusting a man who'd once served in the American military, but the young man, whom Ali called Reza, countered that Major Hassan, the Army psychiatrist who'd shot and killed thirteen unarmed soldiers at Fort Hood, had proven himself to jihad. The woman remained silent, taking directions from the car's GPS device, and occasionally double-checking with the men on the route to take. There was no mention of anyone following them.

After twenty minutes, Jake stirred and moaned aloud. Most men of his fitness level wouldn't be conked out that long, so as soon as he let them know he was conscious, they shut up. All except for occasional cursing from Ali and Reza. Every few seconds, Ali elbowed Jake in the stomach and chest while the others said nothing.

Jake endured the painful jabs as part of this initiation. The hood covering his head was a thick cotton, light enough to allow in air but too heavy for him to see through. Inside the dark car, he was completely dependent on his hearing. After a while, the car slowed and stopped. Jake heard a metal gate creak open, the car moved, and then the gate closed. The car moved again, then stopped. Car doors opened.

Some kind of storage yard?

Moments later, Ali and Reza were dragging him under his arms, his big sneakers scraping on cement. It had begun to rain sometime during the trip up to San Bruno, and the cement was slick and wet. More creaking and squeaking and they lowered him to a dry but cold concrete floor. The bottom of the hood slid up his face as he stretched out on the cold floor, lying on his side and moaning for effect. The hood slipped up farther as Jake rested his head on the concrete. A rim of light below the hood indicated an internal light in what Jake guessed was a large storage locker.

He allowed them to push him into a corner but gave a half-hearted show of resistance when he felt a metal shackle snap around one of his ankles. Using only a quarter of his strength, he let Ali and Reza overpower him. Only after he submitted by bending over on his knees and touching his forehead to the concrete floor did they remove the plasticuffs—he could hear a knife cut through the plastic strap. When they allowed him to move his arms to the front of his body before cuffing his wrists again, he thanked them in Arabic. All the while, the mullah fed him a litany of rubbish.

"Samir, son of Islam, you have been with a kafir, an infidel, and now you must prove your total obedience to Allah and to his divine Messenger, Muhammad, peace and blessings be upon him. Prove to us that you are worthy of helping us."

Jake remained silent, determined not to let Samir surrender too quickly. They would sense a trap if he did. Amad must've given a signal, for Jake heard the two younger men attach the chain that shackled his ankle to what he inferred was a metal support beam along one of the exterior walls. He groped about, tracing the chain back to the wall, and realized he had a radius of motion about one-hundred-and-eighty degrees . . . maybe five feet in either direction. A feel with his hands reassured himself of a nearby bucket filled with water. Another bucket was empty. His toilet? They were treating him like a dog. Ali's and Reza's laughter penetrated his hood. A big foot kicked him in the shin.

"Come closer, Ali, and free my hands. I'll choke the laughter out of you, you slimy bastard."

What followed were Amad's harsh scoldings directed at both men, who apparently backed off. Their behavior confirmed the British mullah was indeed calling the shots. The older man approached, preceded by his particular odor of tobacco and musk. Jake sensed him standing nearby and calmed down.

Ah, the surrogate father.

They either knew Samir's background, thanks to Fariq, or they'd decided to use the old torture routine. One guy tormented, the other soothed. All he had to do was cooperate and things would go easy on him. In this case, the mullah was his *friend*.

"You see, my friends. For this brother of ours, kind words speak louder than threats or harsh treatment. He's an intellectual, after all, a man of science. We must appeal to his intellect, his reason, and test him accordingly. You see, Samir, my lost son, what I demand of you is understanding, approval, and total obedience. But in order to attain such a level, you must be humbled."

Amad seemed to have turned aside and whispered something about *merchandise*. The others apparently receded into another part of the storage room, but all Jake could hear were low mutterings about fifteen feet away. They were behind something, for their voices were low and muffled.

What else was in this storage room?

Suddenly he remembered that he still wore his watch. They'd certainly looked it over, but had let him wear it, once they'd seen the Qur'anic verse on the back. They'd taken Samir's cell phone and had obviously searched him for wires or weapons. The watch had stayed. Relieved beyond words, Jake sat on the floor and calmed down. He'd wait them out, then see what he could discover.

"That's correct, Samir. Sit back and think. Consider your situation, your father and his fate. Why is the world astonished," the mullah intoned, "that we fight America? Is our resistance not a natural reaction against a nation that has pursued a policy of imperialism and terror against the nations and peoples of Islam? America is two-faced. They welcomed your father, then killed him. They profess to tolerate all religions, but they actually resent and fear us. We who believe in Allah as Lord, in Islam and in Muhammad as Prophet and Messenger, we know our religion refuses lowliness, humiliation, and degradation inflicted by the infidels. How could we not act otherwise when we know that the earth belongs to Allah—not to either East or West, not to a philosophy or a way of life other than the narrow and true way of Allah."

Amad was pacing back and forth in front of Jake as he sat shackled to the metal post, hooded, wet, and cold. His chest ached and his head pounded, a residual reaction to the volts of electricity that had surged through his body. His hearing remained acute, however. He could hear the rain beat softly on the metallic roof, other small noises in the background.

One thing was certain. This was not a temperature-controlled storage room. Whatever the *merchandise* was, it could take a cold environment and humidity.

"To quote Chapter eight, Verse thirty-nine, of our sacred Qur'an, *And fight them so that temptation might end and the only religion will be that of Allah.* And to quote from the Verse of the Sword, that every true Muslim learns by heart in childhood, *Fight and kill the disbelievers wherever you find them, take them captive, harass them, lie in wait and ambush them, using every stratagem of war.*"

Jake's head throbbed, lightning streaks of pain shooting behind his eyes, but it seemed that Amad had wound down temporarily. He raised his knees and propped his shackled arms upon them, hoping that the tech van was receiving Amad's preaching — typical long-winded Al Qaeda proselytizing. The talking points of Al Shumukh, Al Qaeda's online propaganda machine. If all had gone well and the surveillance van was somewhere nearby, the tech would have recorded the entire event from the moment that Jake had stepped into the car.

If the van, Mike Jordan, and Linda Brown had lost the tail, well . . . he was up shit creek without even a paddle.

Of course, he had no way of knowing. The watch had a one-way transmitter and he hadn't dared to wear an earpiece or wire.

"The basic goal of jihad, Samir, my son, is to raise the Word of Allah, to diminish the power of the tyrant, to extend the rule of Allah upon the earth. If the Muslim intends to accomplish this with jihad, and his soul desires you gain spoils from the infidels after breaking their power and domination over the earth, then there is no sin in that if Allah wills it. Finally, we ask Allah to make the fighters of jihad constant, to give them victory and the capacity to endure and to sacrifice, just as we ask Allah to bless us with His seal of goodness. We ask Allah to make our deaths a testimony of martyrdom on His path, just as He has granted the warriors who carry the Sword of Islam the highest levels of Paradise at His behest."

A protracted silence fell as the mullah's preaching wound down. Jake felt that Samir was expected to say something in a contrite tone of voice.

"I hear you, Sheikh Amad. You speak the wisdom of Islam. I have been lost for years. Especially since the senseless murder of my father."

"Your humility is a good sign, Samir, but I doubt your sincerity. You're American born and you've been spoiled. A day or two in dark seclusion will help you meditate upon your failings as a true Muslim. To quote Chapter six, Verse one-hundred-fifteen, *Perfect is the Word of your Lord in truth and justice."*

Truth and justice. You wouldn't know truth and justice if it bit you in the ass, you Islamofascist lunatic.

Jake squeezed his eyes shut, willing the shooting pains to stop. When they wouldn't, he cried aloud, not pretending but distressed for real. He'd been tasered before, but this time his physical reactions spiked into real distress. The queasiness of his stomach returned and erupted. He lurched over, lifted the hood over his nose as best he could, and vomited on the floor. He heaved and heaved until his guts felt yanked out of his belly. Then he sank back down on the concrete floor, the cold concrete almost a relief on the side of his face. A peek under the scrunched-up hood revealed wooden pallets on the floor, holding . . . crates? What was in those crates?

What the hell are these assholes planning?

If the FBI was recording the scene, he had to stave them off. They'd think he was hurt and come rushing in with the cavalry, prematurely ending Jake's undercover work. Under interrogation, the mullah and his crew would clam up tighter than abalones at low tide. He drew up his shackled arms close to his face.

"Don't come any closer. I stink but I'm okay." Then more loudly, "Really, I'm fine, Sheikh Amad. I'm feeling better."

In his hopes that Amad would interpret his words as spilling over with shame and remorse, Jake curled into a ball and turned into the wall. There was no pretense to the way he felt, however. His stomach continued to cramp with spasms. He was wet and cold and his head and chest throbbed, and there was nothing he could do about it. He felt as helpless and as vulnerable as a baby.

His sickness spurred the sheikh into a rant, followed by a spate of panicky instructions to his underlings. The mullah apparently feared that he might go into cardiac arrest, upsetting his plans for using Samir. Reza yanked off his hood, allowing Jake more air to breathe. A hypodermic needle flashed in the young man's hand. Jake's weakness left him too weak to resist.

And so for Jake, the lights went out.

Again.

When Saturday morning brought more rain but no sign of Jake, Meg was spurred into action. Still in her nightgown, she made coffee and called Jake's parents. He'd given her their Culver City phone number in the event she needed help from them. A woman's voice answered and Meg identified herself.

"Oh Meg, Jacob has spoken of you so often. He's supposed to bring you for Thanksgiving dinner. We're all looking forward to meeting you. I'm Jacob's mother. Please call me Beth."

"Yes, he told me about Thanksgiving. Thanks, Beth, I'd love to come. And, of course, I'd love to bring something to add to the table. Coming from Texas, I've learned to make a very good sweet potato pie."

They chatted a little before Meg launched into her concern over Jake's sudden silence. He hadn't answered his burner cell phone in a little over twenty-four hours. Not like him. Perhaps no reason to panic, but she was panicking anyway. She knew something was wrong.

Beth said, "We got a call from someone with the FBI field office in San Jose. That's up in Silicon Valley, San Francisco Bay Area. From a woman named Linda Brown. She said she's serving as liaison with Jake's family, so we can call her anytime. She told us that Jake's on assignment and can't communicate with anyone for the time being. She assured us that he's in no danger, that he's being monitored, whatever that means. Maybe they're watching him on a camera or listening to him somehow. It's all very mysterious but I trust Jake to call for help if he feels he can't handle a situation. He's very resourceful. And tough, as you well know."

Meg wondered about that. He was tough all right. Jake had suffered several close calls while investigating her grandmother during their motorcoach tour in Ireland. He'd been shot in the thigh by some neo-Nazis called Celtic Wolves and nearly trampled to death by one of the prize stallions at the Irish Stud Farm in Kildare. She'd seen his stoicism first-hand but she bet his family had never learned of any of those exploits or really knew all the dangers he faced while undercover.

"I worry about him," she confessed to Jake's mother, her voice cracking a little. "Will you call me as soon as you hear from him?" She thought a moment. "Better yet, can you give me Linda Brown's phone number? I'll call her myself. Just for reassurance."

Jake's mother did and added that she would be in touch either way, whether she heard directly from Jake or the woman in the San Jose FBI office. They rang off.

Meg sipped her coffee.

San Jose FBI field office. Linda Brown. A phone number.

This might be one of her worst ideas, she told herself, but she couldn't stop herself from filling up a small weekend bag. And tossing her Lady Smith and Wesson on top. Her German classes could wait.

Within half an hour, she was in her Dodge Durango, heading north on the Four-O-Five.

CHAPTER SEVENTEEN

Hours later, Jake floated to consciousness. He had no idea how long he'd slept. Whatever drug was in that injection had served to relax his muscles, relieve the pain in his chest, and even elevate his mood. Perhaps a cocktail of pain killer, muscle relaxant, and tranquilizer. Whatever, it did the trick. Even his head felt clearer. His stomach was almost back to normal except that hunger pangs now gnawed at him.

Jake sat up in the dark and groped about. His left hand touched a heavy wool blanket. Someone had taken pity on him, shivering with chills and clammy with sweat after puking up his guts. He'd never before had such an adverse reaction to being tasered—probably a sign that the stress of this assignment had gotten to him. At least the damned hood was off and his arms were still shackled in front of his body, not behind his back.

He stood up and moved his legs. Prickly needles ran up his legs to his thighs, making him swerve with unsteadiness. Bending over, then squatting a couple of times, restored the circulation, and some of his strength returned. His shackled right leg wouldn't budge much, so he bent over and traced the chain holding him in place to the metal wall. One end was linked to his ankle and the other end attached to the wall by heavy hasps and fastened with keyed padlocks. If he had a file, or his lockpick kit, he would have made short shrift of both.

He stilled and took inventory, patting the pockets of his sweatshirt and pants: He had his transmitter watch but no cell phone or apartment keys or Samir's wallet. A slow sweep of the storage unit picked up no blinking lights in the corners or near his spot alongside one wall. No security cameras inside the unit, evidently, but he suspected that there were several outside. The jihadis could have left a mike inside to pick up sounds within his jail cell.

With that in mind, he bent over his watch and recited in Arabic the couple of Qur'anic verses he'd memorized. As he wound down, he cupped the watch under his chin, simultaneously turning into the wall.

"Stand down. I'm okay, continue to stand down." He raised his head and muttered loudly the same verse, then repeated his order in a whisper, "Stand down. I'm seeing this through to the end."

If Acting SAC Mike Cho Jordan got the message, then Jake could expect continued monitoring but no interference.

To his extreme left, a straight-line sliver of light caught his eye. Most likely coming from underneath an interior door, the light was bright in comparison to the stark darkness of the storage room. An oddly shaped object stood upright by the door. Drawing up the heavy wool blanket, he tied two corners together and tossed that end of the blanket toward it, about a five-foot distance. Like throwing out a fishing net.

A couple of tries, and the far end of the blanket snagged what turned out to be a broom handle. It fell over with a soft plop. Slowly, inch by inch, he dragged the broom to him. Then holding on to the straw bristles, he swung the wooden handle around the right side of the door jamb. A light switch would be there—he had to swing it up just so. That wasn't working, so he moved his grip to the wooden handle and let the wider straw bristles do the job. By the third swing, he managed to catch the old-fashioned light switch lever. On went the overhead light, coming from a powerful, naked, fluorescent bulb in the center of the large storage room.

A quick scan of the room picked up no cameras or mikes. Now Jake could clearly discern the shapes and sizes of the wooden crates stacked on heavy wooden pallets. Each crate was approximately five feet long, three feet wide, and four feet deep. There were about sixteen in all, each stack of two crates supported by its own pallet and arranged in two long rows. Along the far wall were ten four-foot-high metal drums, odorless as far as Jake could tell. Alongside the two rows of crates were five cardboard boxes about three feet wide, four feet long, and about two feet deep. Most of the boxes were hidden by the stacks of crates, so Jake couldn't make an accurate count. He thought he saw the number one hundred on one of the boxes, so one hundred times five.

He stretched the length of the chain holding his ankle to the wall, cursed it and peered at the Arabic and English print on the cardboard boxes and wooden crates. The English labels on the crates said *The Holy Koran* — the Anglicized version of Qur'an — and the number, five hundred in all if his math was correct. The English on the cardboard boxes read *Prayer rugs for The Cordoba Mosque, San Miguel, California* and the Arabic number five on one of the boxes.

Prayer rugs, my ass. Copies of the Qur'an, like hell.

Number five? The fifth Cordoba Mosque? Could the boxes be filled with firing mechanisms and detonating caps? Could the crates hold Russian or French military-grade plastique? One hundred kilos of plastique would fit in each of those crates. He was speculating, of course, but add the ten drums, filled with a gasoline accelerant, and you'd have a deadly weapon of mass destruction.

So why did the mullah and Ali need Samir, microbiologist and biomedical scientist with supposed access to live anthrax? They already had their fireworks. Jake frowned. There were still too many unanswered questions.

But — and this was a huge *but* — if Jake as Samir could gain their trust, he'd eventually find out. More importantly, he'd learn what their target was.

And when.

Aloud, he recited a verse of the Qur'an, then turned to the wall and muttered, relaying the information about the boxes and crates via his watch transmitter.

"The target's nearby. I'm thinking the airport less than ten miles away. When? Soon. All the more reason to stand down. I've got to find out exactly where and when."

Noises broke through his thoughts. Using the broom handle, he swung again and turned out the light. He slid the broom over to the door and listened in the darkness. Loud male voices rose, then receded before the area fell silent again. He was right. This was a public storage unit.

Would they be foolish enough to store explosives in a public facility? *Who knows, with those fanatics?*

Jake crept over to the bucket of water and scooped up enough to quench his thirst. How long were they going to keep him caged up here like a pathetic dog? Did they truly believe this was how to win hearts over to their cause?

No, they won hearts in part through intimidation, force, and the circumstances of poverty and illiteracy. Brainwashing, misplaced religious zeal, and revenge sucked in the rest.

One thing was certain. He'd never again go to a zoo or animal shelter without empathizing with the pent-up creatures there.

He wished Amad, Ali, and Reza would return and rough him up. Even malicious human contact was better than this dark, lonely silence. And the uncertainty of what else they had in mind.

CHAPTER EIGHTEEN

Exhausted from eight hours on the road, Meg spent the night in a motel close to downtown San Jose. The Federal Building was closed on Sunday, so she called Linda Brown, introduced herself, explained her relationship to Special Agent Jake Bernstein, and that she'd got the liaison's phone number from Jake's mother. Ms. Brown told her to stay put and she'd join her within the hour.

Meg kept calling Jake's burner cell, all her messages going directly to voice mail. After one such call, the coffee going down met the bile coming up, making Meg swallow down the resulting nausea. At least she'd be getting some information soon. However, not for the first time, Meg regretted interrupting a certainly sensitive operation at a critical juncture. Jake would probably be furious when he learned what she'd done. She bent over and gnawed the polish off five fingernails.

Stupid, stupid, stupid!

She swore at herself in French, Spanish, and her most recently acquired German. Soon she was at work on the other five nails.

At ten AM sharp, an older woman in her sixties with short blonde hair entered the coffee shop, followed by a young Asian man closer to Jake's age, maybe mid-thirties. Both were casually dressed in jeans and sweater, the older woman wearing a tweed-wool fedora hat that didn't quite go with her outfit. They consulted the man's iPad before introducing themselves. Acting Special Agent in Charge Jordan indicated that they take seats in the corner. There were two other patrons in the large shop, so the agents seemed to have no problem with this meeting venue.

Special Agent Jordan had thick, black hair worn in a military butch. His height matched hers, five-foot-nine, she noticed as she stood to shake hands, but he bore a powerful, muscular build on a sturdy, wide frame. His handsome face was fixed in a scowl while Linda Brown's speculative expression was more sympathetic.

Again, they studied Meg's passport photograph on the screen of Jordan's electronic tablet. Without preamble, he produced a mobile fingerprint scanner no bigger than an inkpad. Meg's heartbeat ramped up. Were they going to arrest her? Interfering with an undercover operation was probably against the law, something she hadn't considered before.

"Just verifying your identity," he said with no emotion. Surprised, and a little intimidated, Meg sat silently and let the agent scan her right thumbprint. A minute passed while Linda went for coffee and Jordan waited. When verification came back on his tablet, Jordan's shoulders relaxed as he sat back in his chair.

"Okay, Miss Larsen, tell us why you're here."

Meg started and stopped a couple of times, suddenly overwhelmed by her untenable position. Feeling more than a little silly and intrusive, she nevertheless sat tall in her chair and made a stab at explaining herself.

"Jake and I . . . Well, we have a relationship, a very close one. I know he's undercover and can't talk right now, at least not to me, but I'm so worried about him. I was there that night he was shot by one of the Celtic Wolves in Ireland—you see, his last assignment was investigating my grandmother. You probably already know that. I mean, you have my file, my photo, and my fingerprints. So you probably already know what happened in Ireland and Germany with those Neo-Nazis. Jake was hurt again after being tasered and they threw him into the pen with El Cid. That's one of the Irish Stud Farm's stallions. Jake almost got trampled to death. Anyway, I know he thinks he's this invincible warrior who's dedicating his life to truth and justice. And he is, of course. He's sacrificed a lot for this . . ."

She was rambling, she knew, and probably not making much sense. Winding down, she inhaled deeply and turned to Linda Brown. Agent Jordan hadn't moved a facial muscle during her little speech. Meg doubted he'd even heard her.

"What can I say?" Meg added, her hands on the table, palms up. "I'm in love with the guy and I'm worried sick about him. I drove all the way from San Diego to find out if he's okay. I knew you wouldn't tell me on the phone."

"And we won't be telling you in person, either," said Agent Jordan.

Meg's heart sank. Tears welled in her eyes and spilled over, causing her to swipe an impatient hand over her cheeks. She tried to stifle her emotions but to no avail.

"Is he hurt? D-dead?"

Jordan remained unmoved. Linda Brown looked at him and touched his forearm.

"I've got an idea." The pair withdrew to an area by the bookcase display of coffee beans and K-Cup boxes and turned their backs to her. Jordan stood with his arms akimbo, then crossed them over his chest while Ms. Brown did most of the talking. A few minutes later, they both returned. Jordan swept back the side of his sweater, revealing his holstered Glock pistol and gold badge. Meg noticed that Linda Brown wore no gun or badge, and she couldn't help but wonder why.

"All right, Miss Larsen," said Jordan sternly. "I'm allowing you to remain in the custody and under the supervision of Miss Brown. She's with our Special Support Group and helps us in situations like this. But there's one proviso."

Meg shot him a hopeful smile. "Yes?"

"As soon as you're satisfied that Special Agent Bernstein is alive and well, you must return to San Diego. My office will give you forty-eight hours to make that assessment and then off you go. If you reveal any details of this undercover operation to anyone, I'll personally authorize a warrant for your arrest. Are you clear on this?"

She nodded at him vigorously.

"She's all yours, Linda. I have to get back. Jake's been checking in every few hours. So far, so good." He looked Meg square in the eye. "Nice meeting you . . . I hope."

He walked away, and Meg watched him get into a nondescript tan sedan. Another man backed up the car as Agent Jordan raised a cell phone to his mouth. Then they drove away. Meg sighed with relief. She'd just passed some kind of test.

"Whatever you said, thank you so much," Meg effused. The woman plucked off her tweed fedora and pointed to Meg's long ponytail.

"Put your pretty hair up underneath this hat. We'll change your looks a little, just a tweak. You're now my niece, visiting from Texas, and you're staying with me. I won't-can't let you out of my sight. Not while you're here in Silicon Valley."

Meg nodded and did as she was told.

Late Sunday night, Meg absently twirled the pasta tubes in the sauce that Linda had given her. While her stomach grumbled with hunger, her esophagus felt so restricted there was no way she could swallow. Over twelve hours had passed. And while Linda had received an update five hours ago—and all was well with Jake—there had been no word since then.

Linda looked at her with a crinkled expression of pity. "Hey, no news is good news. Jake was certain they'd release him tonight, maybe up the ante with another test. He gave orders to stand down. The code word for *Storm the beachhead* is *storm*. If he says that—"

150

Linda mashed her lips together and returned to her pasta bowl. Meg watched her chew, mouth closed, wishing the woman could reveal more. It was obvious that Jake was being held captive somewhere, trying to prove himself to a bunch of fanatics, make them believe he was a devoted follower of jihad. Why they needed him, she wasn't sure. The danger of undercover work was convincing others that you were the real deal, that you were one of them and could be trusted.

A distant sound of a door closing drew Linda's attention to her laptop. The local FBI office, she'd explained, had insisted on posting a hidden, security camera in Jake's living room.

"He's back!"

Meg jumped up and went to snatch a look at Linda's laptop. She caught only a blur of movement, the back of a man, a turn of shoulder. "Are you sure it's Jake?"

"Oh, yeah, looking like death warmed over but that was Jake. I left a note for him to come over when he could. Bring the dish back — I sent over some brownies on Thursday, so it'll appear normal if any neighbors are looking."

Meg sputtered in her excitement, "I-I really want to go over-"

"No. Strict orders. You can't go into his apartment. In fact, you're not supposed to go near him. If you jeopardize this op, after all the money and man hours put into it, they'll arrest you and charge you with obstruction of justice, interfering with federal law enforcement officers, and a slew of other things. And I'll be fired." Linda restrained Meg's arm. "Now sit down and eat. Or watch TV, read, clean your gun — Yeah, I saw it."

Chastened, Meg went over to Linda's stylish crimson red Ultrasuede sofa. She ran her hand over the smooth surface and thought of Jake's suede jacket, the one he'd worn that weekend in San Diego. He was a careful dresser and liked being clean.

"He'll want to take a shower, clean up a bit before he comes over."

Linda nodded in agreement and forked another bite of pasta. "He doesn't know you're here, Meg, and I'm not supposed to let you into his apartment. Just in case one of the suspects shows up at his door or is planted nearby. Seeing you there would wreck everything. He's sacrificed so much to make it this far. You'd blow his cover for sure. An FBI team is on watch at the park, so please don't make it difficult for me."

"No, I promise I won't." Meg's voice caught as she fought back more tears. This FBI liaison-consultant, or whatever her real role was in this operation, had done enough for her. More than enough.

A half hour ticked by like falling grains of sand in an hourglass. A sudden rap at her door and Linda was there in a flash. "Samir?"

"Yes. It's me, Linda. Returning your plate."

As soon as he walked in, Meg lurched to her feet. His head swung in her direction and his mouth hung open in shock. A quick look at Linda seemed to reinforce what he was surmising. The older woman nodded, then shrugged.

"Jordan said it was okay. I'm supervising her."

Jake's dark brown hair was still wet, plastered down on his forehead, temples, and neck. He wore a white tee, tucked into his faded blue jeans, and a navy-blue fleece jacket. The dark circles under his eyes, the planes of his hollow cheeks shadowed with two days' facial growth, blurred his once neat beard and gave him a grizzled, haggard look. A broad smile, however, brightened his expression.

He held open his arms and Meg dashed into them. They embraced tightly and kissed. Kissed a second time more deeply. She wound her arms around his neck and rubbed her cheek against his hairy one. Nuzzling his cheek and feeling his beard abrade her proved his presence was real. Tears sprang to her eyes, unbidden and unwanted.

"Did they hurt you?" she asked.

"No, not much. Just starved me." He sniffed the air and glanced over at Linda Brown's dining table. "I could eat a horse! What's that you're having?"

"Pasta," Linda said, "To be exact, Rigatoni San Remo. Come here and have a bowl."

Meg held him around the waist while he stood and wolfed down a bowl. Linda shook her head in exasperation.

"For God's sake, sit down. Let the boy go and let him eat. Jake, take a look at this folder of surveillance photos. Four young men showed up at Amad's rental house in Saratoga. They were there for one night, last night, then were followed to an apartment in the East Palo Alto neighborhood."

Jake looked up, his mouth full. He chewed furiously. "That's not far from the airport. Or Genentech, or Levi's Stadium or the NASA hangars." He gazed unfocused at the tabletop. "Shit, that's it. They're studying the entrance gates, the ebb and flow of the crowds, the security details of all these possible targets."

Linda sat down across the table from Jake. "I was there in the van, listening to some of your transmissions. Those crates and boxes. The ten metal drums. Now these four men show up and contact this cleric. Are you thinking, four martyrs for Islam?"

"Possibly. I'm not sure yet but I don't think Amad or Ali have martyrdom in mind, not for themselves, anyway. They're the brains behind it all."

"Levi's, like the jeans?" asked Meg. She draped an arm around his back and watched him eat.

Jake sat down and pulled Meg down beside him. "It's a football stadium. In Santa Clara. Home of the San Francisco Bay Area Forty-Niners."

While he ate, this time with furrowed brow, Meg massaged

the nape of his neck. She wished she could protect him for all time, this brave warrior of hers.

"I'm glad you're not angry"—she broke off as she stared at the photos in Jake's left hand. "Oh my God, those four guys. That's Alejandro and his roommates. How—"

Jake stared at her gawking at the surveillance photos. "You mean, those four Hispanics at your apartment building in San Diego? The ones you said never left their apartment?" He faced her. "Did they see me that one weekend? When I went down to see you?"

She couldn't tear her gaze from the photos. Everything was beginning to make sense now—their behavior, their reticence to socialize with the other grad students in her apartment complex. They weren't really Hispanics after all.

"I don't know," was all she could manage to say.

The strange expression on Jake's face was swiftly shuttered. Instead, an inscrutable mask took its place.

"Well, let's hope not."

Linda filed through the dozen or so candid photos. "You're sure, Meg? You know these men? Take a closer look."

She did, just to satisfy the woman. Her answer didn't change. Linda's frown conveyed everything.

"I have to report this to Jordan."

Jake nodded morosely. Meg could tell he was already regretting that one weekend of indulgence. She wondered if he would blame her.

Linda shrugged. "If they stay up there in South San Francisco, maybe your paths will never cross. By the way, Jake, why did they let you go? How did you—rather, Samir—win them over?"

He gazed at the two women, but his hooded, dark eyes settled on Meg. Because he hesitated, she knew he dreaded what he had to reveal.

"I promised to kill someone. With my bare hands."

CHAPTER NINETEEN

L inda Brown looked stunned. "What?"
"Who?" asked Meg.

Jake could tell by her expression that she expected the target to be another Islamist terrorist. He hesitated before deciding to tell her the truth. There was no avoiding it.

"You," he said quietly.

She smiled and began to giggle. "Oh, Jake, stop that."

"Meg, I'm not joking." His hand settled on her shoulder and caressed it. "They've ordered Samir to kill his kafir girlfriend." He couldn't say *unclean*. "His infidel girlfriend, so she won't tempt him away from his holy mission. Mainly to prove that he's totally obedient to the cause, totally bending to the will of Allah . . . and all that bullshit."

The humor wilted from her expression like last week's roses. Her hand slowly rose to her mouth.

"You're not joking?"

He shook his head, saddened by her shock. Incensed, too, that flying down to see her that one weekend had resulted in this complication. Putting Meg in danger was the last thing he wanted. He'd protected his family. He should've protected her also. Remorse and guilt flooded him. He covered by hugging her to his side.

"Don't worry. We'll arrange something. I know just the place. That beach by Torrey Pines, the end of the park path we took that day down to the beach. They want Fariq to witness it and report back. We'll stage it with the help of TacOps and agents from the San Diego field office."

Tactical Operations agents were the behind-the-scenes support groups that created undercover identities, planted bugs and hidden cameras, and took part in covert entries to gather evidence. They also helped stage fake identities and situations, like disappearances, kidnappings, and murders—whatever was needed to fool the suspects.

But Meg was a civilian. She stared at him with such fulminating disbelief that he thought she'd haul off and slap him one upside the head. He hadn't meant to sound so cavalier about staging her murder. After all, any number of things could go wrong but he'd done something like that once before and the deception had gone off without a hitch.

"They want it to look like an accident," he went on. "So the cops won't suspect me and draw attention to the mosque or my work at—" He glanced over at Linda Brown, whose eyes were as big and moist as Meg's.

Shut up, Bernstein. "—well, never mind. We'll keep you safe, Meg, but you may have to go into hiding for a while until this mission's over. We'll square it with your profs so you can continue your classes online from a safe house. Just until the op's over and done with."

Sympathy for her situation and for her naivete lanced through him. It wasn't her fault that she'd stumbled innocently into a viper's nest. Obviously distressed, she pushed him away, lurched up and went over to the sofa. She sat, staring unseeingly at the clasped hands in her lap.

Give her time to digest this, you fool.

He turned back to Linda Brown. "Which reminds me, I need to make some calls from my secure phone. I'll leave you two alone."

Linda had heaped another helping of pasta into his bowl until he'd given the signal to stop. Now, seeing Meg withdraw, so shaken, had taken the edge off his appetite.

"You two need to talk," Linda advised. "Better to do it tonight. No one's going to sleep anyway. I heard from Acting

156

SAC Jordan that the TacOps guys redid your apartment lock so there's no chance the bad guys'll break in, is there?"

"No, the failsafe lock's in place," Jake reassured the older woman. He'd used his old key but just had to make four clockwise revolutions in order to unlock it. All of this had been put into place while he was trussed up in that storage unit.

Linda frowned at his second untouched bowl of pasta and sighed. It looked like she'd made enough pasta and sauce for a team of agents.

"Take the bowl with you and try and eat some more. Make your calls, Jake, and then come back. I'll switch to your place for the night so you two can talk and . . . settle matters."

Jake looked again at Meg's frozen posture. She was still processing the gravity of the situation and her own unwitting role in it. If anything was a deal breaker in their relationship, this involvement of hers would certainly be it. Already, he could feel her slipping away from him. Damn . . .

This fucking job.

Back in his own apartment, Jake retrieved his hidden secure cell phone and encrypted laptop from the case behind the refrigerator. He'd hidden away all the tools of his trade in case the mullah and Ali decided to pay another call to his apartment before the TacOps team replaced the lock. From all appearances, and according to Jordan, Ali hadn't been there. He sensed the time frame of the mullah's plot had shortened considerably since the arrival of the four men. Clever, a sleeper cell of four Hispanic students, going through the motions until they received the signal to take up the Sword of Allah. He wondered how long they'd been in the country. That would be easy enough to find out. He'd bet their student visas had expired, too. The State Department seldom checked up on expired student visas. Their ineptitude made Jake see red.

As Jake typed his report, he wondered if those four men were on the TIDE, the Terrorist Identities Datamart Environment, a list of about half a million individuals. Or the TSDB, the Terrorist Screening Database, from which consular, border, and airline watch lists were drawn. That list had close to half a million names too. The TSA's no-fly list of about four-thousand people wasn't sufficient to cover all of the potential threats identified by various government intelligence agencies.

Even when the so-called *Underwear Bomber*, Abdulmutallab's father, had warned U.S. officials in Nigeria that his son had fallen prey to radical Islam, he was put on the TIDE list. The State Department, however, didn't pull his student visa, issued almost two years earlier. A near deadly oversight, as it turned out. Maddening, Jake reflected. Getting the State Department to deny a visa based on an FBI request was almost impossible. The FBI had tried to get State to change their visa policy, to no avail. So the FBI and other intelligence agencies would continue to fight an uphill battle.

It seemed that a few Federal agencies continued to subvert the FBI's attempts at counterterrorism.

One good development. According to Jordan, TacOps, which also initiated court-approved covert entries, had been intercepting all of Amad's and Ali's cell phone calls, email messages, and other laptop entries, and had bugged the rental home in Saratoga as well as the rental car they used.

Surveillance teams, hidden bugs, and cameras were in place at the Saratoga home and the public storage facility — and would soon be installed at the East Palo Alto apartment — so that Amad, Ali, and the four men in the sleeper cell wouldn't be able to fart or take a piss without the surveillance teams knowing about it.

The masterminds, Amad and Ali, nevertheless, had been very careful.

"I think it could be Levi's Stadium in Santa Clara," Jake told Jordan as soon as the acting SAC came on the line.

"I agree it's a strong possibility," said Jordan, "Why else would those four suspects move to East Palo Alto? Not exactly a prime tourist or student area. They're still within thirty miles of San Francisco International. And the Bay Bridge is close by. Also, Stanford University. Any guesses on dates?"

"Soon. I think, shortly after Samir proves himself. They want Samir for their plot, but they're not saying what that plot is." He summarized for Jordan his plan for faking Meg's murder. The acting SAC agreed that involving the San Diego field office was necessary.

"Next weekend, huh? I'll get the TacOps guys into that storage unit and talk to the San Diego SAC. Get him on board with your plan. How's Meg taking it?"

"Not well," said Jake. "After this op's over, the only thing she'll want to see is the door hitting my backside."

Jordan actually chuckled. "You might be surprised. For my girlfriend, the danger's a turn-on."

Jake didn't think Meg was one of those women. How many times had she said that she wanted a normal life with a career, husband, kids? But she'd also insisted that was down the road a bit. For now, she wanted to be with him. How long that lasted was anyone's guess. Maybe until next weekend.

He struggled to refocus. "Jordan, see if TIDE or any of the watch lists has those Hispanics or their aliases." He thought a moment. "The mullah might just be jerking Samir's chain, but I think they wouldn't go to all this trouble unless they wanted him to stockpile what they think is live anthrax. It wouldn't take much to kill hundreds of people but . . . I think explosives are the key to their plot. I think they want a big bang. A mass attack like Nine-Eleven. Levi's would provide the largest kill zone."

There was a moment of silence on Jordan's end as they both

seemed to digest and visualize the attack. Levi's Stadium, filled to capacity with over sixty-eight thousand spectators, news media personnel, football players, and staff. A horrible loss of life in the thousands if enough explosives could be smuggled in.

But how? Stadium security would check every backpack and cooler. Every delivery van or truck would be inspected.

Jordan cleared his throat. "I'll apply for a court-approved covert entry into that storage unit. The local TacOps team is good. They'll be in and out and the suspects won't know a thing."

"Once you have the video proof of explosives, hold off on the arrests. This scheme is part of a larger plot. I need to hear from the CTC chief about the other four Cordoba mosques and undercover agents. This may be part of a massive diversion for some other kind of attack. That cleric is one clever, manipulating bastard."

Jake considered Jordan's original question about dates. "Jordan, are the Niners playing in town every weekend this month?"

"Hold on, let me check."

Jake heard the man's tapping at his keyboard. Jordan came back on with a loud harrumph. "Checked their schedule. They're playing away games for the next two weeks. After that, for crissakes . . . the Sunday before Thanksgiving Day. They're playing a televised home game at Levi's. Niners against Tampa Bay. The Sunday after Thanksgiving, they're away in New Orleans."

The import of his words stabbed through Jake like an ice pick. Cold rivulets of fear and dread ran from his stomach down through his guts.

The Sunday before Thanksgiving Day. Was nothing sacred anymore? A memory surfaced. Sitting with his brothers, his father, and Grandpa Nate—not quite understanding

American football and asking Jake in Berliner German to explain each play to him. All the Bernstein men watching the Forty-Niners and the Oakland Raiders butt heads Thanksgiving week. That entire week with families coming together from all over, football reigned supreme in the hearts and minds of every American male. A bonding of excitement that transcended everything, even the blood they shared.

Jake blew air out of his cheeks. "It'd fit their twisted view of America. Their hatred of all things American."

Was this part of a larger plot? Were all five Cordoba mosques involved? Were the other cities' professional football teams playing at packed stadiums that same day? Were all five mosques hosting visiting mullahs from abroad? And if so, had these mullahs already activated sleeper terrorist cells lying in wait near the other four cities? Were they all acting in concert to coordinate five separate but catastrophic attacks at five different stadiums?

"Those sons-a-bitches," hissed Jordan. "Something just came through from Tech. That British cleric and his pal have been ultra-cautious but this morning, we intercepted a call to United Airlines. They booked two seats on tomorrow's nonstop, ten AM flight from San Jose to Dallas. Return flight is on Sunday."

Jake scrubbed a hand over his weary face.

"Must be why Amad told me Fariq was now in charge of Samir. They told me they want Samir to do the deed by next weekend. If he does it, and it's witnessed by Fariq, they'll approve Samir's involvement. Meg's gotta return to San Diego tomorrow."

"If they want Samir for the anthrax vaccine, hope you have a plan in mind," said Jordan. "You know we can't get authority for the real stuff."

"I know." Jake's thoughts lingered on the two women next door. "Can you send Linda Brown down with Meg? She's so shook up by this whole thing, and she seems to trust Linda."

"No problem. I'll send Linda and another female agent. They'll keep her calm and help set things up with the San Diego field office. You know, we're short-handed with Frank in the hospital and most of our local agents doing surveillance on these suspects."

Jake rang off and took another deep breath. It was three AM in D.C. but night-duty agents in Terry's Intelligence Division would take the encrypted call and unscramble it for Terry's eyes first thing in the morning. Up the chain of command to the CTC chief and all his underlings.

Damn.

Jake finished his written report and sent it to the CTC Chief, Harlan Peterson. His next call was to his boss, Terry, at Headquarters in D.C. His heart raced with urgency.

He rubbed his sore chest and pressed the heels of his palms against his tired eyeballs.

It was going to be a helluva long night.

Meg opened her eyes as Jake walked into Linda's spare bedroom. She sat up on the bed, still dressed in her cargo pants and wool knit sweater. The bedside lamp was on, but the drapes were drawn against the cold. Although the rain had stopped hours ago, the gloom of the night had seeped through, seemingly into her very bone marrow.

"Linda's going to sleep next door," he began, "but if you prefer, I can call her back. If you don't want to see me, I'll understand."

Jake had trimmed his beard and was now wearing a cream-colored, cable-knit pullover sweater with his jeans. This time, he no longer seemed dazed with hunger, the food having restored him somewhat. Although his demeanor appeared settled and resigned, Meg knew better. His stoical words belied his feelings. She could see the pain in his eyes, the defeat in his posture.

"No," she said wearily. "I came all this way to see you, see if you were okay. Come over here."

He sat down next to her on the bed. His dark eyes were downcast, as if he dreaded what she had to say. Her poor warrior had suffered at the hands of the enemy. There was nothing she could do now but console him. For the moment, she lacked the words. He nodded in a self-deprecating manner.

"My mother says the only thing harder than being a soldier is loving one. I guess she nailed it."

Meg liked the ironic humor in that. "Your mother's very wise. And very nice, by the way. She invited me over for Thanksgiving Day."

"Let's hope I can make it."

That dose of reality sobered her. "Did they hurt you? Should you see a doctor?"

He shook his head but held up his sweater and T-shirt to show the large square bandage that covered most of his right pec. "I put an antibacterial cream on it. The Taser punctures don't really hurt anymore."

"You're a Taser magnet. This is the second time you've been tasered in . . . how many months?" She saw the dark bluish-green bruises on his torso, too, but said nothing about them. She wished she could've been there with her .38 revolver.

Rage swept over her and she closed her eyes for a second. She opened them when he lifted her chin with a forefinger.

"As opposed to a babe magnet? You called me that once. Right now, I don't feel like much of one."

He smiled lopsidedly and her heart did a little jump. His handsome face and sense of humor obliterated the Samir-visage and shined through his disguise. There he was, Jake Bernstein, her protector and savior from those Neo-Nazis. Strong, stoic, brave. He was her moral challenge and reminder to always seek the truth. The bitterest truth was better than the sweetest lie, he'd said once.

"You draw *me* in." Her arms reached out and she clutched her warrior to her breast. "Oh, Jake. What have I gotten myself into? Should I be scared out of my mind?"

"Of me? Never. Don't worry, the situation is under control. Don't be concerned. You'll have an adventure to tell your grandchildren someday, but they probably won't believe it."

If she harbored any lingering concern or doubt, his kisses and caresses soon obliterated them.

CHAPTER TWENTY

The microbiologist at An-Vax greeted Jake at the second-floor elevator. "The receptionist said you were on your way up. You look like hell," said Todd Wallinski. "Like you tied one on this weekend."

Jake shot him a half-smile, half-grimace. "Something like that." The guy wouldn't believe him even if he told him the truth, how he'd endured two days and two nights shackled to a dark, cold metal storage unit, stinking of urine and vomit, with only a bucket of fetid water to drink. No, this civilian scientist wouldn't believe it.

Todd led Jake to his cubicle, where Jake's empty desk awaited him. The younger man looked refreshed and satisfied, as if he'd had a much more pleasant weekend than Jake had. Ah, the peace of mind of civilians, Jake thought enviously.

"Sorry I'm late." Jake placed his briefcase on the floor next to his desk, "Had to see a friend off." He took out his laptop. All for show, of course, but he had to maintain cover. Just a validation biologist doing his weekly reports on lab protocols.

Todd, wearing a white lab coat, took a moment to sit by Jake's desk. He looked a little sheepish. Clearly, the man had something on his mind.

"Look, Agent Bernstein, you might be getting strange looks or the cold shoulder from the rest of the Quality Control staff. The office scuttlebutt is that you're an undercover FDA officer. You know we can't move our vaccines out of here without FDA approval. They think you're here to screw things up.

165

If that happens, we lose our jobs."

A new wrinkle in his cover job, but how much of one, he had no clue. Jake kept silent and waited.

"So don't take offense," Todd went on, "if they give you the cold shoulder. It's not personal. I wish I could tell them the truth. That you're FBI, not FDA."

Jake waved a hand dismissively. "Making friends around here is the least of my worries. You have no idea, man, what's coming down." He gave the young man a pointed look. "Wish I could tell *you* the truth." He thought a moment and pulled out a notebook. "Todd, I need to ask you some questions, and some of these questions will disturb you. Remember, I'm asking them with national security uppermost in mind."

Todd frowned. "Sounds serious."

"You bet it's serious. Here's the deal. If I, Samir Maalouf, got ahold of live anthrax bacteria in powder form, what kind of delivery system would be most effective?"

Todd's frown cratered to a scowl. "Well, I suppose a sprayer of some kind. What you hear in the news about anthrax powder in envelopes going through the mail is not effective at all. You might infect a couple of people, but a terrorist wants to kill hundreds or thousands. Right?"

Jake nodded. The scientist was smart and likely knew where Jake's train of thought was going.

"The more people you want to infect and potentially kill, the larger the delivery system has to be. The live spores must be sealed in airtight glass or heavy plastic vials, but they can be stored at room temperature. The live spores can survive up to minus twenty-degrees Celsius, so these buggers are extremely hearty and resilient. They can survive in most forms, which of course makes them even more deadly. But I'd think the ventilation system of a closed area would be an effective delivery system. Even a crop duster plane in an open-air venue would be effective, because the powder would be heavier than the air and would sink and cling to surfaces."

Jake's thoughts raced to Levi's Stadium, still convinced that the open-roof stadium completed in 2014 was the target. Lots of surfaces there, including the bleachers and the grassy football field. Bordering the South Bay, the stadium was not often buffeted by cold breezes off the bay because it was situated more inland. However, any wind across the valley swept to the east, where the highly populated cities of Oakland and Milpitas and San Jose lay. Airborne spores wouldn't just infect the stadium of sixty-eight thousand but would have a potential reach of thousands more along the eastern shore.

Todd gave an ironic grin. "The good news is that you—I mean, Samir—wouldn't have access to live spores. Attenuated, or dead, bacteria is what we work with here. And you've seen how we handle that stuff."

"If any of the staff is approached by a Middle Eastern-looking man, do they know not to reveal that important fact?"

Todd stood up to leave. "Oh yeah, you bet. We all sign non-disclosure forms. We just say we're making anthrax vaccines. Most people who aren't microbiologists don't understand the fine details. Just as well, I suppose. Gotta go. I'm wanted in Lab Four."

After Todd left, Jake checked his notes. Several questions prompted him to make a few phone calls to private airports and two calls to a couple of heating and air conditioning businesses. He'd stop at a hardware store on his way back to the apartment and ask a few more questions, posing as a homeowner who wanted to clean his vents. He had to sound convincing about the delivery system, for Amad and Ali were no fools.

A call came in on his secure cell phone. It was Acting SAC, Mike Cho Jordan.

"Our TacOps guys broke into that storage unit early this

morning. Guess what? Except for your little jail area, the place was clean. They examined everything—the crates, the boxes, the metal drums. Which were empty, by the way. Prayer rugs and Qur'ans in the crates and boxes. Not a gram of Semtex, no firing mechanisms, no detonators. *Nada.* With no physical evidence, we can't move forward on this. We don't have probable cause. There's conspiracy to kidnap and detain but Samir would have to bring charges. That would defeat our purpose, wouldn't it?"

Shit! That damned mullah's sly as an old fox.

"Okay, dammit," groused Jake, disappointed. "What about the ten drums?"

"They'd say the mosque needed them for trash. The drums are clean, have never been used."

This operation was going to drag out longer than he anticipated. It also meant he'd have to go through with Meg's staged murder. The very thought sent shivers around his skull. His stomach clenched with anxiety. Another reason why his appetite had vanished.

"I hope they put RFID tags on the crates and boxes, just to track where they end up. Just because this shipment is clean doesn't mean others will be." RFID, or Radio Frequency ID, tags the size of a grain of rice, similar to pet ID tags, were often used to track the routes of contraband.

"Yeah, they did. Standard procedure in cases like this. TacOps says they can't tag the drums, however. The metal's too smooth."

Jordan's efficiency impressed Jake. The man's history as a DEA agent had come in handy. It was as if the man always anticipated Jake's next move or question.

"Good. Maintain surveillance on the East Palo Alto apartment. The explosives might be in storage near those four guys. Which makes more sense, of course. They'd want to be close by to guard the stuff, which could've been moved in place weeks or even months ago. There's got to be old warehouses in the area along the bay." His thoughts leaped ahead. "Also, see if any of their aliases show up on cargo ships, on the crew manifests. Wouldn't surprise me if one or more of those guys accompanied the explosives shipment over here, assuming there are explosives somewhere out there. Maybe they paid off the ship's captain and some custom officer and we can shake up somebody."

"Right, I'll get on it." Jordan cracked one of his rare chuckles. "Frank Rodriguez is on the mend and out of the hospital. He's going nuts at home and he's just itching to take part in this investigation. I'll put him on this. He's a good IT man. Another thing, I spoke to the SAC in Dallas. They and the undercover agent are keeping close tabs on this Amad and Ali, taking names, who they're meeting with, where they're going. They're holding so-called Islamic workshops with a group of youths, mostly high school kids. Think they're recruiting them for jihad?"

"Maybe. In my last contact with CTC, I was told my undercover counterpart in Dallas is making connections with those teenagers and trying to win their confidence. We'll see what breaks on that score, but there could be another sleeper cell now in position around Dallas, one that's been activated in the past few weeks. I know NSA's tracking the mullah's cell phone and laptop for any unusual chatter. As they're doing with the visiting mullahs in the other three cities. New York, Chicago, Miami. There seems to be consensus on the timeline. We have a month at the most, maybe weeks. If you need more manpower, call the CTC chief Harlan Peterson. He regards this op as top priority."

"Good to know, Agent Bernstein. Everyone's totally on board."

"Okay. Keep tabs on the mullah and Ali in Dallas and when they return. They have to make further contact with their sleeper cells at some point. Either physically or

169

electronically."

"Okay, I'll monitor that."

"Mike, I've been racking my brain trying to figure out their endgame. Is it blowing up a packed football stadium-three weeks from now? An airport next week? A commuter bridge? Or something completely different? It's driving me crazy, wondering if I'm overlooking something. My girlfriend's now a target and half the time I'm not thinking as clearly as I should."

Having admitted aloud what had been bothering him for days, Jake grew even more pensive. Usually his analytical mind led him in the right direction, but lately—hell, during this entire undercover operation—his emotions kept muddying his thought processes. There was another mental block that plagued him.

Like all Americans, he believed in and served his country, to support those rights everyone held sacred, including freedom of speech and expression and the freedom of religion. Not that he was a fan of Islam. On the contrary, he believed it was a medieval religion that fostered autocracy and rigid, superstitious thinking. Not to mention violence against women and non-Muslims. What twisted his guts at times was the pretense of being a Muslim. Somehow, he felt like a traitor to his own Jewish roots.

This emotional turmoil affected him. He knew it. The struggle to maintain objective and analytical reasoning had taken its toll.

He shook off such moribund thoughts. They accomplished nothing. Jordan remained silent, probably embarrassed at Jake's admission about Meg. Then, like a burst of sunlight from between a jumble of clouds, the insight hit him.

"I may be wrong, Mike, but I think what they have in mind is a two-fold operation. An initial panic situation set off by relative amateurs like Samir. Then followed by a calculated attack carried out by pros—"

Just then, a call came through on Samir's phone, which Jake carried in his right-front pants pocket. He rang off with Jordan before taking it. Fariq's gravelly voice made Jake's blood run cold.

"Samir, my son, I understand we're taking a trip down to San Diego Friday after prayers. Do you have a plan in mind for your last and most critical test of loyalty? The sheikh doesn't want any mistakes that will connect you to the kafir's death. Your role in his divinely inspired plan is vital, so we want you to succeed."

Jake had to suppress a shiver of contempt. "I've got an idea. It'll look like an accidental drowning."

"Hmm, let's hope so. It is not wise to disappoint the sheikh."

No shit. "Don't worry, Fariq. My plan's foolproof."

"*Inshallah*," interjected Fariq.

"Yes, Allah willing."

Yeah, God willing, Meg wouldn't be hurt. But she might end up hating him for the rest of her life.

Cold comfort.

"Goodbye, Samir. Until Friday. *Salaam alaikum.*"

"*Alaikum salaam.*"

The very thing he dreaded most was about to happen.

CHAPTER TWENTY-ONE

M eg strode down the dirt path leading to the wooden
stairs, the closest access to the secluded beach below the
cliff. This area of Torrey Pines State Park was usually heavily
trafficked during the summer months, but hikers had all but
abandoned the beach path in autumn. Students were back in
school and retirees tended to avoid this path because of its
steep trail. And, more importantly, it was eight o'clock in the
morning.

Wearing sneakers and a warm-up suit, Meg kept her eyes
fixed on the footpath. In parts where it banked off into foliage
and sandstone cliff, the path could be treacherous. That was
not the reason, however, that her heart kept a steady, loud
drumbeat in her chest. All of her survival instincts were on
alert and flashing red. She wasn't stupid. Despite Jake's reas-
surances and the San Diego FBI agents' verbal rehearsals over
the past few days, she knew anything could go wrong.

Above her to her right, a middle-aged man with gray hair
and beard stood on the crest of the cliff, silently gazing out to
sea. Another Middle Eastern-looking man, much younger,
joined him and said something. It was impossible to hear any
conversation either up here on the cliffside or down at the
beach, for the thunderous crashing of surf blotted out all human sound. She glanced up at them, not more than thirty
yards above her, and they briefly looked at her.

They wanted her dead. They knew nothing about her, but
because she was a kafir — she'd looked it up, an unclean infidel — they wanted her dead. And they wanted Samir, her

supposedly deeply religious Muslim boyfriend, to do the deed to prove his loyalty to their jihadist cause. What kind of human being would test another person in such a way?

Coldblooded fanatics.

She didn't know if she wanted to scream or weep. It would have been so easy to just cut and run, screaming her heart out. But she'd committed herself to the plan, and others had committed themselves as well. A part of her understood why she had to do this, but another part of her conjured up a different scenario. As though she'd wandered by mistake into someone else's nightmare. Maybe this was how all the victims of 9-11 felt as their planes approached the hijackers' targets. What *was* this madness all about? How could this happen? Why me?

Suppressing the urge to raise her middle finger at the two men, Meg continued down the path until she came to the wooden stairs. A metal pipe railing guided her down the steep stairs until her sneakers touched sand. Beyond two small dunes, Jake stood next to a blanket and picnic hamper. The ruse he'd used for drawing her to this beach on such an early Saturday morning was a romantic rendezvous with hot coffee and scones.

She'd brought along her own bit of rebellion. The San Diego FBI agents had instructed her to carry nothing but her cell phone and car keys. Screw that! If those jerkoffs on the cliff pointed guns at her, she'd come prepared. In her right-hand zippered jacket pocket lay her snub-nosed .38 revolver, loaded with five bullets. She knew that Jake couldn't pack a weapon for this particular scam, but they'd told her an FBI sniper was somewhere nearby just in case.

Well, she'd packed too. Just in case.

She slowly unzipped her pocket as she slogged her way across the sandy beach. Jake turned to greet her, a funereal expression marring his good looks. He wore the same creamy cable-knit sweater she'd delighted in peeling off him just six days before. His bearing was different, more rigid and upright, than Jake's usual loose-limbed posture. As Samir, he was doing a lousy job of acting the part of a killer of infidel girlfriends. Or maybe not. She'd never seen him as Samir.

Still, he greeted her with a light kiss and a tentative smile. Even so, he seemed unable to look her in the eye. Understandable, if Samir was minutes away from murdering her.

"Meg, they can't hear us. I'm not wearing a wire and the waves are too loud. So we can talk . . . but briefly."

"Okay. What's in the thermos?" They sat down close together on the plaid blanket. She rubbed her hands together as if she were cold. Actually, the air was only sixty-five degrees Fahrenheit but the ocean water was much colder. She was dreading the cold water. "Arsenic?"

He smiled and leaned over her. Just two lovers having a little early-morning picnic on the beach.

"Barbiturates in coffee. Enough to knock you out before Samir dumps you in the drink."

"How thoughtful of him. Must remind myself to get another Muslim boyfriend in my next life." She flung an arm around his neck and kissed him seductively. "Just playing the part so it doesn't look like I suspect anything."

Jake pulled away and busied himself with the thermos. "Don't worry. The TacOps guys replaced it with just coffee while we breakfasted at the IHOP. Halfway through the thermos you should collapse, fall asleep, do what you have to do to look like you're unconscious. The rest is the hard part, I'm afraid. Whatever you do, don't look back at them. Pretend they don't exist. They're just here to watch."

"What if, after you kill me, they try to kill *you*?"

"They won't. They need Samir." He poured her a mug full of coffee and urged her to drink. She did so and as she snuggled against him, she indicated her open zipper pocket. They turned their backs to the cliff as they faced the ocean breakers.

"How can you trust them? You said yourself you couldn't, not even if they're convinced you're Samir."

"I have to play it by ear. Gut instinct—" His expression changed—he must have seen the butt of her revolver sticking out of her pocket. "Meg, what's that—your gun?" Jake propped an arm behind her back to shield the contents of her jacket pocket from the men on the cliff.

"In case they try to shoot us. Or you, Jake. They're not expecting you to carry one. Take it—you're a better shot than I am anyway. You are, aren't you?"

His mouth had thinned to a taut line. He found no humor in what she'd done. "It's going to fall out when I pick you up."

His cheeks flushed with she didn't know what kind of emotion. Anger? Anxiety? While she made a pretense of gazing at the breakers rolling and crashing on the sand in front of them, she drank the coffee. Jake snatched her revolver and hid it in the picnic basket wedged between them.

"I'm so sorry," he hissed into the steady ocean breezes sweeping up the beach. His teeth set on edge, a muscle in his jaw ticked up and down. "This whole fucking op has gotten out of control. It's not supposed to come down like this. You're not supposed to be involved."

He raked a hand through his dark hair, then covered his eyes. "What the fuck am I doing? This is wrong. I can't do this. Meg, I can't do this. I can't put you through this."

She drank more coffee, anxious to get this whole charade over with. Jake was on the verge of panicking and backing out. Then where would that leave her? And him? And the undercover operation? And all the people he was going to keep from getting killed? She refused to think about any other course of action.

Too late to back out now.

What did her grandmother do when her grandfather got

weak and weepy? When he, though an Air Force Colonel, couldn't find the steel, the backbone, to do something that ran counter to his humanity. Like blow up an enemy munitions factory full of North Korean workers? Or napalm a village in Vietnam? Granny would start pushing his buttons and make him mad. Anger and pain always galvanized a man into action. Her grandmother should have been an army general. She had the steel to get it done.

She drank another mug of coffee. Well, maybe Meg had the same kind of steel. After all, her Gran was one of the most successful of Nazi spies. She was never caught. Not until Jake came along with his good looks and smooth patter. And that granite determination to uncover the truth. Was justice done? How could an old woman's torment at the very end of her life have satisfied anyone's sense of justice?

Mustn't think about that now. It wasn't Jake's fault. He was just doing his job. Like now . . .

Meg sipped more coffee and gazed out to sea. Ten yards beyond the water line, a huge boulder rose from the sand. That was where Jake would take and dump her. That boulder and what was near it were so important.

What if something went wrong? What if . . .

Playing her part, she leaned against Samir's wide shoulder. Her head went slack and she shut her eyes. She couldn't bear to see the look of extreme pain on his face. Her voice took on a hard edge.

"Jake, after this is over, don't ever call me again. I never want to see you, talk to you, have anything to do with you. Ever again."

"Meg, don't . . . We'll get through this. This'll be over soon."

His plea touched her, but she had a part to play. The San Diego agents were betting that Jake wouldn't go through with it, the fake murder. One of them had said an FBI Headquarters analyst would be too soft. Another one had argued that

Jake was former SEAL and would finish the job. They'd told her only so that she could get him to see it through. Now she understood what they meant.

"I'm sick of all this, Jake. It's over. Now, for chrissakes, get this over with."

He said nothing as she flopped forward across his lap. For what seemed like five minutes, Jake said nothing to her nor did he touch her. Finally, she felt her body lifted by two strong, muscular arms. She stayed limp, letting her head loll backwards, her long ponytail swinging under her.

"Meg, listen up. The cold water will shock you. Your instinct will be to kick out, flail your arms. Don't move. Stay limp."

Good. Jake was in control again and on task. She felt the drag of his legs as he waded into the water. At one point, a wave broke upon them and he almost lost his balance. He ripped loose his favorite curse. "Sonuvabitch!"

Water sprayed upward, bitingly cold to her face. He was bending over, using the boulder as support.

"Meg, take a big breath. Now!"

He was right. The cold water shocked her. Like an electric current shooting through her, she stiffened involuntarily and squinted her eyes as he lowered her under the water and held her down. With all her might, she fought to calm herself, to not struggle against the weight of his strong hands. She reached out and touched the boulder with her right hand. It was slimy with lichen but it reassured her.

Jake's hands gripped both her shoulders and held her down, making her panic. She began to resist and struggle. One leg kicked out and she clawed at Jake's hand. Every instinct inside her fought to survive. She struggled to surface until —

Jake's hand let go as another man's hand grabbed her right arm. A hand brushed her face just before he pressed a mouthpiece against her lips. As instructed, she opened her mouth just enough to blow out water, then let the diver insert the mouthpiece. She used her free hand to situate the mouth-piece more securely, then began to suck in oxygenated air. Jake's other hand didn't let go of her until she was in the full grasp of the scuba-diving FBI agent.

Together, she and the diver floated around to the far side of the boulder, Meg opening her eyes in the briny sea. When her eyes began to sting, she closed them, said a little prayer, and gave the scuba diver her full trust. He dove further down, clearing the boulder, pulling her with him. The current was strong, but the agent had the advantage of a lifeline that tugged them both around the promontory and into open wa-ter. The diver's hands positioned hers through loops in this lifeline. Meg concentrated on sucking air in through the mouthpiece. Nearby, she could hear a boat propeller churn-ing the water.

Minutes passed. Her body froze and turned numb, as-saulted by the tumbling surf, but the diver held her fast in his arms to the lifeline. She envied the scuba diver his wet suit as her bulky clothes dragged but didn't slow their momentum through the water.

One moment terrified her when one of her hands slipped loose from the lifeline. The diver reacted quickly and har-nessed her shoulders with his body. This part was not re-hearsed, but the steady tug and pull of the lifeline comforted her and kept her from panicking. Also, the diver's presence helped distract her from the freezing water. As long as he held her, she knew she wouldn't drown.

Nevertheless, the waves continued to buffet them like limp clothes in a washing machine. The primal roll and tumble of the ocean waves made her angry, so much that she found her-self believing what she'd told Jake in parting. If she survived this, she never wanted to see him again.

Screw him! Screw the damned ocean!

She was done with him. Done with it all.

Just when Meg's resolve to endure another chilling moment of this rescue began to crack, the diver pulled her to the safety of a jetty. She surfaced with the diver and looked around her, gasping as she pulled out the mouthpiece. She wiped her eyes and swept the hair from her face. Orienting herself, she realized they'd floated to the south side of the park, around the promontory where the cliff and huge boulders marked the northern end.

The diver ripped off his mask and mouthpiece and smiled. "You okay, Miss Larsen?"

She nodded. The skiff that had towed them waited and bobbed alongside the jetty. Linda Brown's look of concern greeted her. Two other agents from the San Diego field office scurried about to pull her, the diver, and the lifeline into the boat. From the diver's thumbs-up gesture, they'd accomplished their task. During their entire underwater journey, they had remained hidden from view of anyone on the northern cliff, including the watchful eyes of the two men.

"You did it, Meg!" Linda threw a blanket around her. "You did it!"

It's over! Thank God it's over.

But not for Jake.

Goodbye, Jake. Stay safe.

CHAPTER TWENTY-TWO

Jake withdrew into himself as he rode in the back of the rental car. Fariq's frequent sidelong glances with Reza served to provoke Jake into low mutterings that sounded to his own ears like growls. He couldn't help himself. In the picnic hamper underneath the cloth napkin lay Meg's loaded .38 revolver. It took all of Jake's concentration to stop himself from pulling it out and shooting the two men in the back of their heads. The world would be better off, he rationalized. But the mission would be blown and more people would die.

Silently, he fumed.

Stay focused.

Meg's gone. My Meg is gone.

Focus, dammit, focus.

In their motel room, Fariq stuffed his overnight bag with toiletries. The man's fastidious care of his sparse head hair and beard apparently drove Reza nuts. The young, skinny punk, Ali's enthusiastic recruit from the mosque, had ridiculed the older man for being so vain. Fariq had borne the taunts for two days in stoic silence.

"Do you think the condition of your beard's going to make Allah himself welcome you to Paradise?" Reza laughed. His own dark beard was cropped and trimmed, like Jake's.

Jake's back was to the men as he considered the problem of Meg's gun. He couldn't transfer the contents of the picnic hamper to his sports bag, for then he wouldn't be able to get the sports bag past airport security. The TacOps guys had bugged their motel room earlier that morning when they switched the coffee in the thermos, so Jake knew they were monitoring everything that was said. He whipped around as a solution struck him. While Fariq darted furious glances at Reza's continued taunts, Jake ignored them both.

"I'm going for coffee in the lobby," he announced, hoisting his sports bag over his shoulder. The hamper hung from his other hand. "I'll leave this basket there."

Reza swung on him and narrowed his eyes. "So why take your travel bag?"

Jake smirked. "'Cuz I don't trust you not to steal something from it."

"You son of a whore! I'm the one who doesn't trust *you —*"

Fariq was quick to intervene. "Reza, he proved himself today. Leave him alone!"

The younger man snarled at the interference. "The sheikh and Ali gave me authority on this mission. They ordered me to watch Samir. I'm not taking my eyes off this dirty, kafir-loving devil!"

Jake's mouth twisted to one side. All week he'd itched to take this punk down a peg or two. Ever since the little coward had kicked him in the gut while Jake was shackled in the storage room. With relish, Jake took a fighting stance, feet apart, one slightly in front of the other, bouncing lightly on his sneakers.

"Bring it on," Jake challenged.

Fariq backed up into the bathroom doorway, his expression oozing irony. He was as sick of Reza as Jake was.

Reza Phares, so full of himself that Ali had chosen him, whipped out a rib-sticker—a four-inch switchblade. A moment later, he charged into Samir. Jake, faster and stronger and hard of body, sidestepped him easily, holding off the guy's charge with a well-timed shove. He spun around and side-kicked the back of Reza's knee. The skinny thug went down, bounced off the edge of one of the beds, and landed on his back, stunned. In a flash, Jake kicked the blade out of Reza's hand, then stepped down on the man's throat.

"You want to die, Reza? I'll gladly put you on the fast-track to Paradise. Give me one more reason. You've already given me two."

Reza could only gurgle underneath Jake's shoe.

"Sorry, couldn't understand." Jake applied greater pressure. More gurgling from Reza, his eyes bulging with fear. "Not much fun on the receiving end, is it, asshole?"

Fariq shot Jake a warning look and shook his head. Remember the mission, the look said. For some reason, the sheikh needed Reza to play a part in the mission. Jake wished he knew what that role was, what the big picture was. Fariq knew, but he had revealed nothing so far. Jake was running out of patience.

Jake pressed harder on Reza's throat while he threw Fariq a questioning look. *Give me more, dammit.* The older man's face broadcast genuine alarm.

"He's needed to drive one of the EMT vans," said Fariq. "The sheikh's plan requires six vans. Reza has agreed to martyr himself for Allah's cause. The woman, Fatima, too."

"Tell me more," Jake snapped, his big sneaker not moving an inch. Reza's gurgling intensified and he began to weep. His hands gripped Jake's ankle but couldn't budge its hold on his throat.

"They told me," Fariq hurried, "they want to use the anthrax dispersal in the stadium to set off a panic, which would trigger a call out to emergency vehicles. First responders— ambulances, EMT's, fire trucks, police vans. In the pandemonium, six vehicles slip in, vehicles that'll blend in. Loaded with six-thousand pounds of explosives."

"Which stadium?"

"The one called Levi."

Jake nodded. *I was right.*

He released Reza's throat and bent over to retrieve the punk's knife. *How the hell did that get through airport security? Or did this scumbag come across the open southern border?*

He scrutinized the handle. By pressing the top of the handle, the blade retracted into what looked like a large pen. Jake tossed the fake pen into his sports bag.

"When?" He grabbed the picnic basket and his sports bag.

Fariq's chest rose and fell. He glanced down at the young punk still lying on the floor, gasping, then lifted his dark, smoldering eyes. "That, Samir, I don't know. Truthfully."

Jake wondered about that. Ignoring the pathetic coward on the rug, who was clutching his throat and coughing his lungs out, his gaze locked with Fariq's. Whether the middle-aged man was telling the truth or not, Jake determined to find out. For the moment, he knew he couldn't press Fariq any further. Eventually, Jake would get it out of him. Yeah, he'd deal with Fariq. Then Amad and Ali. All of them.

"Okay. Make sure this asshole doesn't follow me or, so help me, I *will* kill him."

With that final warning, Jake left the room. In the lobby, two men in jeans and dark blue windbreakers hunkered near a coffee machine on a long counter. Jake set the basket down on the counter.

"For Meg. Don't be surprised what you find in there. She means well." He paused to get his voice under control. "Tell her I'm sorry." Brusquely, he added, "Thanks for your help."

One of the men nodded in reply. Nothing more was said. The men took the basket and left the lobby, but Jake knew they'd hang around and continue surveillance. Jake poured himself a Styrofoam cup of black coffee and drank it slowly, bringing himself under control. He thought of Meg and her snub-nosed revolver—her pea shooter—and couldn't help but smile. A stabbing pain quickly followed and he had to catch his breath.

It's not over, Meg, not by a long shot. I'll make it up to you.

Fariq and Reza waited silently by the rental car. The younger man shot a hateful look in Jake's direction but kept silent.

Jake said nothing as he got into the back seat for the ride back to the airport.

CHAPTER TWENTY-THREE

Jake held his head in his hands, his elbows propped on the table in Todd's office at An-Vax. A moment ago, he'd studied the calendar on the wall. Today was Thursday, November twelfth. The Forty-Niners would be playing at Levi's Stadium that night. Four days had gone by since his staged murder of Samir's kafir girlfriend and he'd had no word from Amad or Ali. Not even Fariq.

What had gone wrong? Had his scuffle with Reza jammed up the works? His head throbbed from lack of sleep, from stress, from worry.

Perversely, his mind wandered back to his last lovemaking with Meg over a week ago. She'd welcomed him to her bed in Linda Brown's spare bedroom, treating him like a wounded warrior about to return to combat. He had to admit he'd taken advantage of the situation, milked it for all he could. Shamelessly. For along with her genuine sympathy and concern came pleasures of the flesh and soul.

After shedding their clothes, he'd reveled in her silky skin, tasted every inch of her flesh, breathed in her unique blend of citrus and lavender and musk. Even her long hair smelled of sunshine and everything good in the world. And her mouth, once he'd licked off all of the lipstick, tasted of peppermint and desperation. She'd explored him as thoroughly as he'd roamed over her body. They couldn't get enough of each other, each one sensing it would be a while before they'd have another private moment.

He was getting aroused, but instead of quelling the

memory, he immersed himself into it. The warmth flooded his mind and body and the memory of shared ecstasy with Meg stopped the ache in his heart, at least for a time.

"Hey there, Jake, I got those canisters — ."

Jake jumped in his seat. Shit!

"Man, you look like hell," said Todd Walinski, a wry smile curving up one side of his mouth, "You must've tied one on this weekend."

"Didn't sleep much. The job, y'know."

The young man's face fell, reminded apparently of the gravity of Jake's mission. "Oh yeah, I almost forgot. I've come to think of you as Samir, our fellow microbiologist. Who doesn't do lab work but writes reports all day." He set a stainless-steel canister the size of a liter of Coca Cola on the table. "It's hermetically sealed and filled with the baked powder from our ovens. Minus the attenuated anthrax, of course. I can get you a couple more like this in the next week."

Jake wrested his mind away from lovemaking with Meg and scrubbed his whiskered face with both hands.

"Baked powder?"

Todd turned the canister around so that the universal sign, the Hazardous-Materials diamond, could be seen.

"Actually, the by-product of our process without the addition of the dead bacteria. It looks like the real thing. I added the Haz-Mat warning sticker for effect. My boss, the owner of An-Vax, okayed it."

Remaining seated, Jake examined the lid and seal. Felt the weight of the canister. Very light. It looked like an innocuous, large, silver metal thermos but with a Haz-Mat diamond. Too small, however, for what he'd had in mind for a crop-duster delivery system.

"How could I open it if I wanted to attach some kind of a sprayer?"

"The real thing? Very carefully. The spores, if the canister contained real live or even attenuated anthrax, would seep into the air and kill anyone who breathed them in. Within minutes, an hour at most. Remember, the spores are hardy mothers. They can survive almost any kind of environment, dry or wet. You'd have to wear a Level Four Hazmat suit. The whole uniform, down to the double gloves and booties. Everything sealed. No cuts or holes." One of Todd's hands punched the air for emphasis. "Also, anyone else in the plane, such as the pilot of this crop duster, would be infected."

Jake nodded solemnly. He'd bet the jihadis had discovered that bioterrorism was not as facile a tactic of war as they'd once thought.

"Would four liters of the real stuff be enough for a crop-dusting plane to scatter around a field or town?"

Todd's face drained of color. "Holy shit! Is that what they're planning?"

"No, just a hypothetical question."

The young scientist appeared to swallow hard. "Four liters of anthrax powder, depending on the effectiveness of dispersal, wind conditions, and proximity of settlement—I mean, does it float off or settle immediately? Is the target a closed, contained area? And depending on the population in the vicinity, I don't know . . . four liters might be enough to kill hundreds. Maybe thousands in a closed-off area. Within thirty minutes to an hour. Wind factor would be vital, of course. And seepage potential." Todd frowned but remained thoughtful. "What kind of environment are we talking about?"

Jake had to risk confiding in the scientist if he was going to give a convincing argument to the Islamists. "An open-air football stadium."

The young man looked ready to faint on the spot. "Shit, you mean local stadiums like Levi's or the Oakland Coliseum?"

Jake nodded as Todd lowered himself behind his desk with the stunned look of a naïve civilian.

"Levi's Stadium is so open, and the winds off the Bay so prevalent and strong, a crop-dusting spray is certainly not an effective delivery system."

Jake had to resort to military jargon to get his point across. "Hypothetically, Todd, what would be the most effective delivery system for maximum kill potential?"

In response, Todd could only stare hard back at Jake, as if he'd only just realized the terrible scope of the enemy's potential. The look of disbelief followed by true alarm and horror was a look that Jake had seen several times, even among seasoned politicians on the intelligence and military appropriations committees, the ones who should know better.

"I don't know. I was at Levi's Stadium last Sunday. They played a damn good defensive game against the Jets." He hesitated as he pondered the problem. "The most frequented and contained areas would not be the bleachers in the open air but the restrooms and concourses where the food booths are. The Press Box and VIP rooms. The team locker rooms."

Jake took notes then looked at the stainless-steel canister standing on the table.

"Can I borrow this? And I'll need a few more to pull off this . . ." He almost said *trap,* as his mind envisioned a spider web. " . . . this operation."

He glanced down at his watch. Fifty minutes until his meeting with Rodriguez and Jordan. Hell, he'd been daydreaming about Meg for nearly twenty minutes. He was losing it.

Bad time to lose your focus, Bernstein.

Todd looked as though he wanted to vomit. "Do you know when? Where?"

"No, not the whole picture. Our best guess is the stadium. When . . . we think soon. Our aim is to stop it before it happens."

"Holy shit, I hope so."

"Can you keep this information under wraps?"

The young scientist nodded, his face as dark as a thunder-cloud. Completely understandable, Todd's reaction of horror. Jake felt he owed the information to the man for all of his help. The scientist had played a crucial role in Jake's undercover operation, and he found himself trusting the man all the way. Besides, more civilians needed to know how often the American intel community had to uncover and battle these terrorist plots. The struggle was daily, ongoing and brutalizing. It made you mine deep corners of hate that you never knew were there.

"So, can I borrow one of those canisters? And do you have a special box I can transport it in? So it looks crashproof? I've got to take it in my car."

"Yeah, I do." Todd frowned. "It's all yours. Good luck in convincing those bastards it's the real thing."

As in all clandestine meets, Jake did a counter-surveillance sweep after he left the secluded back employee parking lot of An-Vax. Fifteen minutes later, he was sure he hadn't been followed. Surprising, considering the fact that the punk Reza had spent every evening in the park across the street from his apartment complex. Jake would never have known this if his second-floor balcony didn't overlook that very street and park. Guess Reza wanted his rib-sticker back. Or maybe he wanted a third round with his nemesis, Samir.

Since Sunday, Fariq's man in the green car had followed him to work every morning but wasn't there hours later when Jake left and circled around to the front of the commercial building. Why they kept surveillance on Samir, he didn't know. His only possible conclusion was that despite everything, they still didn't trust him.

Not a good thing. And maybe the reason for Amad's and

Ali's disappearing act from the mosque. At Wednesday evening's service, Samir had approached the mosque's founder, Sheikh Mahmoud Hijazi, and inquired about them. According to the mosque's mullah, the two men hadn't returned yet from Texas.

To the contrary, Jake knew Jordan's trackers had kept the two in their crosshairs ever since they stepped off the plane Sunday night. They hadn't left their rental house in Saratoga all week. The FBI bugs had picked up a lot of coded chatter in Arabic over cyberspace in emails and Facebook. Both Amad and Ali used their smartphones 24/7. Clearly, the two men's frequency of communications had spiked, leading the FBI and CTC to surmise that attacks were imminent.

Jake's pulse raced at the very thought. They *had* to be stopped. But first, they needed to know all of the players, the exact location . . . *and* the exact date.

Jake drove five miles south to north San Jose. To pass the time, he listened to a Talk Radio show discussion about the history of Thanksgiving. The host mentioned the local exhibition college football game at Levi's Stadium at ten in the morning on Thanksgiving Day. The Sunday before that, the Forty-Niners would be matched up against their NFL South rivals, the New Orleans Saints.

Did it matter which team was playing? Either day — the Sunday before or the holiday itself — the stadium would be filled with football fans. Thanksgiving Day was twelve days away, Jake thought. Would that be enough time, from the terrorists' points of view, to pull it all together? Coordinated attacks in five different American cities? Only if they had a lot more help than what Jake had seen so far.

The parking lot of a family fitness center was half empty at this hour on a Thursday. Mostly housewives dropping their toddlers off in the nursery while they went to work out. He carried his sports bag into the men's locker room and proceeded to change clothes.

Dressed in his favorite Navy-issued sweatpants, white T-shirt, and Nike sneakers, he grabbed the Ralph Lauren towel — white with a blue stripe — from inside his sports bag a reminder of Meg. She'd given the towel to him that weekend in San Diego, a whimsical gift she'd bought one day when she was thinking of him while shopping. His mind wandered to more pleasant memories.

He found himself still staring at it minutes later when Jordan appeared, followed by Rodriguez, limping on a walking foot-cast with the aid of a cane. Frank's right arm was in a bent cast, covered with signatures and well wishes in a variety of felt-tip pen colors. There was even a large pink daisy and a canary-yellow smile figure on the front.

"My kids. Trying to cheer me up."

Jake gave him a man hug and shook Jordan's hand. They took seats on the two benches, the two SAC agents facing Jake.

"Sorry I couldn't visit you in the hospital. They've been on my tail like fleas on a dog."

Rodriguez shrugged. "Totally understandable. Linda Brown sent a box of homemade brownies on your behalf. She just returned from San Diego, said that whole experience down there gave her the willies. Hope we don't lose her. The Special Support Group thinks she's one in a million. Sounds like Meg's cooperating, though, and she's lying low at the San Diego safe house. The local newspaper in San Diego ran an article about the disappearance of a college coed named Meg Larsen, reported by an anonymous source. However, at Meg's request, the Feds made a discreet contact with Admiral Snider, her uncle, and his wife. Also, Meg's brother in San Francisco, to apprise them of the situation. The local PDs on board with this, so everything's cool."

Cool? Everything's definitely not cool with Meg. Her semester of work, down the tubes. I'm sure she's pissed as hell.

Jake blew out air in a heavy sigh. Frank looked as though

he was about to say something but Jordan gave him a warning look.

"What's the update on those four impostors?" Jake changed the subject.

"Hispanic aliases. Even the ringleader, this Alejandro Torres. He has a history with a Moroccan terrorist group affiliated with Salafist militias. He's suspected of providing support to the Moroccan thugs that blew up the train stations in Spain in 2009. Nasty guy. Also, he's a pervert. The Spanish authorities want him for rape among a slew of other charges."

"Probably why he's a candidate for *shaheed* – martyrdom. He's outworn his usefulness." Jake shook his head. "How the hell did we give that bastard a student visa?"

"He subverted the system by getting a student visa to Mexico first before applying for one here. You know how lax the State Department is."

Beating a dead horse, that was. "Okay, what have your men picked up? Have those four gone to any warehouses in the South Bay area?"

They had to be storing their vehicles some place in the neighborhood of their apartment. The location of the vehicles to be used in the stadium attack was key to the conclusion of their investigation.

Jordan piped in, leaning over his knees. "That's the devil of it. They've left their apartment to go buy groceries, do some sightseeing around San Francisco—Fisherman's Wharf, Coit Tower, Lombard Street, the usual tourist sites. They've been to Levi's Stadium once. Last Sunday's game. Paid scalper's prices for four tickets. Another team tailed Reza and that woman, Fatima, to the stadium the same day. There was no sign they crossed paths with the four guys, but all six were there. Same time, same place. So looks like we've got the target and the drivers. Now we need the vehicles and the explosives."

Jordan paused in his briefing when one of the fitness trainers walked into the locker room. Rodriguez flashed his FBI badge and the man left.

"They've even gone to some night spots," Jordan continued. "Bars, strip clubs. Acting like normal, single guys. No visible income except a weekly trip to a bank for withdrawals. We tracked those wire transfers back to a French bank that's suspected by INTERPOL of money laundering for Hezbollah and Al Qaeda interests in Iran. Four thousand a week. A lot of bucks helping these guys. But no visits to any warehouse or dock in the vicinity. No garages or storage facilities."

"They're living it up before their suicide mission?"

Rodriguez posed this question, locking eyes with Jake.

Jake pondered the four men's strategy while scratching his beard. The sooner he was rid of all the facial hair, the better. He hated it and all it stood for. A memory flickered.

"Have those four shaved their beards?" Jake asked.

Both Jordan and Rodriguez nodded. "Even Reza," Rodriguez added.

This newest information was revealing. The six suicide drivers at the stadium on the same day. Now they'd finally verified the location. Another point—time was short. The men had shorn their beards. To a jihadist male, this act was a sign of commitment.

"Just what the nine-eleven jihadis did," Jake said, "before converging on New York and New Jersey from various places around the U.S. and Europe. They wanted to make sure to throw off any suspicions. Their handlers told them to act like normal American men. Shave their beards, wear Western clothes, act American. But not every American guy goes to a strip joint. It's not normal for four guys to live together, not have jobs, and still rake in four thousand a week. It shows they don't understand Americans and the way we live. They're doing what their handlers tell them to do based on stereotypes and caricatures."

Jordan, in that inscrutable, understated way of his, gazed at his hands for a long moment then raised his dark eyes. He spoke calmly as though he were discussing the bookies' odds on the next Forty-Niner game.

"Another thing. I sent TacOps back to that public storage unit. The metal drums are gone. We don't know where. You recall, we couldn't tag them with RFIDs without tipping off the bad guys."

Bad news, but it added support to their theory of explosives.

Frank Rodriguez, in obvious pain, shifted uncomfortably on the bench. His insistence on staying involved testified to his dedication, Jake thought.

"Are you thinking what I'm thinking?" Rodriguez asked. "There's another sleeper cell that's collecting the vehicles and making them ready. Converting them into EMTs or ambulances or whatever. These four Moroccans are just the suicide drivers. They either don't have the brains, or they don't have the skills to convert plain cargo vans into mass-killing machines."

"I think you're right." Jake stood, venting his grim anxiety through restless energy. He paced a little, then stopped to place one big, sneakered foot on the bench before rubbing his face. An idea had struck home.

"Frank, Mike, we need to cast a wider net. I cross the Dumbarton Bridge every day. That cuts my commute to An-Vax in half. Why wouldn't the terrorists consider doing the same thing? Stake out an East Bay location and use one of the bridges to commute back to the west side and up to the stadium. Expand to the East Bay. Scout out the machine shops, chop shops, auto mechanics, detailers in the East Bay. They can transport explosives across the San Mateo Bridge, or even the Bay Bridge."

Rodriguez and Jordan glanced at each other, their eyes widening. Jake knew what they were thinking. A huge area, San Francisco Bay, west and south bays. And now the East Bay. Thousands of mechanics to survey. Maybe hundreds of auto shops to check out in the next few days. Spending so much time with that storage unit in Redwood City had cost them valuable time. And maybe that was part of the plan.

Taquiyya. A diversion. So typical of the Islamists.

Jake pressed on. "Focus on owners with past run-ins with the law, maybe, or connections to Islamic or other Middle East organizations. Also, that bank. Maybe there's another account with an alias we can track."

Jordan stood, also, clearly ready for battle. Another wrinkle in their investigation, rather than deflating him, had galvanized him into action.

"Okay, I'll get on it. Frank, your men—just stay on those four Moroccans. Stick to them like glue. This strip club they go to, maybe we can plant a female agent there. Sniff out a day and time, at least. You have one in mind?"

Frank nodded, smiling and standing with Jordan's assistance. "The hottest Feeb in Northern California."

"A real babe, huh? Just don't introduce her to Jake here," Jordan quipped, "I want to meet her first."

Their joke cut the tension in the air and they all chuckled. Jake's thoughts turned to Amad's and Ali's recent trip to Dallas, and the latest from the CTC, which continued to coordinate the undercover operations in all five cities. His job was to keep the local field office SAC informed.

"Word back from the Dallas field office is that Amad and Ali met with several different groups, supposedly Qur'anic study groups. One group of teenaged boys was disbanded when one of the boys was killed while walking home from school. The cops think it was a drive-by shooting and a case of mistaken identity. Maybe a hate crime. The undercover agent in place thinks differently. That same boy had given his parents a thumb drive that he claimed Sheikh Amad had given him. The parents reported this to the mosque's sitting mullah, who then did the right thing and called the police. The thumb drive was full of Al-Jazeera news videos and Al-Shumukh propaganda shit from Al-Qaeda. The local cops questioned Ali, but he denied giving the thumb drive to the boy. The next day, the boy was shot. The other three boys have clammed up and their parents have hired lawyers."

Jordan snorted noisily. "And the other group?"

"Disaffected men, miscreants. The undercover agent has them under tight surveillance. But it's a similar thing to our problem. Another cell, in charge of the explosives and converting the vans, remains in the dark."

"And lies in wait," Rodriguez added. "What about Houston as a port of entry for the explosives?"

"That's exactly what the Dallas field office thinks. I think Amad sent some kind of secret signal to that group of jihadis. Either someone's en route with the explosives or they're already here."

Samir's cell phone buzzed. Jake held up a hand to quiet them before answering. It was Amad, himself. After the usual *salaam alaikums,* the cleric broached what Jake knew was really on his mind.

"Samir, habibi, can you meet with us ikhran after Friday Fajr?" The usual Friday prayer service at six-thirty at the Cordoba Mosque in San Miguel. Amad was requesting a special meeting with the brothers.

"Certainly, Sheikh Amad. Where?"

"Ali and I will drive you there after the service. Fariq and the others will be coming also. Bring your delivery plan with you. Are you with us, brother, in body and soul?"

Jake had no problem guessing which delivery plan Amad was referring to. Todd's stainless-steel canister with the Haz-

Mat diamond would come in handy and might shake them up a bit. Might shake some information loose.

Show-and-tell time.

"Yes, I am. I'll be ready with the plan. See you at Fajr. *Shokran, shokran.*" He rang off and pocketed the phone. Rodriguez's and Jordan's stares bore holes into him.

"Tomorrow night, after the mosque prayer service. Well, guys, this is finally showtime."

"Wire? Weapon?" Jordan asked. Anxiety creased both his and Rodriguez's faces.

"No, can't risk it. Just the watch. But stay close."

Jordan pointed at Jake's chin. The underside of his chin, the fleshy part, was covered with thick, dark whiskers. "You bet we'll stay close, but, Jake, we can do more."

Rodriguez nodded in assent. "Coming here, we were talking about a biometric microchip. It's got GPS along with ID. Hey, we're in Silicon Valley. Might as well take advantage of it."

They were right. The watch was not enough. It could be stripped off him, especially if he were tasered again.

"Yeah, let's do it," Jake said. Unconsciously, his hand flew up to his chin. "When?"

"Tonight. Linda Brown's trained to insert it. Your beard'll hide it and you can always say you cut yourself."

Tomorrow was Friday the thirteenth.

Not a good sign, but they had no choice. They had to move forward before it was too late.

CHAPTER TWENTY-FOUR

Jake bowed over his prayer rug and murmured aloud the *Shahada*, the first of the five pillars of Islam, the Islamic Declaration of Faith, the first being, "There is no God but Allah, and Muhammad is His Prophet."

The visiting British mullah conducted the service that night, intoning the verses of the Qur'an in Arabic and then translating them afterward. His velvety baritone wafted over the assemblage of subdued men while Ali stood stiffly at Sheikh Amad's side. Jake couldn't help but wonder what these men would do if he lunged to his feet and exposed the mullah and his assistant for what they really were.

They would stone him, or the Americanized, twenty-first century version of stoning. Oh yeah, a staged drive-by shooting. Make it look like a hate crime. And if he revealed that he came from a long line of German Jews on his father's side? Would they behead him, like the American journalist, Daniel Pearl? These men beside him on their prayer rugs, they looked like typical ethnic Americans, but were they really? Did they think like most Americans? He couldn't help but wonder about the influence of Islam on their psyche.

Soon he was filing out of the men's prayer room, avoiding any contact with the women in the hallway. He couldn't be seen to smile or even make eye contact unless the women were relatives of his. No wonder the jihadis were so successful in recruiting Muslim males. The poor bastards were bursting with sexual frustration.

Someone tapped his shoulder. Ali sneered at him.

"Meet us in the back parking lot in fifteen minutes."

Jake nodded and wandered off to the banquet room where the men were sipping sweet tea and scarfing down cookies and pastries. He spotted Reza, Fariq Al-Nasreem and his assumed bodyguard, one of the husky muscles Jake had seen that night in Fariq's restaurant. Fariq came over and greeted him with "Salaam alaikum". Jake returned the greeting and cast him a false, friendly smile.

"So, Samir, are you ready?"

"Yes. Do you know where we're going?"

"The back room of my restaurant, Kabul. We'll have dinner and then go over the plan."

That reply disappointed him. He'd hoped to be taken to the auto shop, garage, or warehouse where the cargo vans waited for conversion to weapons of mass destruction. "Will everyone be there?"

"I suspect so. Sheikh Amad said to expect twelve."

Jake did a quick mental calculation. Including Fariq and his man, that meant another man would be joining them. His heart began to race. Could this be the auto shop owner? Or the one who transported the explosives from Dallas?

"Watch yourself, habibi." Fariq lowered his voice. "Be careful not to give yourself away. Don't ask too many questions."

Jake stared hard. *What did he say?* Before he could react, however, they were joined by Fariq's man and a frowning Reza. As a unit, they moved silently to the hallway which led to the rear of the building. Fariq indicated an older model green sedan, the same sedan that had followed Jake every morning to An-Vax and then disappeared. Probably one of several in Fariq's fleet.

Anticipating the carpool arrangement, Jake had parked his rented Explorer in the rear parking lot also. He made his way to the car, lifted the hatch, and pulled out a small cardboard box. Carrying it to the green sedan, he noticed Reza and

199

Fatima getting into Amad's and Ali's rental car, the same black, four-door sedan that had taken an unconscious Jake to the storage unit in Redwood City.

By contrast, he was now traveling as an equal. The drive over to Fariq's restaurant on the El Camino Real was short and silent.

What the hell did Fariq mean? *Be careful not to give yourself away.* Jake's gaze kept reverting to the back of Fariq's head. *Who is this man?*

Inside Kabul, Jake barely touched a morsel of his lamb kebab, rice, and cilantro-laced salad. He purposely avoided Fariq's frequent looks and, instead, kept glancing back at the cardboard box he'd placed behind him along the side of the wall. There were ten at dinner, the two vacant chairs at the end of the table raising for Jake a host of questions. Fariq's bodyguard stood behind his boss, his arms crossed over his leather-jacket front. His eyes roved continuously over the four strangers at the table.

The four Moroccans were the surprise guests, Alejandro their obvious leader. Everything that Amad or Ali said, Alejandro translated into their Moroccan dialect, a blend of Arabic and colonial French. Apparently they spoke little English and their Spanish, from what Jake could tell, was rough and spotty. No wonder, according to Meg, none of them except for Alejandro would come out and converse in Spanish with her.

To Jake's great relief, Alejandro gave no obvious indication that he recognized Jake as Meg's visitor that one weekend in San Diego. But that did not stop Jake, recalling what Meg had told him about the guy's strange behavior that day the four had left, from itching to grab the man's throat and hang him up to dry.

At one point, Amad and Ali gave the six *shaheed* a veiled toast and applauded their courage and devotion. Everyone drank their cups of sweet tea and echoed, "Inshallah!"

Jake's eyes strayed back to the two vacant chairs. So were two more men going to join them? Neither Amad nor Ali implied that anything was amiss, and Jake decided not to act too curious. *Watch yourself . . .*

Though he had no idea why, he was going to heed Fariq's counsel. Reminding himself that Fariq was vetted and trusted by the San Jose field office, and that the middle-aged man had revealed more to Samir last weekend than he needed to, Jake chose to wait and see and meanwhile say nothing.

The man was either playing a dangerous double-agent game on Jake's team — like Jake was — or he was a very crafty mole in league with the jihadis and playing the FBI for fools. And maybe playing extra friendly with Samir to smoke him out.

"Let's adjourn to the back room," announced Ali, pushing his chair back. He gave the cardboard box on the floor a pointed look and told Jake, "Bring your box."

Minutes later, the entire dinner party of ten stood around a large wooden cabinet in a room that appeared to be used as an office. Fariq's restaurant business had to be successful, for his office was well appointed, dark wood bookshelves lining each wall. A desk and chair sat in one corner along with a myriad of electronic equipment, but the matching cabinet in the center of the large room dwarfed the other furniture.

On the cabinet's dark granite countertop lay a bird's eye sketch of Levi's Stadium, taped at the corners. A brightly lit, overhead lamp illuminated the carefully drawn, black-on-white drawing on the dark countertop. Jake could see there was another layer of paper underneath, indicating the second main level of concourses surrounding the rings of bleachers and the football field in the center. The ground level view was visible on the top paper, including the number of aisles that intersected the main circular concourse. There were ten drive-through entrances and exits wide enough for emergency, cargo, and maintenance trucks.

The number struck Jake. Evidently, six of those entrance-exits sported iron gates that could be opened and closed by gatekeepers manning them during the game. Using a wooden ruler, Ali pointed out the gate number assigned to each of the drivers. All six nodded, bowed their heads and muttered, "In-shallah."

"The timing of this is critical. All six of you must arrive and enter the stadium at the same time. If you are stopped before you can enter the archways leading to the ballfield, show the fake IDs that will be inside the van. That will get you through the gates to the outer perimeter of the stadium walls. If you are prevented from entering the stadium itself, then you have our permission to detonate the bomb inside your van. That will cause deaths and even more chaos and should destabilize the structure of the stadium. But our main purpose is for the vans to gain access to the field, or as close to the bleachers as possible. Whatever happens, each of your sacrifices will serve a purpose and be sanctified."

The cleric asked for questions. Alejandro and Reza followed with a few. The woman, Fatima, apparently the slave to Reza's wishes, kept silent. Both Amad and Ali responded, the mullah in quieter, measured tones than Ali's more passionate inflections. Jake leaned over the table, his left hand positioned so that his transmitter-watch caught everyone's voices. He'd listen more carefully to the recording of this strategy session later, but what they were saying was enough evidence to put all eight of them away for at least twenty years. Fariq was uncommonly reticent. What *was* his role in this plot? Facilitator? Recruiter? Financial supporter?

"To cause the crowd to become alarmed and to panic, thus sending out a call for emergency vehicles, our brother, Samir, has a plan."

Jake carefully unwound the bubble-wrap and lifted the

stainless steel canister out of the box's Styrofoam cradle. He set it on the top of the wooden cabinet, on the edge of the drawing, its Haz-Mat diamond facing the center of the countertop. Once the gathering noticed the symbol, a few gasped audibly.

"This contains a liter of live anthrax in powdered form." He saw everyone shrink away from the cabinet. No one wanted to become a martyr just yet, he thought drily. "This is an airtight, sealed container, so no need to be frightened. I sealed it myself in the lab."

"You brought that thing in the car?" Fariq cried in disbelief, looking outraged and stepping back a couple of feet.

"I handle live anthrax every day," Jake said mildly. "Although it's usually in the lab and when I'm covered head to toe in a Level Four Hazmat suit. What I'm trying to show here is the extremely delicate manner in which this kind of bacteria has to be handled. If I broke the seal, everyone in this room, and most likely half the customers in the restaurant, would be dead in one hour." He paused to absorb the effect this information had on each one, especially Amad and Ali. It was clear they already had an inkling of this deadly bacteria's effects on the human body, so Jake went on. "A very hot fire, caused by an explosion, would kill most of these bacteria if the fire consumes the area where it has been spread. I'm saying this so that you understand that whatever anthrax powder I disperse can only be effective *before* the bombs are set off."

Ali let rip a rapid stream of Arabic at Amad, glowering all the while. Jake now knew that it was Amad's idea, not Ali's, to bring Samir's expertise with handling anthrax into the equation. He imagined that Ali's argument had been for guns and bullets instead. Let loose a machine-gun assault inside the stadium. However, such an attack would be limited and cut off swiftly by roaming armed security personnel inside the concourses. For the first time, Jake realized that Amad's actual manpower might be limited to just the six drivers. Unless this other secret sleeper cell proved to be sizeable in number.

"I've studied the problem," Jake went on. "And I've concluded that contained areas, like restrooms, locker rooms, the VIP rooms, and the Press Box, are the most likely targets for dispersing the bacteria. Fifteen to twenty minutes before the game starts, I'll make calls to the Press Box, Security, and local law enforcement, announcing that live anthrax powder has been planted on the site. This would spike the fear, panic, and confusion. I could plant the powder early that morning, disguised as a maintenance worker."

"How would you accomplish that disguise? How would you smuggle those containers inside the stadium past security?" Amad asked.

"A friend of mine at the gym works for the maintenance company that cleans the stadium," Jake lied. "I convinced him that I needed some extra money, so I'm on call to sub for him anytime I ask. Smuggling in the canisters? In the maintenance carts, along with the Hazmat suit and face mask. It'll be tricky to plant the stuff, but I think I can do it."

"That's crazy," Ali smirked. "Are you ready to be a shaheed, pretty boy?"

Jake stiffened. *Watch out. He's trying to bait me.* "I'll try not to be, but if something goes wrong and Allah wills it . . ." He let his voice trail off, letting the obvious speak for itself.

His face now dark red, Reza banged his fist on the counter. "I don't believe you! He's American military. He fights like a Special Forces soldier. I tell you, Ali, he's an FBI informant!"

Fariq reacted with alarm. "That's not true! My men have followed him every day for months. He has done nothing to betray us. Sure, we know he was once in the Navy, and that one weekend with that kafir showed he's a man with physical needs. All that has changed and he has proven himself by killing the infidel. Reza, you saw yourself what he did to prove himself loyal to us. I'm convinced your distrust springs from jealousy and nothing more!"

Alejandro was now staring at him, a speculative look curling down his mouth, as though trying to recall a distant memory. Ali launched into a tirade of Arabic with Amad, both men fiercely confrontational in their debate. Fariq's bodyguard came to the doorway but his boss waved him off. The middle-aged businessman shot Jake a warning look. *Say nothing.*

Jake waited for the commotion to die down. This kind of power play was typical of Muslim men and probably men in general. Who would emerge on top as the big dog was anyone's guess, but Jake took a step back, legs apart, and lifted the canister in his hands above his head. As if he needed to remind them that he could destroy them all with one broken seal. All heads turned his way. The woman cowered and covered her face.

Jake needed to ramp up his persuasive pitch. "I'm telling you, Sheikh Amad, Ali. I can do this. After a few people see the powder and begin to bleed through their noses, ears, and mouths, panic will break out. It's the most effective way to cause terror. People will drop like flies, and security won't be thinking clearly. They'll wave on through any emergency vehicles that show up." He swung and tucked the canister under his arm. "You don't want my help, come up with your own scheme."

Ali calmed down and, along with all of the men, looked at the mullah, waiting for his final word. The turbaned cleric calmly stroked his ragged, graying Salafist beard and stared hard back at Jake. Amad's dark eyes then whipped to Fariq's gaze across the cabinet.

"Fariq, habibi, you're Muslim Brotherhood. Your father and older brothers, honored officers in the Brotherhood. In your youth, your brave acts of revenge won great notice and acclaim. Now I ask you, what do you think?"

Muslim Brotherhood? Did the local FBI uncover that tidbit in Fariq's background check? Jake's heart raced. *What the hell don't they know about this man?*

As Ali and Reza muttered beneath their breaths, both Amad and Fariq ignored them and turned toward each other to make their assessment of Samir's plan.

Fariq spoke first. "It's audacious and bold but it could work. Samir is capable and has proven his loyalty and willingness to be a martyr. As he said, if Allah wishes it, along with many others he will not survive."

The mullah bowed slightly in Jake's direction. "Then I sanctify his plan." The smile he directed Jake's way was tinged with irony while Ali's and Reza's faces darkened with rage.

Jake exhaled deeply and set the canister back on the granite countertop. With a disgusted sweep of his arm, Amad indicated that Jake should put it away in the box. Which he did.

"Samir," Amad added. "We shall need at least five of those containers. Four others you will ship overnight to four addresses that Ali shall give you."

Jake kept his face a mask. "I've stockpiled three others in my locker at the lab," he lied. "I can get them from the lab tonight and ship them wherever you like. But I'll need more time to put together the fifth one. A couple of days."

The mullah looked pleased. "Good. You see, four other targets in Satan's country are involved. The other teams shall have need of your bacteria before next Friday. With seals intact, of course, so they can plant the powder first. Other *shaheed* are prepared to do what they have to do to plant the deadly bacteria."

"My sheikh, they'll have their canisters in time." Jake bowed in turn and placed his hand over his heart.

Apparently, the fact that four stadiums in four other cities would be attacked was news to the six potential martyrs of *jihad*, resulting in excited murmurs around the cabinet. They would have one more week to prepare. The time frame was shorter than he thought.

As Jake returned to the countertop, the back-alley door slammed shut. Two bearded men, tall and husky, entered the room.

"*Salaam alaikum,*" one of them announced loudly.

CHAPTER TWENTY-FIVE

The two heavyset, beardless men, at least six feet in height and with dark, thick moustaches, entered the spill of light and greeted Amad, Ali, and Fariq. The five men hugged and kissed each other's cheeks in the Muslim male way. Fariq ordered his bodyguard, in Arabic, to call the waiter for tea. When the visitors lit their cigarettes, others followed suit. Before long, the room's air hung heavy with smoke.

The visitors scanned the room, their gazes weighing each one in turn. The first man's glance lingered on Samir before moving on to the others. The six shaheed appeared a little puzzled but obviously excited by the arrival of the two new strangers. Clearly, these strangers' roles in the attack were crucial, and both Amad and Ali treated them with the respect due them. Almost immediately, the taller and huskier of the two leaned over and whispered to Ali, who then passed on the message to the mullah. Amad smiled broadly, hugged the man again and kissed his cheeks.

Jake surmised this sudden lovefest had a lot to do with the vans being readied for their deadly cargo. His stomach clenched and twisted. The need to discover who these men were and the location of those vans and explosives was visceral.

Fariq introduced the two men around the cabinet island before stopping in front of Samir Maalouf, followed by more greetings of *Salaam alaikum* and *Alaikum salaam*. Wahid and Hameed were their names, as Fariq introduced them, but no family names were given. Jake suspected the names were aliases. A few minutes of courteous Arabic inquiries ensued before Fariq tossed Samir his car keys.

"Put that thing back in the trunk. And while you're at it, bring my car around to the back." Implied was Fariq's desire to leave his restaurant soon and discreetly.

Jake nodded his assent, silently regretting that he couldn't leave his watch behind to continue transmitting. He threaded his way through the restaurant, wondering all the while if Fariq had another reason for temporarily getting rid of Samir. Now that he knew *where* the attack was to happen, he needed to know exactly *when*. And where the vans and their deadly cargo were now being stored. This was vital information that could have been transmitted had Samir been allowed to remain. One of the newcomers must have conveyed something to Fariq or Amad, or vice versa, an indication that Samir could not be fully trusted.

No sooner having parked the green Camry in the rear alley, Jake noticed a dirty, mud-splattered, white Ford F-250 pickup with an extended cab parked alongside the high brick wall separating the strip mall from a residential area. The FBI surveillance van was nearby on that side street, its sign bearing a local electrical company. He hoped that Jordan and his techies had picked up everything up to the point when he'd left.

Anxious to return to the meeting, Jake got out and strode to the rear of the pickup. He gave a description of the truck into his watch, then bent over to rub the mud that obscured the license plate number.

"Hey! What the hell're you doing?"

He looked up to see a barrel-chested, dark-haired man in his forties rounding the extra-long bed of the pickup. Another man was standing behind him. They wore the aggressive expressions of men accustomed to physical confrontations. Jake hadn't seen them emerge from the shadowy alcove by the back door.

"Uh, I dropped my cell phone." Jake pulled it out of his slacks pocket and held it up in the palm of his hand. "Fariq told me to move his car back here. We're having a meeting inside."

The two men exchanged a glance, then one of them advanced. "Arms out."

"What?" Jake took a step back.

"We're going to frisk you," the man growled, "We don't know you from Adam. Now spread!"

American-born musclemen, Jake concluded, deciding not to push the issue. Apparently they were with Wahid and Hameed inside, the rest of the second sleeper cell now finally out of hiding. These guys had to be followed that night back to wherever they'd come from. That was vital. He had to let the van know. Unfortunately, they'd covered up the rear license plate and most likely the front one as well.

The shorter, barrel-chested guy gave him a thorough but rough pat-down. Jake kept his temper under control and endured it, training his eyes on the second man a few feet away. They were both obviously packing.

"So who were you talking to?" the guy asked.

"Talking on the phone. My pal at the Sharks game."

"San Jose Sharks, huh? They're playing tonight, Abdul?"

"Fuck if I know," the second guy snarled. "Okay, let him go. I know Fariq's car. This prick wouldn't have the keys unless Fariq wanted him to."

Jake passed through the rear door of the restaurant while the two enforcers took guarded stances on either side.

Wahid and Hameed turned and displayed toothy smiles as Jake walked in. Fariq joined them in their mirth.

"You've met the two gorillas?" Fariq said as he took a drag from a skinny cheroot.

"Yeah, thanks for the heads-up," Jake muttered. Amad and Ali grinned in their beards as Ali gave the rolled- up drawings to Reza, the apparent point man of the six shaheed.

Fariq offered a cheroot to Jake. "Strange, I've never seen you smoke."

"Had asthma as a child. Bothers my lungs," he explained, declining with a gesture of apology.

"Well, good news," said Amad. "The vehicles will be ready by Wednesday and you said the other four cities would have your containers by next week. We've had a change in plans. They must be in the others' hands by Wednesday. The Sunday before the American Thanksgiving is our new target."

"Why next Sunday?" Jake asked.

Fariq shot him a look of caution before acquiescing to the mullah's leadership.

"The five stadiums in question will have games that day, all at approximately the same time. One o'clock Eastern time, noon Central time, and ten o'clock Pacific time. We want a simultaneous attack, so this new development works to our advantage."

Amad nodded to Ali, who approached Jake with a piece of paper. "Here are the addresses to which you shall send the other four containers. Make sure they're wrapped sufficiently well and the couriers are reliable. We don't want the seals broken before they can be in place. They must arrive at their destinations by Wednesday."

Jake nodded, folded and pocketed the sheet of paper without reading it. "*Nam.* Thanks be to Allah, your plan will be successful."

"May the Prophet, peace and blessings be upon him, guide you in this endeavor." Amad then held up his hands, facing the others, as he intoned a verse from the Qur'an.

"Good and evil are not equal. Repel evil with what is best until the one whom you have enmity with is transformed into a passionate friend."

"Even if those evildoers must enter the Paradise of Allah to be transformed," interjected Ali.

"If you are killed in the cause of Allah or you die," recited Amad, "the forgiveness and mercy of Allah are better than all that you amass. And if you die or are killed, even so it is to Allah that you will return."

Everyone assembled placed hands over their hearts and bowed slightly in the mullah's direction. A moment of silence passed before Amad and Ali straightened.

"The meeting is over," declared Fariq. "*Allahu Akbar.*" God is great.

"*Allahu Akbar,*" chorused Jake and the others.

"My role is over," Fariq told Jake matter-of-factly as they pulled into the mosque's rear parking lot. "You must do, Samir, what you have to do."

Before sliding out of the back seat and heading to his rented Explorer, Jake asked, "What do you mean, Fariq, your role is over?"

"Just that, my friend. I'm a facilitator. Nothing more. I must take a business trip next week and will be gone for at least a month or two. Be careful with those bacteria. I hope to see you again. Under other circumstances."

"You bet." Jake frowned, "And thanks for your support, Fariq."

"I was all too happy to assist you." The older man then waved his driver on.

Too bad the FBI was going to arrest him, just as soon as they rolled up the others, the whole bunch of these violent fanatics. Jake was beginning to like the older man. He couldn't figure out the man but, wealthy or not, Fariq was going to spend the rest of his life in prison.

Jake climbed in his Explorer and rushed back to Fariq's restaurant, lurching to a stop on the side street where the FBI surveillance van had parked. It was gone. So was the Ford pickup.

Popping open the burner phone that he retrieved from under the driver's seat, Jake called Jordan in the van.

"Are you following that white Ford pickup?" he burst out.

"We were. They lost us going north on the One-o-one, the Bayshore Freeway."

"Shit!"

"My sentiments, exactly," said Jordan. "On the bright side, they peeled off, we think, around the Burlingame area. So that might narrow down our search. What was on the door signs? We never could get a fix on them."

"I just took a glance, and the alley was dark, but I'll bet it was bogus. A clever deflection."

"Oh yeah? What was it?"

"Homer's Hunting Guns and Ammunition. No phone number or website."

"Hell, at least they have a sense of humor. We'll check, anyway."

"They're American born, second or third generation. Ex-military, maybe. Three names, Abdul, Wahid, and Hameed. Probably aliases. The last two, Wahid and Hameed, were tall, big men, resembled each other. Could be brothers or cousins."

"Well, that narrows it even more," Jordan said sarcastically.

Man, it was going to be another long night.

CHAPTER TWENTY-SIX

"Sorry, Agent Bernstein, no luck. We ran checks on over two dozen body, paint, and detail shops in the South San Francisco, Burlingame, and San Mateo areas. A white Ford pickup matching that description was reported stolen Friday and was recovered late that same night. But no mechanics or body shop workers or detailers even remotely resembling those guys you described. Not in the South Bay."

That was Jordan reporting four days later on their search for the four jihadis who had converted cargo vans into killing machines.

Jake was back at An-Vax, putting in his time and collecting the five canisters of anthrax-free, baked biologics. He had to send out four of those canisters to the list of contacts in four cities—Miami, Dallas, Chicago, and New York City. Of course, his reports back to the CTC Chief and his boss, Terry, had found their way to the assigned undercover agents in those very cities, and the appropriate field offices had been notified. All four agents in those cities had already zeroed in on their own targets, but the exact date surprised them all. Apparently Thanksgiving, which everyone assumed was the actual target date, was changed to a simultaneous, coordinated attack on the Sunday before Thanksgiving Day. The news made everyone scurry to head off the attack and make plans for a coordinated plan of their own, a dragnet of suspects set for that Sunday morning.

The priority was the same for all five teams—find the explosives before they were set off and avoid civilian casualties.

The microchip imbedded underneath Jake's chin never ceased to irritate him. He scratched the fleshy, whiskered area almost unconsciously. Something Frank Rodriguez said in the locker room the other day nagged him. About the attractive female FBI agent.

"I've got to be a driver," he told Jordan on the phone. "That might be our only chance to find out where those vans are." He paused, wondering if what he was about to propose was such a good idea. So many things could go wrong . . . "Jordan, that female FBI agent in San Francisco, the one all the men drool over —"

"Nope, you're not meeting her. No way. Not till I get a shot at her first."

Jake chortled deep in his throat. The joking eased the tension in their voices. "One of the drivers, Alejandro, can't seem to curb his impulses. He's wanted for rape by Spanish authorities. And from what Meg said, he can't control himself. What if he's picked up for attempted rape and they suddenly need another driver? I'd volunteer my services."

Silence, but by now Jake was accustomed to Jordan's quiet as the man worked through the plan mentally before commenting.

"Not a bad idea. Are you thinking last minute, like Saturday night?"

"You got it."

"Okay, I'll see about it."

Three hours later, as Jake was driving over the Dunbarton Bridge, heading west back to the South Bay Area, he glanced to the north. The San Mateo Bridge was visible on this bright, clear, cold day, a major link between the West Bay and the East Bay. Just north on the East Bay was Alameda, the former home of one of the most important Navy bases during World War II. An extensive shoreline was littered with abandoned warehouses and old commercial buildings and shipyards, some of which were undergoing tear-down and restoration projects. How feasible would it be to lease one of those warehouses for short-term auto storage?

From the SUV's side pocket, he pulled out a laminated, folded map of the entire San Francisco Bay Area. As soon as he exited the Dumbarton Bridge, he stopped at the curb. He studied the map for a few minutes, frowning, and then punched in Jordan's number again. "Expand your search to the East Bay. San Leandro up north to Alameda. I think they'll cross over the San Mateo Bridge from the East Bay."

"Why not the Bay Bridge? It's closer to Levi's," countered Jordan.

"Too busy, too unpredictable, the traffic flow. The construction on the Bay Bridge has caused a lot of jam-ups. Even emergency vehicles have a hard time getting through. Along the East Bay's shoreline, there are lots of abandoned warehouses, factories, commercial buildings . . ." Jake prayed to God that he was right. Stress shot another ripple of aches through his brain. "Worth a shot, Jordan. Burlingame is just north of the San Mateo Bridge on the west side of the Bay. That pickup could've double-backed to the bridge easily."

A grunt was audible over the line. He needed more manpower, Jake knew. The guy was feeling the effects of stress too. For taciturn Jordan, the grunt was the equivalent of a scream.

"Okay, we'll expand the search to the East Bay."

"Good man," Jake said tersely. "Let's just hope I'm right."

The stress was getting to him, for even he felt like screaming. A deep, primal, lung-burning scream.

Samir's cell phone buzzed loudly and Jake jerked up in bed. Had their plan worked? He'd lain awake most of the night, wondering, praying, swearing aloud his frustration. He looked at the phone's screen. *Sonuvabitch.* Ali's British-accented English was almost unintelligible in the urgency of his tone.

"Samir, we want you to be shaheed. Allah's calling you to prove yourself one last time."

Jake pretended to be groggy. "W-what? Who is this?"

"Ali," the caller announced, his voice laden with impatience. "Alejandro, one of our drivers, was picked up two hours ago by the local police in South San Francisco. Arrested for attempted rape. I cannot believe he would do such a thing to jeopardize our mission." What ensued was a stream of Arabic epithets that made Jake grin. "We need you to step forward and do the right thing. You must take his place. Look deeply into your heart, Samir. Allah is calling you to take up his sword and enter the kingdom of Paradise. Are you ready to receive His glory and love?"

Their plan had worked!

He didn't want to sound too eager, however, so he temporized. A moment passed. "I want His love and glory. My life is dull and monotonous. Pointless . . ." He trailed off, then continued, "My father . . . he deserves this honor. I will avenge my father's murder in this way, in Holy War. Will Sheikh Amad sanctify this?"

"Yes, of course. You shall do fine, Samir. Go to the stadium and spread that deadly powder. Carry out that part of the plan as you explained it to us. Then report to this address by eleven o'clock."

Jake was disappointed to hear it was the Hunter's Point apartment address. Still, it was another step closer to discovering the location of those cargo vans and the explosives.

"Samir, inshallah, you shall be with Allah this very day. Allahu akbar!"

"Nam, shokran. Yes, thank you! Allahu akbar!"

217

Jake, his voice shaking with the excitement of their operation coming to a head, called Jordan to set the last steps into motion. Jordan and Rodriguez were working hand-in-hand on the operation, for every man in the San Jose field office was needed.

"Follow us closely. Wherever Reza takes us is where those vans are. We'll need the sheriff's bomb squad and SWAT team as backup. Also, by noon pick up Amad, Ali, and Fariq."

There would be a special military tribunal for the masterminds, Amad and Ali, and whoever else in the other four cities was behind the planned attack. Fariq had played a role in supporting the operation.

Thanks to the Military Commissions Act in 2006, it was now a war crime to lend financial or material support for any act of terrorism. If he were Convicted of this crime, Fariq would get at least five to ten years in prison, possibly longer. Masterminding a terrorist act would get Amad and Ali at least twenty years in Guantanamo or another military prison not quite as luxurious or accommodating. Or possibly rendition in one of the government's black ops prisons. Each man carried a trove of knowledge of radical Islamic groups that the CIA would kill for.

"Roger that. Another thing, Agent Bernstein. We've turned the microchip implanted in your chin back on. It's our most sophisticated mini microchip transmitter. It transmits up to two thousand feet, about half a mile. TacOps and Frank will be monitoring it in the surveillance van. My other men and I will follow you in other cars, so we're not going to lose you, bet on that. We'll need about thirty minutes, after we find out which county the vans are in to gather all the backup squads. The bomb squad will take at least twenty, SWAT a little less. I've notified all the Bay Area counties and their sheriffs, so they're on alert. They know something big's coming down. Oh, and once you're in place, we're going on radio silence."

Good man, Jordan. He'd thought of everything.
"Okay, then we're all set."
"Good luck, Jake."
He suspected he'd need more than luck that day.

At one minute past eleven that morning, Jake parked at the curb in a seedy East Palo Alto neighborhood — urban blight mixed with run-down apartment buildings and old commercial buildings.

Five shaheed met him as soon as he turned off his engine. The woman, still wearing her hajib, silently slid behind the driver's seat of Reza's car, which was parked nearby. The four men had shaved off their moustaches and beards. They looked even younger than their average age of twenty-five.

Reza approached him, his hostility reverberating in waves, but Jake ignored that. Not having shaved his beard, he wondered if the guy would remark about it.

"Samir, you drive these three. Follow me and stay close. We're going north and crossing the Dunbarton Bridge." Reza paused as he looked over Samir's face and clothing. "Did you plant the bacteria in the stadium? And why haven't you shaved? Ali told us to shave."

Jake suppressed his excitement. His guess proved correct. It *was* the Dunbarton Bridge in San Mateo County!

"Ali said nothing to me about shaving. And yes, this morning with that cleaning crew. I had access to all of the men's bathrooms on the main concourse, so I had time to change into the Hazmat suit and scatter the powder. Left the canister there in a garbage can by one of the food booths."

"So where's that Hazmat suit you said you had to wear?"

Jake lifted the rear hatch of the Explorer. "In there. Want to take a look, Reza, so you can put your doubts to rest?" The man peered inside a box, made a sour face and harrumphed. "So much for the brotherhood of Allah, huh?" added Jake sarcastically.

Reza stepped back while the three Moroccans climbed into Jake's Explorer. "When I see you in Paradise, begging Allah for forgiveness for your kafir ways, is when I claim you as a brother."

Jake shrugged. He slid behind the steering wheel and waited for Reza to get into the car with the woman. Had he known he would be driving his car, he would have planted a transponder instead of enduring the discomfort of the microchip. Didn't matter as long as Jordan didn't lose their tail.

Reflexively, he knuckled the underside of his chin and rubbed the scar with his thumb. A medical adhesive had closed the wound, left uncovered so that Jake could laugh it off as a shaving cut. Half a mile coverage. If they lost him, he and this whole operation were doomed. Still, he never acted without a backup plan just in case, but he hoped he wouldn't have to resort to it. Underneath the Hazmat suit, he'd placed his Glock pistol with a spare magazine. If worse came to worse . . .

The microchip had better do its job, he thought, and surveillance had better be as tight as a leash on a pit bull. Outwardly, he put up a calm front. Inside, he felt twisted and coiled, like a rattler ready to strike.

He kept Reza's silver Honda in view as they traveled north on the Bayshore Freeway and took the ramp onto the Dunbarton Bridge. Jake glanced at the rearview mirror. The three Moroccans wore expressions of glum resignation. He almost felt sorry for the bastards until he reminded himself of the innocent people these three intended to kill in the name of jihad.

On the eastern side of the Bay, they entered the Eight-eighty, the so-called Nimitz Freeway, named after Admiral Nimitz, the World War II Navy hero. Reza's car sped up north through Fremont, Hayward and San Leandro. When the Five-eighty merged, Reza's silver Honda slowed down and took the Marin Boulevard exit. Ten minutes later, the woman driver, Fatima, took a road that paralleled the Amtrak train tracks. They headed toward the East Bay shore, past warehouses and older industrial parks that had seen better, more prosperous days.

A spur off the dead-ended paved road, a graveled frontage road, led to the right going north. As the East Bay shore appeared to his left, Jake noted the succession of derelict factories and closed shipyards to his right. These bayside buildings, now in disrepair, took up valuable real estate. Each bore For Sale signs in front.

Reza's car came to a stop in front of a locked gate. A ten-foot high chain-link fence ran around the perimeter of an enormous warehouse. The faded sign on the front indicated the worn steel-and-wooden building once housed a boatyard, where boats were once winterized, repaired, and stored. Weeds sprouted everywhere in the graveled driveway. One old, splintered boat hung upside-down from an ancient crane.

Within a few minutes, a tall husky man who Jake recognized as Wahid unlocked the gate and swung it open.

Jake checked his watch. Twenty minutes had passed since they'd left the West Bay. Crossing the Dunbarton Bridge *was* faster than taking the San Mateo Bridge. Heading back south would take them to the stadium in thirty to forty minutes.

"So it looks like an old warehouse on a frontage road across the tracks in San Leandro," he muttered, his left hand still on the steering wheel. "Off Marin Boulevard. San Leandro Boat Works. Whaddya know?"

He glanced over at the three Moroccans, who apparently thought he was speaking to them, their limited English not picking up his intention. One of them grunted in reply before withdrawing back into himself. The other three looked up, suddenly startled as Jake braked behind Reza's car to the left of a huge bay door. Prayer seemed uppermost in their thoughts. In their minds, they were already dead and enjoying the virgins in Paradise. Jake climbed out.

If this op went south, he'd be joining them.

CHAPTER TWENTY-SEVEN

The tallest of the four, Wahid, came forward and stood before a thirty-foot high bay door that resembled a hydraulic garage door. The three other mechanics—if that was what they really were—walked out and stopped in an area to the right of the huge bay door. Two black Chevy trucks were parked there, their tailgates down. The three men joined Wahid and stood like their leader, legs apart, their hands inside jacket pockets.

"Stand in a line," barked Wahid. "We're going to frisk everybody. Hands on your heads. Now!"

Everyone did as they were told, Hussein lagging behind the others in obeying. *The prick's going to get us killed.*

One by one, the shortest and stockiest of the four came down the line and gave everyone a pat-down, even the woman, Fatima, much to Hussein's loud protestations. A few words from her in Arabic settled him down but he continued to bristle after that. Wahid seemed to delight in Hussein's temper tantrum.

"We've put a lot of time into this project," explained Wahid coldly, "and we don't want any problems. We're paid a shitload of money to see this attack go forward and be successful. I'm operating under the sheikh's advice, so no yahoos. Just cooperate and we'll have you on your way soon enough." He checked his watch, prompting Jake to do the same. Three o'clock. "We have work to do before all of you leave at four-thirty."

Wahid signaled the man called Hameed, whom he called

223

"bro." Because of their close physical resemblance and height, Jake suspected he'd been correct when he surmised that the two bearded men were actually brothers.

Hameed hit a remote and the huge bay door rose and disappeared into the two steel tracks high above their heads. They followed the two brothers inside while the other two mechanics cleared the graveled driveway by carrying tools, cases of supplies, and compressors to the two pickups parked in front of another huge bay door. Jake noted that they were getting ready to leave and wondered why. Were these mercenaries ditching the scene before it all came down?

Inside the cavernous warehouse, six white vans sat waiting. All of them bore two different local counties' EMT logos, meticulously painted on. The vans, all facing the bay door, also bore bars of emergency lights and blacked-out side windows. Wahid stood behind one and called them over. He opened wide the rear cargo doors so the six drivers could look inside.

Jake swallowed hard and took a deep breath. The rear beds, instead of bearing gurneys and medical equipment, held stacked gray bricks of RDX-10 explosives, a central detonator device, and wires to each brick. On each side of the crate of bricks were two fifty gallon, metal drums. Filled with accelerant, Jake surmised. He glanced at the others as the reality of their mission sank in. Big eyes stared and jaws dropped. Fatima began to pray.

"Powerful!" Hussein exclaimed.

"You bet," Wahid said, black eyes gleaming, "Each van's carrying five-hundred pounds of military-grade explosives. Three-thousand pounds total. If you guys don't bring down that stadium on the heads of everyone there, I'll be a monkey's uncle."

Wahid left the doors open. "Haven't hooked up the detonators to the remotes yet. Didn't want to accidentally blow us all up. Come here."

His brother, Hameed, stood at the open driver's door. He held a black, hard plastic remote-control device.

"This is the detonator which we will clip to the visor on the driver's side. When the time is right, you punch the button. Only once. There might be five-second delay, so don't panic and keep punching. Punch it once and kiss the world as we know it goodbye and kiss the hem of the Prophet hello. Or whatever you do in Paradise." Hameed darted an ironic glance over to Wahid as he spoke the last sentence.

Two coldblooded, Islamist mercenaries in it for the money. Jake, dying to ask them where the money came from, decided to give it a try.

"This whole setup must've cost a fortune," he ventured.

"Oh yeah, a million smackers each," Hameed crowed. His brother snarled a shut-the-fuck-up kind of growl, causing Hameed to clam up.

We've got to find out . . .

Wahid moved next to his brother after taking a black object off a nearby metal worktable. "Who's running this?"

Hussein spoke up, his chest swelling with pride, his eyes glittering with unabashed zeal.

"I'm in charge. I'll be the last to detonate and I've got orders to kill any one of us who doesn't go before me." His scan of the other five drivers settled finally on Jake. "Including you, Samir. I am to count five explosions, then I set mine.

Wahid held up the device in his hand, a large remote with apparently more battery power. "This is the master switch, which I will give to Hussein. This overrides and controls the other remotes, so if any one of you chickens out, he'll make sure you don't escape. Does everyone understand?"

The five drivers under Hussein's control nodded solemnly. Jake glanced over at the metal worktable. Another large remote, the exact same size and shape as the one Wahid handed to Hussein, remained. Hameed moved over to the worktable and snatched it up while Jake turned his gaze back to Hussein, who seemed oblivious of the second master switch.

"Anything goes wrong, Hussein has the master kill switch," reminded Wahid. He turned to his brother and rattled something rapidly, which sounded a lot like Pashto, a Pakistani dialect. As a Navy SEAL eight years before, Jake had heard the language spoken often while doing a tour of duty in Lahore. He couldn't understand the dialect but could recognize it when he heard it. In Arabic school, they'd reviewed the various Middle Eastern dialects.

Jake tucked away that bit of information, along with a sense of growing alarm. If these four mechanics left before the vans, only to face a blockade of sheriff's deputies and SWAT team trucks, they had the power to blow the place up. All their evidence up in smoke, the case against them would weaken.

"Go over there." Wahid pointed to a clear area on the concrete floor where six folding chairs stood in a ring. "And then wait. There's hot tea on that table. Hameed and I have to connect the detonating wires to the firing mechanisms. The vans'll be ready to go in about thirty minutes."

The six drivers sat silently until the woman jumped up and crossed the room to a commercial container. She poured a Styrofoam cup of tea and brought it to Hussein, who nodded at her. He appeared unconcerned that she would soon be ending her life. The three Moroccans, spying a large, stained area rug on the cold concrete, approached it and fell to their foreheads and knees to pray. Reza sat, sipped his tea, and stared at Jake.

Finally, his careful work completed, Wahid gestured to Reza and the other two mechanics waiting just outside the bay door. "The keys are in the ignitions. Once these two vans pull out, there will be room for the others to follow." To Hussein, he added, "Good luck. *Salaam alaikum!*"

"Allahu akbar!" cried Reza, his hand over his heart.

"Yes, *allahu akbar,*" said Wahid. He pointed to the bay door. "Keep this open. We'll come back tomorrow and close up everything. Over there on the table is a police scanner and, next to it, a radio broadcast from Levi's Stadium. The crowd's already there, waiting for the game to start."

They could hear the dull roar of the stadium crowd in the background. The anonymous calls about the anthrax were to be made at four sharp. The police scanner emitted static and occasional cops checking in. But Jake knew the SWAT teams and deputies would maintain radio silence during the blockade. In case Jordan needed more time, Jake felt he had to delay the four mechanics and keep them from leaving. The deputies and SWAT teams might not be in position.

Jake lunged to his feet. "Wait! Why are you leaving now? It's only four o'clock. We don't leave for another half hour. What if we have mechanical problems? Ignition problems? Flat tires?"

Reza strode to Jake's side. "Shut up and sit down!"

Wahid tossed back, "You won't have any problems. We've double-checked everything. All systems are in prime condition. I tell ya, we're the best money can buy!"

He jumped in the passenger seat as his brother revved up the engine of one of the black trucks. The second one was already halfway down the driveway.

Reza was in Jake's face now. "They can leave whenever they want. You're not in charge!"

"You don't understand," Jake grabbed the man's jacket lapels. "They've got the master switch! They're going to blow us all up!"

"You're crazy! You're trying to get out of this!" yelled the woman, coming to Reza's side. The four Moroccans stood undecided, not fully understanding what was going on.

Reza bent over and retrieved a small pistol from a calf

Donna Del Oro

holster strapped to his leg. He stuck it in front of Jake's face.

"You're going through with this or I'll shoot you in the head right now."

The twenty-two-caliber pistol was a pea shooter, but at close range it could kill a man. The barrel was pressed against Jake's temple as the four Moroccans circled him, Hussein, and the woman. She whipped a switchblade out of her bra which she snapped open. Without hesitation, she held it up against Jake's throat.

"We knew you'd never go through with it," she declared hotly, cutting his skin as her hand shook with rage.

He grew still. Let them think Samir, the scientist, was a coward, all talk and no action. Let them think that Jake, a former SEAL trained in close-quarters combat, didn't have the skills to take these two down. It wouldn't be easy, however, with the rib-sticker digging into the skin in front of his Adam's apple and the cold muzzle of the twenty-two indenting itself into his head.

"Okay, okay," he sighed, holding up his hands. He glanced outside. The two trucks had cleared the open gate of the boatyard. In less than one minute, they'd see the police blockade. Then Jake had no doubt that Wahid wouldn't hesitate to blow up the evidence in the warehouse. And the six *shaheed* along with it.

He began counting to himself while staring down the murderous looks of Reza and the woman. At thirty seconds, he whipped both arms up, grabbed the woman's wrist with his left hand and Reza's wrist with his right. He twisted both outwardly as hard as he could, throwing them off balance, deflecting the man's aim as he fired.

Temporarily deafened, Jake took off at a sprint down the driveway. He slipped once on the gravel as a bullet stabbed him in the shoulder. Hot pain seared his arm, running up and down like liquid fire. Still, his training kicked in and he

228

ignored the pain as he zigzagged his run for another fifty yards. Loud reports shattered the air, but he couldn't tell where they were coming from.

The police blockade? Reza's gun? It didn't matter. He knew what was coming. He ran until he came to the dip in the driveway. He'd noticed a large concrete culvert near a small gully but it was large enough for a man to squeeze into. He dove into it. A moment later, the earth shook with the force of a violent earthquake. Around him rained wood, metal and glass, set afire by the explosion of three-thousand pounds of bombs.

One flaming piece of metal rolled into the mouth of the culvert, so he kicked it away. His ears rang and his right shoulder and arm burned as though someone had plunged a red-hot stake into them. He swore aloud as he rolled over onto his back.

Tears leaked slowly after he heard police sirens approaching.

Damn! That was too fucking close.

CHAPTER TWENTY-EIGHT

Jake woke up to find Jordan, Rodriguez, and Linda Brown hovering over him. Linda set a round tin on the tray by his hospital bed.

"Your favorite peanut-butter chocolate chip cookies. For when you get tired of Jello."

He smiled and ran his hand over his face. For the first time in months, he felt smooth skin instead of hair.

"Didn't know you had a face underneath all those whiskers." Frank shook his head. "Now you look like me, another baby-faced, wounded warrior."

Jake took inventory. He found a cast on his left ankle and foot and another on his right arm, and it hurt like hell to move on his left side. He rolled back to his right.

"Sorry, pal." Jordan smiled. "No more pain killers, according to the nurse, for another hour."

"Jeez, how many? I only felt one."

"You took a bullet in your ankle, your left butt cheek, and right bicep. Better than blowing sky high."

"Did you find any bodies?" He winced as another wave of pain swept over him.

Frank Rodriguez shook his head. "No, just bits and pieces. That was some blast. Windows were blown out up to a mile away. The deputies lost their windshields, for which they're sending the FBI the bill. My ears are still ringing."

"You picked up those two Pakistani brothers and their buddies?" Jake eyed the tin. Immediately, Linda opened it and put it in his lap. Grateful, he smiled at her, selected one and began chewing. *Ah, just as good as a pain pill.*

Jordan nodded. "Oh yeah. They've lawyered up and claiming entrapment. What else is new? Bad news is Amad and Ali flew out early Sunday morning for London. The Brits have them in custody and Justice has filed extradition papers. We'll get them but it might take a while."

Jake swore under his breath. "Fariq? He said he was leaving town. Did you find him?"

Rodriguez and Jordan glanced at each other, looking uncomfortable. Finally, Jordan spoke. "We learned this just yesterday. Fariq—not his real name, by the way—is CIA. One of the deepest moles they have. They send him all over."

"Well, sonuva—" He looked over at the middle-aged woman. "And they couldn't trust us with the information? Is it true he's Muslim Brotherhood?"

"Former Muslim Brotherhood," said Jordan. "His father and brother were killed by a rival extremist group and that did it for him. We have no idea where he's at."

"What about the other four cities?"

"All stopped, everyone arrested. The JD's going to be busy for a while."

Jake absorbed this information and nodded. *Thank God!* All five of them, the undercover agents from Arabic school, had saved thousands of lives. He then gazed up at Linda. "Any word from . . ."

No mental slouch, the older woman knew whom he referred to. She smiled as she offered the tin to Rodriguez and Jordan. The men helped themselves with a flourish.

"Meg's fine. We wrote a letter and each of us signed it, bearing witness to her assistance to the FBI's Special Support Group. Her professors are letting her make up the work she missed, so she's happy." She looked as though she had more to say, but then apparently thought better of it.

"Good," was all Jake could think to say. That familiar ache

had returned to his chest. He frowned at the enthusiasm with which Rodriguez and Jordan were scarfing down his cookies. "Hey, guys, leave me some."

"There's more," Linda said, a wry grin on her face.

"Great, I'm getting out of here."

Rodriguez and Jordan looked doubtful but Linda nodded her encouragement.

"Going home for Thanksgiving," Jake announced.

Just anybody try and stop me.

"No, he gets too rattled in the box," declared his brother, Gabe.

"Yeah, only when they're behind two touchdowns. Otherwise, he's a laser beam."

Gabe and David, his younger brothers, were arguing over which starting quarterback had the coolest head under pressure. Sprawled on the sectional sofa, his father kept patting Jake's leg and muttering, "*Mazel tov*, my boy" in between plays. UCLA and USC were butting heads again on the TV screen, a forty-five-inch job that Jake had bought his parents last Hanukkah. They somehow knew all about the terrorist attack that Jake had played a crucial role in preventing although he'd said little about it, only that he'd helped to stop it. They'd gotten the details from someone but they weren't saying who.

His family, including his brothers, their wives and kids, had fussed over him as though he was a heroic astronaut returned to Earth. The wives and his mother worked in the kitchen—the aromas wafted into the adjacent family room, making the men's stomachs growl. His brothers' kids played outside—all except for Gabe's oldest son, a boy of five who'd just discovered the allure of football. Little Jacob sat on the carpet, tucked between his father's legs.

Jake's wistful gaze kept returning to the cute dark-haired boy, nestled against his father's strong chest. The old ache lingered inside, forcing up the same question. Could he ever lead a normal life? Marry, have kids, a mortgage, pets? Probably not. He couldn't even sustain a serious relationship.

Meg.

As if by uncanny timing, the doorbell rang. When Jake looked up, his mother was greeting someone in the foyer. Two women's voices rang out into the big family room. Jake's pulse sped up and his face turned hot. A moment later, all male heads turned as Meg and his mother entered the room. Jake's eyes locked with Meg's.

His father helped him rise from the sofa, and with the aid of a cane, Jake limped over to the two women. His mother was all sheepish smiles.

"Our special surprise guest!"

Meg looked stunning in tight jeans, a bright blue sweater, and wedge heels. Her blonde hair lay loose over one shoulder in a low ponytail. Gold hoops drew his eyes over her face while she surveyed his two casts, the cane, and the bandage under his chin. They'd finally removed that damned microchip, Jordan revealing that the FBI planned to use them in all their undercover agents.

Her beautiful blue eyes crinkled with emotion as tears spilled over. They came together wordlessly and embraced. Long and hard. He could've stayed in her arms all day. He intended to, all night . . . if she would have him.

Later, they strolled in his parents' garden, Jake doing the best he could with his cane and ankle-foot cast. Meg's arm, wrapped around his back, helped to balance him.

Balance. He needed that in his life, just as he needed her. She looked up at him, her rosy lips curved in a coy smile.

"Your mother invited me to spend the night. In your old room in one of the twin beds. Do you mind?"

He bent closer and whispered, "Or we can find a hotel with a king-size bed?"

"Too big. I'd rather . . . uh, snuggle. If you can manage it."

"That's not the appendage that's broken." He chuckled deep in his throat. "I'm taking time off. Plan to find a warm beach somewhere and heal. Want to join me?"

"Christmas break, for sure. Just say where."

He smiled and tried to hug her with his arm cast. The damned thing just got in the way. There was something he had to get off his chest, however, and from Meg's look, she was expecting it.

"Look, Meg. I'm so sorry . . . that whole incident. I didn't want . . . you shouldn't've had to . . ." He sputtered to silence.

"Hey, that fake drowning—it all made me realize what you people in intelligence and law enforcement have to go through to keep the rest of us safe. Don't apologize." She squeezed his waist, rose up and kissed his cheek. "Linda Brown says I'm a natural. I'm going to join the Special Support Group . . . if they'll have me."

His heart sank. "The San Diego field office?"

"Wherever you are. If you'll take me."

He stopped and looked at her. Was she saying what he thought—he hoped she was saying? Her returned look resounded with *Yes*!

ABOUT THE AUTHOR

A retired high school and junior college English teacher, Donna loves to read, write, travel, and play golf with her husband, Joe. She is a member of Sisters in Crime, and the local chapter, Capitol Crimes, in Sacramento, California.

Bilingual and bicultural, she is an award-winning author, winning the Silver Falchion Award for Best Comedy-Suspense in 2022 for *Saving La Familia*, as well as the 2023 Bronze Award by the International Latino Book Awards.

The author has four series in print: the *Born To Sing* series, the *Jake Bernstein FBI* series, the paranormal-suspense *Delphi Bloodline* series, featuring a clairvoyant artist, and the award-winning *Saving La Familia* series.

Made in the USA
Coppell, TX
09 June 2024

33314954R00133